DEADL

They heard a noise. Or maybe it wasn't a noise at all, maybe it was the reflection they both caught at the same moment, or the way a shadow moved on the asphalt outside the car. Ridge's hand went beneath his sweater and suddenly he was holding his pistol. Cully grabbed her purse, where her own gun slept.

"Start the car!" Ridge whispered. As she twisted the key she saw the other shadows, huge forms of men, and when the BMW buzzed to life she saw them freeze. "Take off!" Ridge shouted.

Before she could obey him the back window shattered from the blast of a shotgun.

Ridge twisted and fired three times through the empty gash of the back window.

Cully hit the accelerator, and the car took another round, this one in the windshield.

Ridge turned again and fired through the now open windshield. He shouted, "The lights! Turn on the lights!"

She twisted the light stalk, and the headlights flared on. Three men stood in the sudden gush of illumination. Two turned and ran, but the third raised his arm, his gun barking, the muzzle flashing. . . .

Bantam Books offers the finest in classic and modern American murder mysteries.
Ask your bookseller for the books you have missed.

Rex Stout
The Black Mountain
Broken Vase
Death of a Dude
Death Times Three
Fer-de-Lance
The Final Deduction
Gambit
Plot It Yourself
The Rubber Band
Some Buried Caesar
Three for the Chair
Too Many Cooks
And Be a Villain

Dick Lupoff
The Comic Book Killer

Meg O'Brien
The Daphne Decisions
Salmon in the Soup

Virginia Anderson
Blood Lies
King of the Roses

William Murray
When the Fat Man Sings
The King of the Nightcap
The Getaway Blues

Gloria Dank
Friends Till the End
Going Out in Style

Jeffery Deaver
Manhattan Is My Beat
Death of a Blue Movie Star

Robert Goldsborough
Murder in E Minor
Death on Deadline
The Bloodied Ivy
The Last Coincidence
Fade to Black

Sue Grafton
"A" Is for Alibi
"B" Is for Burglar
"C" Is for Corpse
"D" Is for Deadbeat
"E" Is for Evidence
"F" Is for Fugitive

Carolyn G. Hart
Design for Murder
Death on Demand
Something Wicked
Honeymoon with Murder
A Little Class on Murder

Annette Meyers
The Big Killing
Tender Death

David Handler
The Man Who Died Laughing
The Man Who Lived by Night
The Man Who Would Be
    F. Scott Fitzgerald

M. K. Lorens
Sweet Narcissus
Ropedancer's Fall
coming soon:
Deception Island

Diane Shah
As Crime Goes By

Paul Levine
To Speak for the Dead

Stephen Greenleaf
Impact

Margaret Maron
Corpus Christmas
The Right Jack

BLOOD OF THE LAMB

RANDALL WALLACE

BANTAM BOOKS
NEW YORK • TORONTO • LONDON • SYDNEY • AUCKLAND

BLOOD OF THE LAMB

A Bantam Book / November 1990

ISBN 0-553-28763-X

Published simultaneously in the United States and Canada

Bantam Books are published by Bantam Books, a division of Bantam Doubleday Dell Publishing Group, Inc. Its trademark, consisting of the words "Bantam Books" and the portrayal of a rooster, is Registered in U.S. Patent and Trademark Office and in other countries. Marca Registrada, Bantam Books, 666 Fifth Avenue, New York, New York 10103.

PRINTED IN THE UNITED STATES OF AMERICA

RAD   0 9 8 7 6 5 4 3 2 1

I would like to inscribe this page to my grandmother, who passed away while I was finishing the manuscript of this book. Such a dedication is awkward, however, because lurking here and there in the novel are depictions of actions and dialogue that would have pained me to place before her gentle eyes.

And yet I know that, even looking down from the battlements of Heaven, she could see these things and be at peace with them. She would give me the benefit of the doubt and believe that I had tried to describe the world as it is and not simply pandered to a taste for the violent and the profane.

And even if she found fault with my choices, she would have forgiven me the shortcomings of my judgment, for there was never a shortcoming in her heart, and she loved me as if there could be none in mine.

And so this novel is dedicated

To the memory of

ELIZABETH RINGGOLD PAGE

PROLOGUE

Caesar Augusto de la Puente took two cigars from the box the Cuban ambassador had given him, tossed one to his houseguest, and leaned back into the white leather of the sofa. He lit the sweet tobacco with a custom Ronson, one half pound of gold and butane, and tossed over the lighter too.

His guest caught it in a manicured hand, decorated with a thumb ring and a Rolex. The guest, keen to every new luxury that glinted before his eye, felt the lighter's heft, and sampled its smooth operation. "Nice," he said. The excellence of the cigar he took for granted; together they smoked nothing but Havanas.

De la Puente smiled. "Keep it! I'll pick up another one when I go to Washington next week for the drug conference."

The two men burst out laughing. The gringos were flying him up on a private jet to attend a conference with other Latin American officials to discuss the suppression of the drug trade. Meanwhile, the man he was sharing his cigars with was the most active cocaine trafficker in Mexico.

He had many names, but was known in the drug trade as Chocolate. Not that he was black; he took pride in his European ancestry and even fancied himself aristocratic, especially when he was sitting, as he was now, with his feet propped on the Minister of Public Safety's polished marble coffee table with his pursed lips blowing a fine stream of blue smoke toward the ceiling of the minister's private villa. He held the nickname because he owned the connections with the black street gangs north of the border. While other suppliers had gravitated toward American distributors who

1

shared their Spanish language and heritage, Chocolate had had the foresight to brave the dangers of distrust and go where the future lay—trading with the blacks—and he had reaped the rewards.

"Where is that little Indian?" Chocolate asked, acting more impatient than he really was. They were waiting for the arrival of Guillermo Montoya, another dealer in the dream-and-death business, and Chocolate was sensitive to any potential slight to his honor.

But de la Puente, who had called the meeting, was just as protective of his own prestige, and said flatly, "He'll come." He smiled smugly when only a moment later the red light on the desk intercom blinked on and flashed twice. De la Puente stood and moved to the window. Down in the courtyard was an armored Mercedes, its bumpers and metalwork all blacked out in Eurotech style. "That's him," he said. He walked to the desk, pressed a button, and moved back to the sitting area. De la Puente wished he had taken the winged-back chair thinking it might make him look more regal. But Chocolate showed no inclination to give up the more impressive place, so de la Puente returned to the white couch and crossed his legs casually, as his guards admitted the visitors.

De la Puente was surprised to see not one but two men: Guillermo Montoya, the man he had expected, and Montoya's brother Alejandro. Alejandro was three years older and three inches taller, and his eyes lacked the flash of his brother's, but he owned the identical flat forehead and high cheekbones. Although the smaller one—barely five and a half feet tall—Guillermo was clearly the leader, stepping into the room first and waiting for de la Puente's guard to close the door behind them before he spoke. But then he only blew out a loud breath and wiped the sweat from his forehead with the back of a brown wrist. Finally he said, "It's hot."

"Doesn't your car have air-conditioning?" de la Puente asked, as though he was concerned.

"It broke," Montoya said, and showed white teeth in what passed for a smile.

Chocolate glanced at Montoya and snickered. It had been

two years since he had seen the little man, and though Montoya's reputation had mushroomed he looked even less dangerous in his Italian slacks than he had when he had worn the loose cotton slacks and peasant shirts of Mexico City. De la Puente's guard, in searching the Montoya brothers for weapons, had made them remove their jackets, and the Montoyas' silk shirts were soaked with sweat and sticking to their chests, showing brown skin beneath the thin fabric.

"A pity! And on such a hot day, too," de la Puente said. "Won't you sit down? Would you like a drink?"

"We can't stay long," Guillermo Montoya said, denying both offers. "We could not have come at all if it had been for anybody else."

"Then we will make our meeting brief," de la Puente said. "We wish to talk about economics."

"Business," Chocolate said, as if the fancier word had needed translation.

"Yes?" Guillermo Montoya said weakly.

"Come closer, please," de la Puente said, "we are all friends here, we are sailors in the same boat." He beckoned, and the brothers shuffled forward and stood with their heads drooping as this officer of the President's cabinet lectured them. "Here is our problem. Economics—business—has its own laws. And we of course do not like to break laws." He chuckled; and then seemed sobered by the gravity of his subject, and frowned. "A law of economics is that when demand increases, the price goes up. But we have been violating that law. Demand for cocaine, especially the rocks, has been rising. But price has fallen."

Chocolate said, "This hurts me." It was impossible to miss the threat in his statement.

"It hurts everyone involved," de la Puente said diplomatically. "And it is impossible for one supplier to maintain a price floor, if he is being undercut by competitors."

Montoya frowned, then his face cleared. "I see! You want to be like . . . OPEC!"

"Yes!" de la Puente said, pleased with the analogy.

"Mexico is not in OPEC," Montoya said, frowning again.

De la Puente wondered how Montoya had stayed alive

so long, being so stupid. "It is only an illustration. What we are saying—"

Chocolate interrupted, looking directly at Montoya. "What we are saying is that I have the blacks and I have left you the rest. I have been generous that way. You operate with my permission. And his." Chocolate nodded toward their host. "We can stop you tomorrow if we want to. So quit underselling me. Now."

Chocolate had said all he was going to say; he looked away again.

Montoya physically ducked, wrapping his right hand over his left wrist like a coolie and stammering, "I . . . am so sorry if I offended . . ." He moved forward, almost bowing. "I thought . . . I did a service. The black and Latino gangs do not get along. I thought by supplying the Latinos I was keeping them happy. If I offended I am truly—"

It happened faster than de la Puente could believe; later he would realize Guillermo Montoya had unspooled the garrote from within his watch. Alejandro Montoya stood over the cabinet minister, daring him to speak, as though de la Puente could have uttered a sound, watching open-mouthed as Chocolate's body slid up the back of the winged chair, dragged by the razor wire around his neck. Blood appeared first in a fine line around Chocolate's throat and then in a sheet like a red turtleneck collar. Guillermo had moved behind, his shoulder to the back of the chair, using all the leverage of his whippy little body to pull the fine metal through the flesh of the bigger man.

It was over in seconds. Guillermo let the body settle back into its chair, only now the head, nearly severed, pitched forward at a sick angle, vivid blood draining from it into a red blossom on the white leather of the chair. Guillermo cleaned the wire on Chocolate's oiled hair and snapped it back into his watch.

"This is the first time I've ever seen him smile," Guillermo said, looking at his victim. He and Alejandro began to laugh. The curved gash in Chocolate's throat looked like a second mouth, drooling red, but de la Puente's eyes did not take in the joke. He gawked first at one Montoya, then at the other.

"Now. Señor Caesar Augusto de la Puente," Guillermo said formally. "Your friend here, who has paid you so much money in the past, I think he will not be paying you any more. You may call your guards if you wish, but I have another suggestion. Would you care to hear it?"

Montoya waited politely for an answer. De la Puente at last gained control and nodded.

"Good!" Montoya said. "Maybe you and I can do some business. And gain together from the . . . economies. Yes?"

"What do you—"

"I will make things simpler. That is another rule of economics, isn't it? The fewer competitors, the higher the price? Now we will have many distributors, and only one supplier."

"But . . ." De la Puente's brain was beginning to work again. "But the blacks don't know you."

"Their last connection . . . smiles on them no more," Guillermo said. He was having a good time.

"But . . . your other people! The Latino gangs . . . !"

"If they disagree with the way I do business, I will give them . . ." He looked at the dripping head, already fragrant with death, and then grinned at de la Puente. ". . . an illustration. Now. Do you want to call your guards? Or should I call in my friend Ricardo Flores, who is an excellent chauffeur, and ask him to give Chocolate a ride home?"

THE FIRST DAY

CHAPTER ONE

After her first patrol, they called her Bull Barrel.

Her name was Scarlet McCullers. At the Police Academy, where she had been at the top of her class, her friends had called her Cully. And two years later, when she made Detective One faster than anybody else they could remember, the guys at the Van Nuys Division would refer to her behind her back as Dickless Tracy. Male cops are no different from other men; the ones who like to talk about balls don't have any.

But soon, they would know her as Bull Barrel.

It had been a summer's day. Her uniform was new, her holster stiff, her pistol cleaned and oiled. Her blond hair was rolled and pinned behind her neck; her green eyes were full of the traffic on Sepulveda Boulevard.

It was 10:18 A.M. and she was at the wheel of a patrol car from the Van Nuys Division. Beside her sat Ragg Wilson. "Ragg" was an acronym for Rough As Goat Guts, as in: "I tell you what, it's gonner be rough as goat guts out there today." Ragg was from Oklahoma and had feet like cow pies. He kept a pinch of chewing tobacco between his cheek and gum. He hated hot weather—sun dappled his skin. He hated cold weather—it made his joints hurt. Clouds, he said, gave him headaches. So every day was rough as goat guts for Ragg. Rookies made life rougher, and Ragg got all of them sooner or later. The supervisor's theory was that new cops with twitchy reflexes ought to have raw nerves deadened a little, and Ragg was just the man for the job.

But when Ragg had laid his watery yellow eyes on Scarlet McCullers, he was not completely indifferent to the job of breaking her in. The Sam Browne belt around her little

waist stretched the new uniform shirt tighter around the
swell of her breasts, and the blue pants wrapped her without
a wrinkle and showed the ripple of smooth muscle as she
walked. She had a narrow chin and pursed lips that looked
angelic, and when the sergeant introduced her to Ragg at
roll call, the old veteran cop drew himself up straight and
sucked in his bloated gut.

Out at the car Ragg had thrown the hemorrhoid cushion
he always sat on into the back seat, and said, "I wish the
night shift would clean up, knowwhuttamean?" He let her
drive, and their first hour out she wrote up a Mexican
gardener's pickup truck for an obscured license plate. He
would have laughed at any other rookie who had pointed
it out, but that morning he found her rookie attentiveness
delightful.

They had moved north, away from the Sherman Oaks
Galleria and toward a hive of prostitution motels, Cully's
eyes wide and darting. The months of training had wound
her brain taut with expectation, and she rolled the slang
terms of the street through her head, as if knowing what a
weapon was called in the real world would make danger
more visible. She thought of the zips, the switches, the
homemade silencers; the categories of pistols, and all their
modifications, like the thickened, weighted muzzles that
dampened noise and recoil and made a regular gun a "bull
barrel." She wondered, like every rookie before her, when
she would first look at death. She hid such thoughts by
chatting and laughing with Ragg; but it's not easy to forget
about killing and being killed when the last thing you do
before going to work is to strap on a gun.

Suddenly the radio came alive with an armed-and-dan-
gerous call: a muscular black male had just robbed a 7
Eleven ten blocks away; he had escaped in a green station
wagon. Ragg picked up the receiver and acknowledged.
Five seconds later Cully spotted a green station wagon,
with a wide-eyed black man behind the wheel. "There!"
she said, and romped the accelerator.

Ragg hit the lights and siren and Cully spun the car in
an impressive one-eighty. Ragg wished he'd kept his hemorrhoid cushion. The guy in the green station wagon

didn't even try to run; when they blew up to him, he swung to the curb. In an instant Cully was out of the squad car, her .38 revolver leveled. The brother in the wagon got out slowly, his hands in the air. He had on dirty jeans and a T-shirt that strained around a bull's neck and a bodybuilder's biceps. Cully was only vaguely aware of herself screaming, "Against the car! Against the car!"

Ragg tumbled out and covered her. Cully moved to the suspect, who was irritatingly cool. "What this?" he said. "I didn't miss no lights."

Cully jammed her pistol into its holster and began to pat him down for weapons. She ran her slender fingers over his arms, although they were bare—she was doing this by the book—and then remembered his rolled-up stocking cap; she snatched it off, crumpled it, and dropped it on the street. She went back to his collar, then traced her fingertips across his chest and down his stomach. The beefy young black man gawked around at this blond angel touching him all over his body. "Turn around!" she barked.

She felt inside the band of his pants, then groped down in search of any pistol concealed in his crotch. The dude rolled his eyes back at her, just as she jumped away, snatched out her pistol again, and screamed, "He's got a gun! And it's a *bull barrel!*"

Ragg jumped, kicking the brother's knees to fold him, tugging him down, twisting him face first to the pavement and shouting, "Spread out, you son of a bitch!"

And all the while the guy was screaming, "Don't shoot, don't shoot! That ain't no gun! That's my *johnson!*"

Before they got back to the station, Cully made Ragg promise—on his mother's *grave*—that he wouldn't breathe a word of this to anybody, and Ragg swore, *swore*, he'd never tell a soul.

The next morning at roll call the sergeant read the roster, booming the names of the on-duty shift from behind a tooth-pick clinched in his molars: "Lowman!"

"Yo."

"Lupton!"

"Aw-haw."

"Maston!"

"Yep."

"McCullers!"

And before Cully could say "Here," the other thirty cops in the room all sang in unison, "Bull Barrel!"

Before that day, her ambition had been merely fierce; after that day it was relentless.

The next time the Los Angeles Police Department offered its written examination in its annual formation of the Detective Promotion List, four hundred fifty-seven patrol cops entered the competition, and when they published the test scores the name at the top was Scarlet McCullers. But the written score was only the first half of the competition, and a lot of guys were saying, sure, she's good with the books —whatta ya expect from some bitch that graduated from U.C.L.A.—but just wait'll she hits the oral exams.

They forgot that Cully's father had been a street cop. They figured this slender young woman who seemed so fragile—beauty always seems fragile—would fold like a tissue in a rainstorm when those tough old dicks on the Examining Board starting asking her the street cop questions. The examiners figured the same thing, and they came at her hard, trying to shake her with fast questions whose real answer was It All Depends . . . . But candidate McCullers didn't flinch; she leveled her eyes and rattled off the legal distinctions and departmental policy of every situation back at them.

Then midway through the grilling she lifted a slender hand and said, "Gentlemen, you're really asking just one thing: Can a woman who's been in the department two years keep her head on the street? Maybe you've heard about me and an incident with the wrong guy in the wrong green station wagon. Let me tell you, that taught me something, and I think it may be the secret of this job: out on the street it's not enough to be intelligent, you've also got to be smart, and you've got to be smart when your heart's pounding in your ears and sweat is turning your pistol grip into grease. What you don't do is get pushed around. What you *do* do is take charge, like I'm doing right now." She paused. "Any more questions?"

They put her at the top of the orals list too, and when she was promoted it was with the second highest composite ranking in the history of the LAPD, and the chief himself came down to hand out her certification.

The promotion to detective did not, however, gain her respect in her division. When Personnel sent over her new shield, it was Badge #288. In the LAPD, two-eighty-eight is the numerical code for oral copulation.

Back at the academy, she had not only excelled in the classroom, but had scored a Top Possible on the pistol range with a .38 revolver. When the department allowed detectives to carry 9-millimeter automatics in an effort to keep up with the firepower of the machine pistols street criminals were now using, she outshot the experts with the new weapons, just to prove she could. But since that first day on patrol with Ragg, she had never drawn her pistol in the field. It was as if she had decided that if she was ever going to live down the name Bull Barrel, Badge #288, she would do it with her brain.

CHAPTER TWO

Beyond the mountains, the sun dipped its hot back into the cool Pacific and colored the western air with a long pink sigh. The pastel light flowed past the sharp edges of the palm trees bordering the boulevard and dazed the detectives in the sedan.

At the wheel, doing his version of driving, was Din Minh Quang, an eight-year veteran of the Van Nuys Division. Beside him sat his new partner, Scarlet "Bull Barrel" McCullers, the new D-I, currently assigned to Vice as a trainee.

Quang was a D-II; in the Los Angeles Police Department, Detective Two is the first rank beyond the Civil Service level, and is a major leap toward a lieutenancy and even a Captain's bars someday. But Quang behind the wheel of a car was always the junior partner. When the Thunderbird they were following jerked out of the traffic and bounced into the shadow of an AM PM Mini Market, Cully ordered: "Go past," and Quang rolled the Dodge through the intersection and darted into a parking space, scraping the curb and punching over a wire trash can labeled "Keep L.A. Beautiful."

"Maybe they can't buy a Thirsty-Two Ouncer in Mexico City," Quang said. But the Mexicans in the Thunderbird were leaning over something—a map. Then they were back into the sparse Saturday traffic. Quang followed them into an upper-middle-class neighborhood in the San Fernando Valley. The houses, buried behind bunkers of bougainvillea, sat far back from the street, and the two Mexicans in the Thunderbird went slowly, reading the addresses on the mailboxes.

Cully reached for the radio, and said, "West on Magnolia."

A voice came back from the van that was following their directions from two blocks parallel. "Check." Then the guy in the backup van added, "Still wearing your crash helmet?"

Quang did not smile and Cully did not acknowledge the joke.

The voice from the van came back, "Hey Quang, you know what they call a Vietnamese with a dog? Huh? A caterer!"

Quang reached for the hand mike, but he couldn't drive and work the radio at the same time so Cully held the mike in front of his mouth and thumbed down the send button as Quang returned, "You know what they call a Vietnamese with two dogs? Huh? A rancher!" Quang looked at Cully and grinned; he was proud of his sense of humor.

The Thunderbird swung into a driveway and disappeared behind a house screened by vines and lemon trees. Quang drove to the next intersection, circled back on the other side of the divided road, and circled again, stopping under the palm trees just before the driveway. He turned off the ignition; Cully called in the address, and they waited.

During the next ten minutes she looked at her watch a dozen times. "This has got to be it," she said.

"I'm not sure," Quang said. He frowned at the radio, wanting it to speak.

"They're not thinking fast enough!" Cully said, with irritation.

"Who?" Quang said; he had been her partner for four months and always had the feeling that in Cully's opinion nobody was thinking fast enough.

"The quarterbacks!" Cully said, meaning Frazier and Morris, the two senior detectives in the van, who were there to swap positions behind the suspect car to vary the tail and make any decision to initiate a bust. "They're wondering if we've got probable cause because we followed these guys out of the airport!" She looked at the radio without punching the send button and said, "Come on, you guys! The courts say matching an established crime profile is probable cause!" Their operation that evening was mostly a shakedown cruise; somebody in the narcotics division had figured that, since Customs had known for years that smugglers display tip-offs—subtle signs of stress, predictable variations from the characteristics of other travelers—local Vice might sniff out drug infiltration routes by tailing some of the people who matched the known patterns, and the two Mexicans they were following were the first pigeons on the program. But now nobody seemed to know what to do next.

Cully looked back to Quang. He did his best to look inscrutable. She snapped open her door and got out. Quang grimaced at her, at the radio and at the backup van now parked across the street. He got out of the car too.

"If we run into anybody, you don't speak English. I'm a hooker who's trying to take you to a party, and we're lost," she said. Quang knew the lie was believable; in the shorts and tank top Cully put on to jog five miles during lunch hour, she looked like an ad for a Hollywood health club; in street clothes she could pass as a thousand-dollar-a-day prostitute.

They strolled down the driveway, past the layers of vegetation sheltering the house. The front rooms were dark. So were those along the side, where the drive curved.

Around the back, among the deepening night shadows, the Thunderbird was parked on the sandy dirt. Next to it was a Corvette. Light glowed from the windows of the house's kitchen. Cully and Quang glanced into both cars, and crept toward the house. They raised their heads and peered in a window.

Around the kitchen table were four men—the two young Mexicans they had followed from the airport, and two young blacks. The Mexicans wore silk coats with pushed-up sleeves, the blacks wore letterman jackets and T-shirts. On the table were eight plastic-wrapped packages and two foot-tall blocks of currency. The blacks had Uzis visible in shoulder holsters. The Mexicans stood with their feet spread, alert and ready to draw; they too had weapons.

Cully and Quang ducked simultaneously; their eyes met. She jabbed a finger the way they came. Quang took a step and turned back when he realized she was not going to follow. "We need a SWAT team!" he whispered.

"We don't have time for that!" she whispered back hotly. The prime elements of a bust are surprise and overwhelming force; or as Ragg would've put it, "Catch 'em with their britches down, with so much firepower the sumbitches wouldn't dare fight." But men exchanging drugs and big money are raw as rattlesnakes, and just as hard to surprise; Cully and Quang had stumbled into position by blind luck. She saw the opportunity—and the danger. "You gotta move the car into the driveway and wave the van up behind you!" Cully whispered. "As soon as they come at you, hit lights and sirens, and they'll think we've got a whole squad! If they do open up with those Uzis, somebody's got to be behind them!"

The male pride in Quang wanted to argue that he should be the one to anchor the ambush in case of a shootout, but unfortunately he shot as well as he drove. He nodded once and scurried back toward the car. Cully reached below her left arm and pulled out the 9-millimeter automatic. She raised her head again and looked in the window.

There was nobody around the table, and it was empty.

Just as she ducked again, pressing her back to the wall, the kitchen light went off. She spun to her left and found herself trapped by an eight-foot fence. The back door to the house opened. The four men, exuberant and jumpy, pumped with the adrenaline of a drug deal, trotted down the steps and to their cars. They did not turn toward Cully, but she understood that in five seconds she would be standing in their headlights, facing their guns.

"Stop!" she yelled, and leveled her pistol, holding open her police shield in her free left hand. The four of them, caught in the open space between the house and the cars, gawked for what seemed to Cully a long time; so long, in fact, she thought they would surrender. But for the drug traders that possibility did not exist; as soon as their brains registered the sight of a single woman in front of them, they reached into their coats. The black closest to the house jerked the trigger of his Uzi before he had the weapon fully out of his shoulder holster, and the gun, burping six rounds per second, ripped a chunk from the rib cage of his partner and put another bullet precisely through the ear canal of one of the Mexicans, as if the slug knew the easy route through his head. As the barrel swung toward Cully, she dropped her badge and fired twice.

The tall black gunman stopped shooting and stared at her. The second Mexican, teeth clenched, with a briefcase in one hand, raised a flashing pistol in the other. She felt the air alive around her head, heard the stream of rounds chewing up the fence behind her. She gripped her pistol in a death choke, and kept it pointed at the Mexican's abdomen as the automatic cranked off rounds. His body whirled and twitched, rolling along the side of the Thunderbird until he slithered off the trunk.

She swung back onto the second black, who still faced her. Her pistol would not fire and she realized it was empty. He seemed to smile.

Cully snatched at her dangling purse, trying to dig out her extra clip of ammunition, when the man looming in front of her melted where he stood and slowly put his mouth to the dirt.

CHAPTER THREE

Lake Hollywood. Fog mingling on the water surface like smoke from the cannons of phantom armies. Mountains on three sides, the Los Angeles basin far below. A May Saturday, abruptly ending; darkness seeping up from the earth. A chain link fence around the lake, joggers huffing on the damp trail.

On the lake point, a dam, and over that, a bridge where lovers talk. A couple there now. The city view dull in the lateness of afternoon, they turn toward the water, as lovers always do. In the water, a pattern. A swirl of substance—hair. A shoulder. A hand.

A corpse.

Doubting Thomas Ridge watched as the forensics man gripped a bush with one hand and stretched out over the water with the other to snag the end of his catchpole on the dead girl's shirt. He pulled her smoothly to more waiting hands, and as they lifted her, water poured from her mouth and nose. They placed her on the stretcher. The coroner laid the bulb of his stethoscope on her chest, as likely as a lump of marble to hold a beating heart.

Ridge walked over and looked first at the face. He would guess she had been in her mid-twenties, and that maybe she had been pretty. Her mouth was open, her eyes shut tight. Water from her hair collected in her eye sockets and coursed like tears down her cheeks.

The inside surfaces of both her forearms were scraped. Ridge lifted the torn shirt from her belly and saw other scratches, white from the water. He climbed back up the bank, to where a forensics photographer was wrestling his way through the hole they had cut in the chain link fence surrounding the entire perimeter of the lake. As Ridge waited he looked up at the barbed wire crowning the fence.

18

After the photographer cleared the hole, Ridge squeezed through and found Connelly, his lieutenant, standing with a man from Water & Power who was saying, "You cut the fence you *fix* the fence, right? Okay? Right?"

"Don't get mad at us," Connelly said, "*we* didn't put the flavor in your drinking water."

As the Water & Power man stalked away Connelly turned to Ridge. "Suicide," Ridge said.

Ridge had been there seven minutes. Connelly had seen his detective's abilities before; but still he looked doubtfully at Ridge and said, "You sure?"

Ridge turned. He was tall and lanky, and his movements seemed slower than they were. But his muscles were strung like piano wire, and Connelly, who had once boxed him in the Police Olympics, knew that when Ridge hit you your head played high C. Ridge nodded toward the bridge. "She did it last night. She hasn't been dead long enough for her body to blow up with gas, and she would have been seen and stopped in the daytime. If she'd had her choice she would have gone in at the bridge, but it's too open, even at night, and there might have been people there, like the two that found her. No," he went on, to himself, as if Connelly wasn't there, "she walked around, probably this way, where the trees are thicker."

Ridge wandered off in the direction he had indicated, and Connelly followed uninvited. A hundred yards around the jogging circle he found what he was looking for: a smooth slope leading easily into the water. The fence there was sheltered but accessible. Ridge stood with his face to the chain link. As Connelly stopped beside him, Ridge pointed down.

Among the pine needles on the other side of the fence lay a button fresh and unweathered, the same red color as the flannel shirt on the dead girl's body.

"Jesus," Connelly said, in admiration. "Doubting Thomas strikes again."

Ridge looked at Connelly, and for the first time the detective's face showed surprise. He seemed bewildered that the lieutenant could believe Ridge had just understood the whole story.

CHAPTER FOUR

Cully McCullers had never killed anything larger than a roach.

She sat in the office of the Chief of Detectives, Valley Division, and shivered. Dugan, her supervisor, had closed the door to shield her from the eyes of her fellow cops, but still she felt they could see her, and she would not allow herself to cry—not in front of the men who had called her Bull Barrel.

The paperwork and debriefing carried them through a change of shift, so that two full units of cops got to pass around word of the shoot-out. By the time she scrawled her name at the bottom of the report, willing her fingers not to quiver, she was a legend.

Dugan, who had leered at her longer and more often than even the most lecherous of the uniformed patrolmen, and whom she had always suspected of being the one who had put the cutouts of a Midwestern policewoman who had posed nude for *Playboy* into her mail slot, now looked dead into her eyes and said, "You want somebody to drive you home?"

Since the gunfire, Cully's response time had doubled, as if behind every question there was another question she had to understand before she could answer the first one. Now she glanced at Quang, and Dugan said, "No, not Quang! I mean, I want you to *get* there!"

"No, no, I'm fine," Cully said. "I'm fine."

She drove, on her own, from the Valley station, south on Van Nuys Boulevard, a street renowned among teenagers as a spot for cruising. On Saturday nights the black-and-white traffic units kept a tight patrol, and when two of the on-duty uniformed cops spotted a weaving red BMW, with its driver vomiting on her leather upholstery, they hit their sirens and pulled her over.

The patrolman came to her window, shined the light into her face, and said, "Holy shit." He went back to his partner, mumbled for a minute, then walked back and ushered her into the back seat. He climbed in behind the wheel and asked for her home address. She did not remember giving it to him, but she must have; with his partner following in the patrol unit, he drove her to her apartment, where he escorted her to her door and waited till she had the lock open, then touched a finger to the brim of his cap, and went back to his partner without even trying to introduce himself; cops can be a lecherous bunch, but they also take care of their own.

Cully locked the door behind him and threw all the bolts. She had left her new automatic at the station because a cop involved in a shooting is supposed to drop off any discharged pistol at the Armory for test firing to verify its operating status for the impending Shooting Board hearing and to insure its safe operation in the future. So now Cully had to feel the top shelf of the hall closet for her father's old .38. Tonight, of all nights, she needed the comfort of a weapon.

Her fingers found the familiar shape of the pistol, enclosed in blue felt, and she pulled it down and unwrapped it. Packed with it was a photograph of her father. The picture was framed but she kept it hidden, for no other eyes but her own. She looked at it now, Big Jim McCullers in his prime.

Her height, her athleticism, the high-cheeked, narrow chin structure of her face, had all come from him. And her smile, with the upper lip arched as if to drop a sassy comment. The way he was smiling in the picture, wearing his dress uniform, with his cop buddies no doubt behind the camera and baiting his blarney. Cully's blond coloring had come from her mother; her father had Irish skin but black wavy hair. Cully and her father made an odd pair sitting together on the couch, her father's feet propped on the coffee table and hers stretched out to copy him, as they shared a bowl of popcorn and watched football on television, and he explained the plays and the strategies, with the same zest he would have shown her had she been a son.

He had taught her to shoot.

Today, with the skill he gave her, she had killed.

She rewrapped the picture and returned it to the closet

shelf. The pistol she took with her into the bedroom, where she slipped off her shoes and drifted into the bathroom. She laid the pistol on the white tile beside the sink and undressed slowly. She moved to the toilet and paused; something was floating in the water. It was a condom.

She flushed the toilet, and watched the limp rubber tube spin in the weak swirl. Eleven months ago she had left the man she had married straight out of college. Five months ago their divorce had become final. Before she married, she had been picky about men. Now, newly divorced, she was still picky about whom she dated, but was no longer picky about what she did with them.

The night before, she had slept with a man she did not love.

As she watched the flush bottom out, and the condom float up again, the self-esteem drained from her core in the same way, and coughed back up a hard little knot of revulsion. She tugged at the toilet handle again, before the tank had time to refill, and the second flush was even weaker than the first. She jerked at the handle again, in a sudden rage at bad plumbing, condoms, careless men, and loveless women.

She grabbed the old .38 and aimed it into the toilet. Big Jim McCullers would have done something crazy like that, killing a condom. But at the moment she was ready to pull the trigger, Scarlet McCullers the policewoman stepped out of Cully's body and saw herself.

She put the pistol down, climbed into the shower, and let the hot water pound her. When she had dried herself she spun two yards of toilet paper onto the unkillable condom, and a new flush finally carried it away.

She sighed, and felt better. She walked back into the bedroom.

Cully stood naked at the foot of her bed, and it was then that she began to cry. Sobs shook her, but she would not let herself make noise; she stretched out upon the sheets and burned the pillow with silent tears.

She drifted that night like a log on a dark sea, her consciousness scraping sawtooth rocks, ripped back and forth between raw alertness and dull oblivion.

CHAPTER FIVE

It was not a night for sweet dreams.

Thomas Ridge sat alone in the leather recliner he had bought himself five birthdays ago. When his wife left him, it was the one piece of furniture she had let him keep, and now the chair was something that could isolate him from other living things. In the apartment below, someone watched cop show reruns, full of gun blasts. The new neighbor in the unit next door, who had introduced herself to Ridge as "an actress/singer," was practicing the theme from *Evita*. Ridge felt encased in a stucco cell, suspended between artificial bangs and "Don't cry for me, Argentina."

He thought of a joke he had once heard . . . . Heaven and Hell aren't actually above and below, but lie side by side, and God and Satan talk shop across the fence that separates them. One day God is leaning on a rail and the whole fence almost falls over; so he says, "We gotta get this fixed." Satan agrees; and God says, "I paid for the repairs last time, you take care of it this time." But Satan says, "Hell no." God insists, "It's your turn." But still Satan says he won't pay. Finally God says, "Listen, either you fulfill your responsibilities or I'm gonna sue you."

Then Satan smiles and says, "Now where are *you* gonna find a lawyer?"

The idea of paradise and torment on the same plane appealed to Ridge. It made sense. Such opposites are so close. Every lie has a truth behind it, and every truth is not far from a lie.

A girl had killed herself. She had climbed eight feet of chain link and torn her abdomen on barbed wire to get to oblivion. Or did she think it would be oblivion?

A cross had hung around her neck.

It was a suicide. Even Doubting Thomas Ridge did not doubt that. And Ridge did not feel alone simply because no one else cared. All the cops at the Hollywood station wanted to talk about was some female detective who had

23

killed four drug dealers that afternoon, and no one else
found the slightest bit of interest in Jane Doe, victim of
self. Ridge did not blame them; they saw too many others
like her every day.

What did make Ridge lonely was that no one seemed to
ask the same questions he did.

Ridge wondered if this dead floater had knelt to pray
before she walked into the water.

Ridge leaned back his head and closed his eyes.

He heard, over and over: *Don't cry for me . . . Don't
cry for me . . . Don't cry for me . . . .*

CHAPTER SIX

At the moment that Scarlet McCullers lay sweating, and
Tom Ridge sat frowning, Guillermo Montoya paced in a
concrete room beneath a pile of rubble in Mexico City,
waiting for news of the emissaries he had sent that morning
to Los Angeles.

And while he paced, his *capitáns* stood in the underground corridor that connected the office building Montoya
owned with the secret room beneath the rubble of an earth-
quake-shattered building and they held a whispered conversation. The four *capitáns*—the men who arranged the
pickups, payoffs, and murders necessary in a smuggling
enterprise as extensive and successful as this one—repeated
over and over the sparse details of what they had just
learned: that Alejandro Montoya and the bodyguard who
had accompanied him were dead. Behind all the repetition
was a single question: Who would tell Guillermo?

Arturo, one of the men in the conversation, wore an eye
patch that was a reminder of how little Guillermo liked bad
news. Arturo once had employed an airline stewardess who
had delivered a satchel of Mexican brown heroin to Los
Angeles but had not returned with the half million dollars
in payment, and Guillermo had plunged his thumb into
Arturo's eye socket when Arturo told him. Arturo had barely
moved, he barely cried out as Guillermo tore out his eye,

for the loss of his eye was nothing against what Guillermo would take if he decided to end their association. His courage had restored Guillermo's respect and hunting the woman down, all the way to the French Riviera, and cutting out her heart in her suite at the Hotel de Paris had restored his favor. But the fact that Arturo was once more a trusted *capitán* did not make him or any of the others anxious to volunteer now to tell Guillermo that his brother had been killed in Los Angeles.

It was Ricardo Flores, who had grown up with Guillermo in the mountain village near the southern border and who had known Guillermo longest of all, who finally agreed to carry the news into the concrete room.

Ricardo walked slowly down the corridor, tapped at the metal door, and entered without a word.

Guillermo stopped pacing and looked at him. Ricardo's brown face had changed; it was now the dusty pale color of a paper sack. Ricardo approached, gripped Guillermo by the shoulders, and leaned to whisper, though he could have fired a pistol and no one else would have heard. He said simply, "Alejandro is dead."

Guillermo said nothing.

He could not allow himself to react. He could not let his most loyal friend see him show anything less than courage.

Ricardo watched him, and grew uncomfortable with the silence. "The blacks did not betray him. They died too. The police do not seem to know who they killed, or why the meeting was being held. It seems they were simply lucky and picked them out at the airport."

Guillermo held back his rage. Rage was to be directed against men, not luck.

"If I lose my own brother," he said, "how will the blacks believe I can deliver a ton of cocaine?"

Ricardo had no answer. He looked blankly at Guillermo's eyes, steady in their anger.

"Call Los Malos," Guillermo said. "Tell them that now is the time for them to bring me Victoria Lopez."

THE SECOND DAY

CHAPTER SEVEN

Cully gasped, confused by the contradictory sense of awaking and the impression that she had not slept. But she must have; here was a bright hazy morning. *Habit. Routine*, she told herself, and sat up on the edge of the bed, switching on the radio to jolt her through her morning exercise.

She showered, dried, powdered, dressed in a clean suit. She made coffee and toast but did not want it.

She didn't remember what she had done inside her car until she opened the door and the smell hit her. She fished out the floor mats, wiped the seats down with disinfectant and wet paper towels, and drove to work with the windows down.

"Bull Barrel!" Ragg Wilson hollered when she walked into the detectives' section, and everybody applauded.

"Knock that shit off!" Captain Dick "Michaelangelo" Fresco yelled from his office. He was in a foul mood; two of his officers were going before a grand jury tomorrow on manslaughter charges over a shooting incident, and this latest street combat between Cully and the drug dealers ("alleged drug dealers," the newspaper said, in spite of the five pounds of uncut cocaine the department's press office displayed) had brought fresh attention to the issue of cops and their weapons. A female detective getting into a gunfight with four men and leaving all four of them dead was generating journalistic comparisons to Annie Oakley and Dodge City, and the captain didn't want the prosecutors in the courtroom tomorrow using this latest shoot-out to ask questions about the congratulations a cop receives from buddies when his bullets have dropped a felon.

So the guys on the day shift waited until Fresco's glass

door had rattled shut, and then they came over and slapped Cully on the back. Someone—she suspected it was Quang—pinched her bottom. She did not find out for sure because before she could turn around Ragg Wilson tousled her hair as if she were a towheaded schoolkid. "McCullers! Quang!" Lieutenant Dugan called. "In my office."

Lieutenant Peter Dugan was a florid Irishman. He laughed at everything, he liked everybody. The promiscuity of his affection for the people in his command bought him contempt in return, but the truth was that he was a fair and able organizer, which is all a police lieutenant need be. Dugan made it easy for his subordinates to laugh at him by clinging to the notion that he was known as Pistol Pete. The truth was more poetic; he was known for the bumpy, capillary-crossed expanse of his proboscis. They called him Rose Nose.

"Hey, kid! How you feel!" Rose Nose bubbled as they walked in. "Hey, listen, I talked to the chief, he says it's righteous, the policy hearing's nothin'! Routine! Rubber stamp!"

"So what do I do now?" Cully asked. Officers involved in shooting incidents, especially fatal ones, were always shifted to indoor duty while their nerves drained voltage.

"It's slow today," Rose Nose said. "The only crime all morning was when Quang drove to work."

Quang laughed at everything Rose Nose said, except for the jokes about his driving. "I'm Vietnamese," Quang said. When the lieutenant didn't connect the point Quang said, "Not Chinese. *They're* the ones who can't drive."

"Gee, Quang," Rose Nose said, "I guess the bumpers on the unmarked cars we give you are just supposed to look like rubber pretzels."

"Normal wear and tear," Quang said in hurtful defense.

"Maybe your driving teacher was Chinese," Rose Nose said. He turned back to Cully. "You goin' to the grand opening?"

Cully had not remembered until now that official autopsies, with homicide detectives in attendance, were required for all corpses the police pick up, even the ones they've made themselves.

"Come on, kid," Rose Nose said. "When you shoot somethin', sometimes it's good to see it dead."

Cully, Quang, and Dugan headed downtown to the morgue, Dugan driving, Quang sullen in the back seat. They parked in the lot of the Central Headquarters building. "Wonder if Woger is here today?" Rose Nose said.

The entrance to the autopsy section of the City Morgue was a double airlock, and even before they were through the second pair of doors Cully smelled the faint fragrance of dead organs.

The four men she had shot the day before were laid out belly up, on four identical, guttered tables. Two gowned forensics workers stood at the head end of the bodies and talked and laughed with the two detectives who had driven the backup van: "Micro" Morris and Bert "Trigger" Frazier.

Morris was a little guy. Frazier was a legend.

Every cop has some kind of nickname; Frazier's used to be Pig. The other cops called him that because, they said, Asshole could'a meant too many other guys. Now they called him Trigger. Frazier liked the name and when he was with a woman he claimed he had won it in macho action involving firearms. But the name was actually derived from Frazier's lack of a trigger finger.

Every police division in Los Angeles had its own version of how Frazier had lost the last three inches of his right index finger, but all the accounts agreed that the incident had taken place at the Dorothy Chandler Pavilion, L.A.'s temple of high culture and home of the ballet and the theater. Frazier was having an affair with a woman he had met when answering a burglary call in Hancock Park. Frazier had taken the call—which turned out to be a malfunctioning alarm system—on a dull night, and found a bored, bosomy redhead still a few years shy of fifty. A woman who had just realized that her corporate lawyer husband was getting more from his pretty young physical therapist than a neck rub twice a week. Frazier, after an impromptu dance in the sheets with the redhead, surprised her by asking her out on a date, and she surprised him by accepting. Being out of his league with a rich broad, Frazier decided to take her to the theater, to prove he was cultured.

Frazier, one of those stocky, slew-footed guys who swings his arms sideways across his belly as he walks, was in a touchy mood on the night of their date; the tickets had set him back sixty-five per, and the tux had been another seventy, and at the restaurant, where she had shown up for their rendezvous driving a sixty-thousand-dollar Mercedes, the juggy redhead had ordered lobster thermador *and* an appetizer *and* desert—not to mention two bottles of French wine. Frazier told himself that for all this money he'd be getting one hellacious blow job after the play.

The opening act was full of long speeches and the redhead kept falling into a boozy sleep, and during intermission she took him out to the lobby and made him buy her two more martinis and then said she was starting to have a headache. Frazier began to get the idea that he might be out a few hundred bucks and still not get the blow job, and he was a little testy when they went back to their seats for the second act.

They sat down, and Frazier looked at the bushy head of the guy in front of him, and in his most polite, cultured, theatergoing way, Frazier said, "Hey you! Jew-boy! You think you could part that Brillo fuzz a yours, so I can see the fuckin' play here?"

So the guy in front turned around, and he had a mustache like a Tartar and eyebrows to match, and the eyebrows were dancing up and down and he said, "Excuse me?"

"I said, mow the lawn, there, Bozo!" Frazier bellowed, and grinned at the giddy woman beside him. He looked back at the guy, who was flushing red, and added, with all the arrogant untouchability of a cop, "Oh, that's right, you people don't do manual labor! Har har!"

The guy in front stood up. "What did you say?"

Frazier couldn't take that kind of a challenge, especially in front of a woman, even if she was too drunk to care. He bounced to his feet. "You better sit down, pal," he said, and jabbed his finger at the bushy guy's nose.

The guy bit off Frazier's finger at the second joint.

The cannibal was never caught. He got away through the crowd, and as it turned out he had paid cash for his theater seats, he was therefore untraceable.

Later versions of the story had Frazier pulling his service revolver and trying to shoot the guy but being unable to pull the trigger; other guys swore Frazier had chased the man, yelling "Thief!" What actually happened was that Frazier, grabbing his blood-spurting hand, lay down in the aisle, and screamed "Mother-fucker!" over and over again.

Publicly admitting that Frazier was an off-duty detective of the LAPD didn't especially appeal to the Office of the Chief of Police, so they talked Frazier out of listing the apprehension of the Finger Cannibal as the top priority of his division's homicide team.

Of course the jokes were relentless:

"It's a good thing the guy was never caught! The trial would'a just been a lotta finger-pointin'!"

Or: "Hey Frazier! You give the guy a knuckle sandwich?"

Or: "Hey bro, how you doin', gimme four-and-a-half!"

One detective even had the gall to suggest that the suspect had already been executed: "The poor bastard's croaked! Death by lethal ingestion!"

Frazier just simmered in his own fury. He staked out the airport on his off hours for a week, figuring the guy looked like a New Yorker and would fly back sooner or later, but the stakeout was futile. And Frazier seemed to have put the incident behind him, except that he would sometimes burst out at odd moments, "There ain't no fuckin' justice!"

Now Frazier hailed Dugan with a big call of "Rosie!" Cully he greeted simply by bobbing his thin eyebrows up and down and touching the end of his nose with the tip of his tongue.

Roger, the coroner, entered the room and smiled at Dugan. "Mornin', Woger," Dugan called.

"Wosie!" the coroner said. "Hey, gweat! You can take the picture!" He tossed Dugan the Polaroid camera they used for taking file shots of the victim. The coroner, one of his assistants, Micro and Trigger fanned out between the autopsy tables so that they made a chain of man-corpse-man-corpse-man-corpse-man-corpse, and then each man reached out and grabbed the hands of the cadavers on either side of him. "Weady, Wosie?" Roger said.

"Weady, Woger!" Dugan said.

"Thwee, two, one . . . Hey!" The coroners and the cops lifted the limp arms in a chain. Quang, seeing the joke, grabbed the dangling fingers of the dead dope dealer on the table nearest him and reached out with the other hand to Cully as Roger said, "All wight!! Hands Acwoss L.A.!"

Cully, stunned, did not resist as Quang took her hand and Dugan snapped the picture.

"*We ah the Wuld! . . .*" Roger sang.

Morris cocked his head back and lolled it in a Stevie Wonder impersonation; Frazier graveled his voice for a little Bruce Springsteen.

Cully noticed for the first time the man standing over a fifth cadaver on a dissecting table at the far end of the room, his back to everyone else. She knew before he turned around who it was: the great Tom Ridge. Dugan had once pointed him out to Cully at one of the detective seminars the department organized every few months. "That's him," Dugan had said. "Doubting Thomas. The best there is. If it beats Ridge, it's unsolvable."

"If he's so good," Cully had asked, "why haven't I ever heard of him?"

Dugan had grinned at her. "You planning on bein' top gun yourself, are you?" He did not wait for Cully to deny her ambition; Dugan would not respect a detective who lacked an ego. But the topic of Tom Ridge kept him from joking; in a sober voice he said, "Ridge doesn't like publicity. Anything that's got to do with media—stranglers, mass murderers, the headline stuff—he hands off to somebody else."

"What do you mean, he hands off? Doesn't he do what the Detective Supervisor tells him?"

"Ridge is a D-Three, same as me. He was the supervisor himself in the Hollywood Division. But a while back his wife left him and he decided he didn't want to supervise anymore. So they made him a floating homicide specialist. He chooses his own assignments, and he likes the cases nobody else wants, the ones nobody else understands."

"Why do they call him Doubting Thomas?" Cully had asked, and Dugan shrugged.

"You know how cops are," he said. "I mean hey, do you deserve to be called Bull Barrel?"

And now Bull Barrel McCullers, who had just served four men up to the coroner's blades, felt herself drawn to the back of this man who stood so quietly at the rear slab of this stainless steel room and separated himself from the garish commotion around him. He was saying nothing, just staring down at the body before him, and when the coroner's assistant asked him a question, Ridge turned slowly and stared at the C.A. for a moment.

Cully had wandered close enough to hear the C.A.'s question: "Whatta you wanna call her?" The morgue ran a surplus of John and Jane Does; corpses were assigned numbers, of course, but detectives found it easier to keep up with the unknowns when they christened them with names. Most preferred to use the names of ex-wives; in her time in the department, Cully had heard of a Cheryl, a Blue Sue, and two Glenda's.

Ridge looked back to the corpse for a long moment, and then to the coroner's assistant. "Call her the Lady of the Lake," Doubting Thomas said.

He turned around. For the first time he seemed aware of the frivolity at the front of the room, the song having deteriorated into raucous laughter. His features seemed unsure how to arrange themselves. Anguish, pity, and a kind of isolation—all and none of these were on his face. Cully had never seen so much happening in anyone's eyes, but she did not have much of a chance to take it all in. Ridge walked slowly from the room, passing each body and detective in turn, Cully last of all. His eyes, a pale blue, held on her for a moment, and then he was gone.

Cully moved to the slab he had just left, and looked down at the body Ridge had been standing over. It was a woman, milky pale. She seemed to be floating, suspended in white water.

CHAPTER EIGHT

Cully wobbled. For a moment, she may have fainted; she lost her balance and pitched forward, groping at the silver table to steady herself. Her vision collapsed into a dark tunnel, but she was still on her feet, and was able to suck air to clear her head. Her left hand clutched something cold and slick, that reminded her of nothing so much as the head of a dolphin she had once touched at a petting tank at Sea World. Her vision cleared and she saw she was holding the shoulder of the dead woman.

Bile pitched into her throat, and she jerked back and staggered again. The four bodies on the front slabs were not people to her. The jokes, the song, the camaraderie of her fellow living officers, had all done what they were meant to do: strip those corpses of any human meaning. But this cold gray thing with the matted auburn hair and the dolphin-slick skin, naked and powerless, had once been a woman, and the horror of that threw a chill into Cully's chest.

Cully walked back up to Dugan. "I've gotta get out of here," she said.

He was laughing, looking at the Polaroids they had taken of Hands Across L.A. But when he saw the bloodlessness of her face he stopped smiling. "Hey, you wanna sit down a minute?"

"No. I want to leave." She would have walked out right then, but her knees were rubbery and she did not want the other detectives to see her stagger.

Roger the Coroner had seen this look on the faces of many young cops, and he responded with characteristic sensitivity. "Come on, Bull Bawwel," he said, "it's good fah you to see the autopsies. By the time we hahwo out the chest cavities and wap their insides in a pwastic bag, they won't be bodies, they'll be canoes."

Dugan, seeing the anger flare into Cully's eyes, took her arm and said, "Me and Trigger and Micro can sign the paperwork, and I can catch a ride back with them. You and Quang wanna just roll on back to the station?"

As she walked out, she heard Frazier and Morris's hard bright laughter.

CHAPTER NINE

"Is it being in the United States that makes you so nervous?" Guillermo Montoya said, "or just all the chocolates?"

Ricardo Flores, driving the new white rental car through Watts, felt the sweat roll down his cheek, even though he had the air conditioner blowing so loudly that it was hard to hear Guillermo speak. Ricardo's eyes darted, checking the rearview mirror, the road, the sideview mirror, the road, the rearview mirror again. "I don't know," he said. "I guess it's what happened to Alejandro."

"Forget that," Guillermo snapped. He wanted to show Ricardo how professional he could be, ignoring the death of his own brother. He had even insisted they take the same flight from Mexico to Los Angeles, to remove any superstition. Guillermo Montoya did not believe in luck. Something had gone wrong and he was going to find out what that something was. He had de la Puente checking through official channels, but in the meantime he had business to conduct, and if trouble came to him, the same way it had come to Alejandro, then he would be ready.

He had ordered Ricardo to drive around on the freeways for an hour before heading for their destination, to make sure the police did not have another accident and follow them from the airport. "Just don't wreck the car," Guillermo joked. "If we get into a fight with one of these monkeys over a dented fender, all we can do is bite him."

Ricardo tried to smile. Guillermo had insisted they travel with no bodyguards except each other, and carry no weapons at all, though Guillermo owned a half dozen of the new plastic pistols that could be carried through any airport security system in the world and never set off the metal detectors. One of Guillermo's suspicions about Alejandro's death was that the security officers in Mexico City whom his brother had bribed to let them bring their weapons aboard the flight had leaked word of their travel to the police in Los Angeles, so this time they carried neither the metal nor the plastic pistols. Guillermo wanted to take no chances. No chances—but here they were in Watts.

"This is it," Ricardo said, as he turned onto the street they had been looking for. He drove slowly but steadily, down through the middle of the block, as Guillermo straightened in his seat. It relieved Ricardo to see that Guillermo was nervous too.

"Drive past, then turn around and park on the opposite side of the street," Guillermo ordered, and Ricardo did as he was told.

They stopped across from a brown stucco house with all the windows boarded up. "It looks deserted," Ricardo said uncertainly. "I thought all the rock houses would be busy this time of day."

"You don't get it, Ricardo," Guillermo said with a smile; he enjoyed lecturing Ricardo as if his *capitán* were stupid. "They are clever. They do not sell from this location; a parade of buyers can only draw attention. Here they gather and distribute, and even that they do wisely. A man from a selling house meets a man from this supply house at a third location. The monkeys do not like jail, they don't like . . . to be in cages."

Guillermo always tried to make jokes when he was nervous. Ricardo knew that about him, but never pointed it out.

As Ricardo stopped the engine, Guillermo stepped from the car, and moved around to the street side so that anyone watching from the house across the street could get a good look at him. He took off his jacket and tossed it onto the hood of the car. He wore a tight polo shirt, and close-fitting slacks; he wanted it clear to any lookout that he carried no weapons. Ricardo performed the same routine, then threw both jackets into the front seat of the car, locked it, and followed Guillermo across the street to the door of the silent house.

There were no windows and no bell, but above the door

was the lens of a security camera, and Guillermo stared into it, and waited. He waited for a full half minute, just staring; finally the door buzzed and opened. Guillermo stepped through with Ricardo behind him.

They were barely inside when many black hands were on them, shoving them both against the front wall. "Who you?" said a muscular man in a T-shirt and a hat like Al Capone's.

Guillermo did not even wince from the barrel of the Uzi poking into the flesh at the side of his throat. "I am a man with three names."

"Yeah?" said the man with the muscles. "What they?"

Guillermo told him three names. Two were runners from Chocolate's old organization; the third was a name belonging to nobody; but unless he told the blacks that name, to show he knew their code, they would kill him.

All the men in the room—there must have been eight of them—relaxed immediately. Their leader grinned. "Man, we been lookin' for you. You got the stuff?"

"I don't got no stuff," Guillermo said, using the English he had learned selling drugs to the G.I.s off the American bases in Panama. "All I got's the names—and some information."

The men in the room were tense again. The air in the room was stale, and littered with cans and empty boxes from fried chicken places; for days they had been waiting for a shipment of drugs from Mexico, doing nothing but killing time, and they were in no mood to be played with. But Guillermo stayed cool. "That right?" the leader said, his voice flat and deadly.

"We got a problem in Mexico," Guillermo said. "A big change. The man who has been supplying you, he is dead now. A new man takes his place."

"What new man?"

"I don't know him," Guillermo said. "I only know a man who knows him. But they send me here to tell you this: You need supply, he can supply. With the same men who supplied you before. They will work for the new man now."

The men in the room just stared at him.

"You need supply. You have none now. The supply will

be as before—except better. Everything else will be as before."

"When do you deliver?" the muscular man said. He was a pragmatist.

"In two days."

"Two days? We hungry now."

"And in two days your customers will be even hungrier. And you can get a better price. And . . ." Guillermo paused, ". . . you might need one. Because this supplier, he is more expensive."

The leader flared. "Can't be! We can't pay no higher price! The Mexicans, they undercut us if we do." He meant Chicanos, but to the blacks they were Mexican if they spoke Spanish, no matter what side of the border they were born on.

Montoya understood that lack of distinction, and accepted it. "The man I work for, he says the Mexicans won't undercut you. This man, he says you trade with him, and the Mexicans won't have a supply. You can have all the business—if you're strong enough to take it."

"You gonna sell to us and not to them?"

"My employer, he thinks this is the best way to make the most money. He has sent me all this way to talk to you because he is taking a big chance, betraying his own. But you are the heart of the distribution, and he is the heart of the supply. So we must make this deal heart to heart."

Montoya smiled. The men in the room looked at each other. They suddenly understood who this man was. When they looked back at Guillermo, it was clear they had agreed to make his deal.

"Things tougher now," the black leader said.

"Yes," Guillermo said. And then he noticed something on the wall. It was a collage of photos, taped against the bare paint. Some were Polaroid pictures, others shots from the newspaper. Guillermo moved over; Ricardo noticed a bit of a strut in his walk. "These your neighbors?" Guillermo said, studying the shots like a connoisseur. He knew they were all cops.

"We keep a lookout," the leader said.

Guillermo noticed one picture in particular. It was cut

from the *Los Angeles Times*, and was the official Police Academy class photograph of Cully McCullers, the one the *Times* had run when Cully had shot the dealers. "So," Guillermo said softly, "this is the *puta* that killed my brother."

And he took a good long look at Cully's face.

CHAPTER TEN

Thomas Ridge did not like to drive in Los Angeles. Once a case started for him—not externally, when he first walked around a murder scene, but internally, when the facts of what he had observed there began to bump together in his mind—his thoughts began to drift; it was as if his brain would gradually turn molten, flowing where it needed to, and the more he was in that state the more distant he was to everything else around him. Driving on crowded streets and especially on freeways became a chore, a dangerous distraction, and Ridge did not like distractions.

He had to force himself to pay attention to the traffic as he wound his way onto the Hollywood Freeway and headed south. He drove the short distance toward the Santa Ana Freeway and missed the Harbor Freeway exit, so that he had to double back, and then got lost in the middle of downtown. But at last he found the parking lot of the Church of the Blessed Sacrament.

The lot was almost empty, but the space marked "Monsignor" contained a black Lincoln, so Ridge parked the department's Dodge and got out. He stared for a moment at the awesome mass of the Spanish spire. Then he headed into the arched alcoves and moved along the pebbled concrete walkways polished smooth by feet and time. He followed the small engraved markers set into the stone walls, pointing toward the church offices.

Ridge found a portly pale woman at a reception table, and said, "I'd like to see the monsignor, please."

The woman studied him. "Do you have an appointment?" Her calendar was open on her desk, and was clear for the afternoon.

"I won't interrupt his golf game," Ridge said casually.

He had guessed correctly; the receptionist's attitude went from defensive to lamenting. "This is his only day off," she said.

Ridge showed her his shield. "I understand about working long hours. I'll only need him a minute."

She hurried through a doorway and reappeared thirty seconds later, smiling. She ushered Ridge into a paneled room and invited him to take a seat. But before Ridge could pick a place on the burgundy furniture, in stepped the monsignor. He was a fiftyish, fit-looking man with smooth black hair, black horn-rimmed glasses, and a broad smile. The cuffs of plaid golf pants showed below the hem of his black robe. He gave Ridge a firm handshake. "Good morning," the priest said. "Can I help you with something?"

Ridge was deferential. "Father—it's proper to call you 'Father,' isn't it?"

The monsignor laughed. "I've been called worse!" He continued to grin as if this were a great joke. But his eyes betrayed him; like many powerful men, he was offended that Ridge was unfamiliar with his office and its protocol.

"Father, I'm here to find someone. That is, I'm trying to find a name. An identity. To go with a corpse. I think she may have been Catholic."

"We'll be happy to help if we can," said the monsignor. "Why do you think she was Catholic?"

Ridge tried to place his accent. Boston, he thought. "Because she should have said, 'Now I lay me down to sleep' And she didn't." Ridge let the comment sit for awhile. "She also wore a cross. The Catholic kind."

Two minutes before, the monsignor had been anxious to leave, ready to get to his golf game. But Ridge's remarks were just a tiny bit annoying, making him want to mix it up. "What, exactly," said the monsignor, pausing a half second, "is a Catholic cross?"

"You know," Ridge said, "the kind with the crucified Jesus. Protestants always leave Him off. Symbol of the Resurrection instead of the Crucifixion. This cross was ornate."

The monsignor stared at Ridge, really looked at him for the first time. "What is it I can help you with?"

Ridge opened the envelope in his lap and reached a hand inside. And now the monsignor saw Ridge's coldness to be a only a curtain, that parted suddenly. The detective's pale eyes brightened with sadness, and when he pulled out the stack of pictures—a run of two hundred from the police photo lab—he looked as if he wanted to apologize. Not to the priest, but to the woman whose corpse was in the picture.

"This is a picture of the victim," Ridge said.

"Victim?" the monsignor asked. "Didn't you say she was a suicide?"

"Suicide is murder, isn't it? In the eyes of God?"

The monsignor's eyes darted up to Ridge's face. "You're not a Catholic yourself, are you, detective." It was not a question, just an observation delivered with a smirk, just enough to tell the cop to show some respect.

Ridge shook his head. "I sorta went to 'em all. When I went." He handed the monsignor a stack of pictures of the Lady of the Lake. "Now I need some help. I figure you must make regular mailings to all the priests in the area, so I wondered if you would distribute these and ask if anybody knows her. If there should be any extra costs, the department will bear them."

The monsignor stared down at the photograph, a full face shot of the girl on the slab, in black and white, before "Woger" the coroner dug a crater into her skull and turned her chest into a canoe. But the bloodless face, the immutable casualness of the dead girl's expression, was more horrifying than the sight of the dissected body would have been.

The monsignor did not flinch; he had seen corpses before. "We'll do what we can," he said.

"Thank you," Ridge said. "If every priest in Southern California gets a look at this picture, then I think we'll find out who she is pretty quickly."

"If she was Catholic," the monsignor said, shoving the pictures back into the envelope and tossing it onto a side table.

It was Ridge's turn to stare at the monsignor, for just a moment longer than he should have. "Well," Ridge said, smiling, but with the muscles around his eyes tight, "even if they don't know her, it won't hurt them to be reminded how ugly death can be."

"We know how ugly death can be," the monsignor said. "I'm sure we see it as much as if not more than you!"

Ridge smiled again, this time with real pleasure. "I just meant it might encourage them, Father, to see that this is the kind of pain they're trying to keep their parishioners from. Thanks again for your help."

Ridge showed himself out of the office. But once in the hallway, he did not leave the church right away. He moved down another corridor, and found the entrance to the sanctuary. Silently, he moved inside the enormous cathedral where pillars wide as a squad car held up a peaked ceiling and stained glass windows broke streams of sunlight into thousands of colored shapes upon the pews. Above the altar, a sixteen-foot Jesus hung on a gilded cross.

Ridge stood there for a long time, staring at His crucified golden agony.

THE THIRD DAY

CHAPTER ELEVEN

Cully wore a business suit, dark blue, the same color as the uniform she had worn when she got the name Bull Barrel. She wore a plain white blouse and a simple yellow scarf, and brushed her hair back from her face, so it would look softer and more feminine than when it was pulled back and braided behind her neck. And she chose dark blue shoes with a low heel; when she stood before the Shooting Policy Board, she thought she should appear as small as possible.

It was the Los Angeles Police Department that had taught her to think that way. Part of her training in the Police Academy was a course called "Court Appearances: Attitude and Dress." They had told her that no matter who was in the defendant's chair, it was the cop who was on trial. They had also told her that no matter who else doubts you, you must never doubt yourself.

When she walked into Van Nuys Division station, and moved into the unfamiliar first-floor corridor of the administrative offices, she was confident. She found a chair outside the room where the board would convene, and sat down to wait. She was fifteen minutes early. The morning paper lay in the chair next to her, and she picked up the top section to browse through the national news. In doing so she uncovered the Metro section, and there, on its front page, was her picture.

CHAPTER TWELVE

At the Lopez Produce Company, between the rail yards of Union Station and the glass towers of downtown Los Angeles, jets of water from high-pressure hoses slammed against the mashed rinds of cantaloupes, the sticky pulp of oranges, the translucent adhesive layer of crushed lettuce leaves, and tore them all from the truck beds.

Esteban Lopez, owner and proprietor, stood on the broad loading dock where twenty tractor-trailors could park at once, and watched his trucks being cleaned. It was his favorite time of day.

Twenty-seven years ago, Esteban Lopez had crossed the border and started his life in America by scraping out the stinking shells of produce trucks as the residue of their morning loads soured in the fierce California heat. And, a small and slender man, Esteban Lopez had done more than scrape. He had bought his own wire brush and his own hose, and worked like a devil to make every truck he entered clean, right to the metal.

He endured the taunts of his fellow *brazzeros* who did not wish to work so hard. When they cut his hoses, he bought more; when they tried to bully him he fought back. His employers made him a supervisor and told him to train other truck cleaners, and he did so; those who worked hard he kept on, those who did not, he fired.

He slaved that way for four years and then told his bosses he was quitting, to form the Lopez Cleaning Company. They laughed at him. Six months later their trucks were stinking and their competitors were gaining business because their loads of produce smelled fresher and drew higher prices.

Now Esteban Lopez had a fleet of trucks, two acres of refrigerated warehouses, a mansion in Encino, a son in law school, and a daughter at U.C.L.A. And at midmorning— the end of the workday for men who begin their labor two hours after midnight—he always ordered everyone in the company except the girls in accounting to get out onto the docks and help with the washing—as he did himself.

He watched the sheets of sudsy water pour from the backs of his trucks and stream toward the drains, where screens caught the solids. Other produce companies might wash directly into the sewers, but not Esteban's; one of the city's mayors had expedited his naturalization, and Lopez took patriotic duty as seriously as he took everything else. He watched with satisfaction his apprentices breaking down crates and his warehouse supervisor getting his day's exercise by pumping the wire brush.

He turned back to inspect the warehouse for the next day's work. He passed through the double airlock of hanging plastic curtain into the dim cold cavern of the main warehouse, and stopped abruptly. Two men stood there, waiting for him.

"Remember me?" Guillermo Montoya said. "I once offered you a proposition, remember?" He smiled.

"Get off my property," Lopez said.

"Whoa, hey! Chill out!" Guillermo said. It was another of his jokes, but Lopez did not smile. Lopez stepped toward Montoya and did not care that Ricardo Flores was beside him; Lopez, even at fifty, was willing to fight them both. "We're going," Guillermo said, showing both palms in a gesture of peacefulness. "I just wanted to remind you that I came to you before. I tried to talk to you as a brother."

Lopez said something in Spanish that meant Montoya was the brother of the devil, and he could go live with him.

Montoya smiled. "I just wanted to remind you," he said. Then he and Ricardo Flores left quietly.

Lopez went about his work, making sure the electric forklifts were hooked to their chargers to be ready for the next day's work, and all the refrigeration units were lubricated. Suddenly he stopped. Fear rose in his throat, and he ran to the telephone to call his family.

CHAPTER THIRTEEN

Men filed by her, into the room. Cully kept her eyes down. It was not characteristic of her. Had she been mostly frightened, she might have countered with defiance; but right now she was angry, and she didn't want it to show.

It was not only the men who were about to judge her use of deadly force that she wanted to hide her face from; it was also the photographer, young enough to sport a full crop of pimples, who was casually peering through the viewfinders of his cameras, one after the other, checking their focus against the contours of Cully McCullers's face.

You've got no right to be mad, she told herself. *The job of the police is to make the public feel secure, and they have every right to wonder at the judgment of the men and women who are legally armed with deadly force. Hell, Cully, you know some of the pigs in your own division; does it make you comfortable that they carry guns?*

But she could not shake the anger. She kept thinking of her father, eaten from the inside out, with nobody asking what gnawed at him, and nobody asking her now about the emotions that had surged through her over the last few days.

"Detective McCullers?"

She looked up; a lieutenant from the chief's office was standing in front of her. She stood quickly. "Yes sir."

"We're a little shorthanded today. Several of the people who were scheduled to attend this hearing were asked by the chief to observe the grand jury proceedings downtown. I've asked a couple of people I feel are qualified to fill in for us, but it's your option whether you want to go on with your hearing today, or postpone it."

"Who are the fill-in judges?" Cully said.

The lieutenant smiled. "Referees, not judges," he said. "Senior detectives. Street people."

"Then they're fine with me," Cully said. "I'd like to get this over with."

The lieutenant nodded and led her into the room. The young photographer followed.

At the head of the room was a table where four men sat. Two were in uniform, two in suits. The man in the gray suit at the left of the table was Doubting Thomas Ridge.

Cully sat down in a chair facing them. The lieutenant took his seat in the middle of the table, and the photographer sat against the side wall and clicked off a series of pictures as if he were invisible and his auto-winder silent. Cully had no table in front of her and felt awkward; if she crossed her legs she would look seductive, so she crossed her ankles instead and sat with her knees pressed together and her hands folded primly above them.

The lieutenant said, "Detective McCullers, would you recount for us the events of night before last, in your own words, please?"

Cully told them; though not by any stretch was the story in her own words. She used the courtroom drone and the formal police jargon, with words like "suspect," "observed," and "situation," and phrases like "following the recommended procedure . . ." The bullets cutting the air beside her ears, the muzzle flash of the Uzis, the slow-motion eternity as she squeezed the trigger of her own Beretta, became: "Returning their fire, I discharged my weapon."

For a full thirty seconds, no one in the room said anything. The men at the table scribbled on the pads in front of them, as if the same words were not in the reports they had read already. All but Ridge. He looked only at her, or down at the table, and wrote nothing.

Then one of the suits, who identified himself as the representative from Internal Affairs, said, "Ms. McCullers—"

"Detective McCullers," she interrupted him.

Doubting Thomas Ridge glanced sharply up at her.

"Yes, excuse me," the man from I.A. said. "Detective McCullers. When you looked through the window, and observed the men at the table, you immediately told your partner to go for backup, right?"

"Not extra backup, just for the rest of our immediate team, across the street."

"Right. There wasn't time to call for additional personnel to join the situation."

"That was my judgment, yes."

"So you gave your partner an order."

Cully paused. "I said, 'You do this, and I'll do that.' "

"But you told him what to do. He's been on the force for eight years, and a detective for three—two years longer than you—and you took charge of the situation."

He's trying to corner you, Cully thought. *You either lie, or you burn Quang.* "I knew he would volunteer for the more hazardous position," she said, "but I felt I was more qualified to stay."

"Why was that, Detective McCullers?"

"I'm a better pistol shot."

"Oh, yes, right!" the man from I.A. said, and poked at the papers in the open folder in front of him. "You do a lot of shooting. Is that why they call you Bull Barrel?"

He's baiting you, Cully. Don't get mad. It's his job. "I do a lot of shooting," she said flatly.

"Your father was a cop. A uniformed patrolman."

"Yes, that's right."

"And you're anxious to prove yourself."

She looked directly at him; she couldn't help herself. "Maybe," she said. "Mostly I'm anxious to do my job, and stay alive."

"Yes, but—"

"The department issued my pistol, and told me to learn to use it. Apparently they were right, because I happened to need it."

"My point is that you may be out to prove yourself a little too much."

"Your point is that I may have sought out or even created a lethal situation. I don't think so, but maybe I'm wrong. There were four other people behind that house when the shooting started, but they're all on slabs at the city morgue. So you'll have to take my word for it, I guess."

"You resent our questioning," the I.A. rep said.

Cully said nothing.

"So you think we should let our officers use their weapons whenever they want to."

"Of course not. You've got to ask these questions." She glanced at the photographer. "Could we get rid of him for a second?"

The presiding lieutenant raised his eyebrows, but he gestured for the photographer to leave. When he had closed the door behind him Cully said, "Gentlemen, you're not asking me what I did, you're asking me what I think, what I feel. You've got no choice except to judge me on that. Okay, fair enough, here it is:

"When violence breaks out, people suffer. My personal sense of justice is that the person who started the violence should be the one who does the suffering. I get paid to obey the law's sense of justice, not my own. Out on the street, with my life in danger, I made a decision that my use of deadly force was justifiable and necessary. *If you agree with it, I'm anxious to stay a cop.* If you don't agree with it, then fuck you."

All the faces behind the table turned red. Cully saw the surprise and anger on all of them, except Ridge. He was biting his lower lip, and trying not to laugh.

CHAPTER FOURTEEN

They had stolen a van for the job, a 1980 Chevy, like surfers use. They wanted to blend in on the campus. For the same reason, they had bought sport coats. Later, Cully would think of this with a kind of pity, that these members of a Latino gang thought the typical U.C.L.A. student was a surfer who dressed like a used car salesman.

Reuben Morales and Jesus Sanchez had brought Jesus's younger brother Angel to drive for them. They directed him along the roads they had scouted earlier and had him stop at a loading zone in a long traffic circle. They told him—for the third time—that if any of the school's traffic patrolmen ordered him to move he was to say "Delivery,

Delivery," over and over and pretend to speak no more English than that.

Reuben and Jesus got out and walked into the sculpture garden. Jesus was thin and slightly tall; Reuben was stocky, with a Fernando Valenzuela kind of round face that made him appear fat when he was not. Both were nineteen, an age that made them elder statesmen in the world of street gangs, the only world they knew.

It was a day like every other in Los Angeles September, hazy and hot. Victoria Lopez was in her designer jeans, lying on her stomach in the grass. Her boyfriend, Chuck "Chaz" Pendleton, rubbed the back of her leg and tickled her inner thigh. They were whispering, giggling, when Reuben and Jesus walked up.

"Hey . . . Victoria?" Reuben said. "Victoria Lopez?"

She looked up. She saw immediately what Reuben and Jesus thought they had concealed—that they were kids from a rough neighborhood. "What?" she said; not like a question, more like a warning.

"Remember me?" Reuben said. "I worked for your father!"

She smiled—a beautiful, cold smile. "Yeah, sure! Great to see you."

"Hey," he said, "isn't this something? 'Cause you know, you know what? I just bought a blue macaw! Hey! You like birds! You like 'em! Don't you?" Reuben had never worked for Victoria Lopez's father, but one of the older members of Los Malos had, and swore for a fact that the girl adored birds.

"A blue one? You've got one?" she said.

"Yeah, just got him!"

"Where? They've gotten really hard to come by!"

"Oh, sure! Man, we got a great deal. Beautiful bird, blue one, wanna see?"

The witnesses—other coeds around that morning— would say later they thought Victoria was suspicious even then, and that Chuck "Chaz" Pendleton looked definitely hostile. But Victoria got up and started walking, and Chaz came along at her side.

They reached the steps and saw the van waiting. Vicky

stopped. Reuben beckoned her toward the van. She started to turn around and Reuben stepped forward, taking her arm. Chaz pushed him, hard, but only pushed him, like two boys in a prep school fight. Jesus, standing behind, opened his sportcoat, pulled a .44 Magnum from the waistband of his pants, and shot Chaz three times in the spine.

CHAPTER FIFTEEN

The review board took an hour to find Detective Scarlet McCuller's shooting of the four men to be within policy. They could have wrapped up the hearing even quicker if several of the board members hadn't wanted to go on the public record with speeches about this young lady's courage and the Department's commitment to its officers in the war against drugs. Within the hearing room they made statements praising her heroism and condemning whatever benighted fools had thought women couldn't make good police officers, and it served as practice for what they would repeat outside, to the news teams that showed up for the announcement of their decision.

Cully didn't hang around for the media show; they had sent her out of the room so that they could arrive at their findings in private, and then had called her back in to announce their decision. When it was over, she left the building by a side door and circled the alley, back into the station.

"All-fuckin'-right!" somebody shouted, and Cully thought, for a crazy moment, that this was an ovation for her. She and everybody else in the station turned to look, and saw the shouter to be Ragg Wilson, in a cubicle several down from Cully's. He had just heard something over the phone, and, slamming the receiver down, stood up and yelled, "They've thrown the charges out! Freed the sons of bitches! Cooper and Nelson! Not guilty!"

Cooper and Nelson were young cops from the sexual crimes section who had tracked down a rapist who knocked the front teeth out of the heads of teenaged girls before he demanded oral sex from them. When Cooper and Morris brought the man in, most of his teeth were broken along with his jaw, and he lapsed into a two day coma before waking up to file assault charges against the cops, who swore they were just using "reasonable force."

This news of the court's dismissal of the charges set off a wild celebration. Bert "Trigger Finger" Frazier jumped on his desk and howled. Micro Morris threw his stack of arrest reports at him, and Frazier swatted at the blizzard of paper like it was tickertape and he had just returned from the moon. Captain Fresco, who had heard the news two minutes before and had been deciding on the best way to inform the shift when Ragg scooped him, stepped from his office, saw the Styrofoam cups, the ballpoint pens, and the booking sheets flying, and only nodded. He didn't like the disruption of his station; although he too thought Cooper and Nelson were innocent, he worried what the court action would mean to the next cop who wanted to break a head. But most of all he looked at his jubilant subordinates and thought, What kind of cops would they be if they weren't happy right now?

Cully, left alone, returned to her cubicle.

Quang was there, studying the manual for the sergeant's test. He looked up as she entered and said, "How'd you do?"

"Okay," she said.

He nodded, and went back to his book. Cully was stung that Quang's casual response was the most interest anybody could show.

Trigger thrust his bald lumpy head into the cubicle and said, "The Fuzzy Taco! Come on! The Fuzzy Taco!" It was a Mexican place, the bar of choice for Van Nuys detectives drinking after shift, and the consensus paradise for knocking off early and celebrating the acquittal of the cops.

Quang looked up from his book, and weighed the political value of his appearance against a free evening of study. "Thank you, but I'd best not," he said.

"McCullers!!" Trigger growled happily, grabbing her by the elbow and shoving her back and forth as he watched her bosom.

"Thanks," Cully said. "I'd better pass."

"Come on, Bull Barrel! Your brother detectives need you! It'll be good for you."

"I'm sorry," Cully said. "Not tonight."

"Suit yourself," Frazier said, and walked away.

In three minutes the entire detective area was deserted except for Cully and Quang. She was staring at her desk when she realized a phone was ringing. She turned and saw it was the one in the big homicide cubicle they called Death Row. With no one else to answer, and Quang lost inside the sergeant's manual, she walked over and answered: "Homicide. McCullers."

"This is Commander Bellflower!" an angry voice exploded. "Get some detectives over to the sculpture garden at U.C.L.A. Now!!"

CHAPTER SIXTEEN

Leonard Bellflower was a commander in the LAPD, with four service commendations in his past and a chance to be chief in his future. There were those who said Len Bellflower's prospects were bright because he was handsome and black, and Los Angeles had a black mayor who had once been a policeman himself; but anyone who said that ignored Bellflower's own abilities. What cops liked best about Bellflower was his honesty: Bellflower had grown up with racism and had overcome it through his whole career, and now that he had succeeded he refused to do the political thing and pretend it no longer existed. Bellflower would tell you what he thought: about prejudice, partners, community bias, or anything else for that matter.

When Cully and Quang arrived, Bellflower was standing on the roof of a squad car, addressing a crowd of three hundred college students who had gathered around the sculpture garden, now ringed with yellow police tape. Word of the shooting had spread through the campus, and the students were frightened. Bellflower's big frame suddenly towering six feet about the car roof got their attention, and he sounded less official because he spoke without a bullhorn. Not that he needed one; he had a voice like thunder.

"Okay!" he boomed, "we're going to get the people who did this. And we're going to get back the girl they took—get her back alive! But you've got to help us. We need everybody who actually *saw* anything—the abductors, the shooting, the escape, anything while it was happening—to come here, to the front of this car. If you didn't see anything, please move back. If you didn't see anything but know somebody who did, please go find them, or tell one of the officers who they are."

Chaz Pendleton's body still lay on the pavement; the scrambling cops had not yet been able to set up enough barriers to screen the view from the crowd. Bellflower barked, "We're going to move the body as soon as we can. But we're not going to move him until we're sure we've collected every bit of evidence that will lead us to his killer. Now get back and let us do our job!" Bellflower climbed down off the car, and the students obeyed.

Cully and Quang pushed through the crowd, up to the big commander, who looked a decade younger than his fifty years when he was in his dress blue with all the bars and braid, but was now in a short-sleeved shirt under a sport coat. Cully and Quang showed him their badges, and Bellflower, a former lineman at U.S.C., towered over them. To the fifty-year-old, burly street cop, they looked like children. "My God," he said. "You my detectives?" He looked away, toward the school's bell tower, and clearly thought, *No wonder this city's fucked up*.

"McCullers and Quang," Cully said. "Guess you can figure out which is which."

His eyes snapped at her. "Smart-ass, huh?"

"Why don't you show us your situation, sir," Cully said.

"Okay, Detective Smart-ass. Here's my *situation*." Commander Bellflower stalked his way through the milling police officers toward the broken form of Chaz Pendleton, and screamed at the men who had still not shielded the body from the terrified eyes of the students.

CHAPTER SEVENTEEN

"Slow down, Angel!" Reuben said. "Slow down!"

"Sí, Angel!" Jesus said, and the boy, sixteen, did what his older brother told him. He fought back the panic and let the van drift into the slower lanes.

They had brought along a crate they had salvaged from a dumpster behind a furniture store, and Vicky Lopez now lay inside it, her wrists, knees, and ankles taped, a rolled sock stuffed into her mouth and strapped in with silver duct tape. Reuben periodically lifted the lid to be sure he could still hear her sucking air through her nostrils.

They swung off the freeway four exits south of their entry point at U.C.L.A. They headed east and turned into an alley. Ricardo Flores stood halfway down the block. When he saw them he opened the metal doors of a grimy double garage in the rear of an out-of-business body shop. He stepped aside and waved them in beside a sky blue van, then closed the garage doors behind them.

When the van stopped, Victoria began to kick. The noise her feet made against the sides of the crate sounded even louder in the enclosed garage. Reuben had not thought of the girl doing such a thing, and he was embarrassed in front of Ricardo, the trusted right hand of Guillermo Montoya himself. "Quiet, you whore!" Reuben spat in Spanish. Still Victoria kicked.

Ricardo stepped up into the van, pulled back the top, and looked down at the girl. Her eyes were wide as a startled doe's; she kept thrashing and trying to scream. Ricardo slipped a knife from his pocket, flipped it open, and slid the blade between her legs. In Spanish he said, "You want to make noise I give you a reason."

The girl lay absolutely still, except for the throbbing of her lungs as she sucked air through her nostrils.

Ricardo smiled and closed his knife. He looked at Angel and said, "Who's he?"

Reuben looked at Jesus. "My brother," Jesus said.

"You said you would use only two of you," Ricardo said to Reuben.

"We needed a driver in case there was trouble," Reuben said.

Ricardo looked at their faces. "And there was trouble," Ricardo said.

"We had to kill a guy," Reuben said. "Some guy, he tried to stop us. Her boyfriend, I think."

In the crate Victoria began to whimper. Ricardo realized how stupid he had just been, to let the girl hear of the death of her boyfriend; she was confused by all the action, and might have been convinced that the shots she had heard hadn't killed anyone, which would have made her easier to control over the next several days. But it was too late to worry about that now. Ricardo stepped to the blue van, popped open its back door, and said to Reuben, "okay, move her over."

Reuben hesitated. He glanced at Jesus.

"What's wrong?" Ricardo demanded, trying to show anger because he knew what question was coming.

"We just wanted to know. Why do we have no supply to sell?" Reuben said.

Ricardo smiled. "The paste has been hard to move. What we are doing right now will fix the problem. Now let's go."

Reuben and Jesus exchanged another glance. "But the blacks have supply," Reuben said.

"Then maybe you should go talk to the blacks," Ricardo said. "But I don't think that would do much good. The man who controlled their supply in Mexico had an accident. A sharp wire got caught around his neck." Ricardo smiled again. "If you don't trust your Mexican brothers to do the right thing for you, then maybe you should do business with the chocolates."

Reuben and Jesus lifted the crate containing Victoria Lopez and slid it into the second van.

Ricardo would be at the border in two hours.

CHAPTER EIGHTEEN

The first order of business in a homicide is to preserve
the crime scene, not just to maintain the original moment
of death, but also to shield its details from public exposure;
the chances of solving a murder are best when the specifics
are known only by the police and the killer. Several hundred
people had seen Chaz Pendleton's body by the time Cully
and Quang arrived, and now it lay like the bull's-eye in a
huge dart board, the yellow police banners forming the
outer perimeter and a splash of bright blood making an
inner ring.

"The dead sophomore is one Charles 'Chaz' Pendleton,"
Bellflower said. "Son of the people that make Pendleton
Pumps. The suspects were Hispanics. We got good descriptions of them, and even the numbers off the van they
were driving, which turns out to be stolen."

Quang had his note pad out and was scribbling furiously.
Bellflower glowered down at him, and forced himself to go
on. "We got a famous-family victim," he said, "killed by a
minority." As Quang kept scribbling, Bellflower exploded.
"Are you listening to me, God damn it?!"

"Oh, yes sir!" Quang said. "It appears that we may have
a possible retribution situation here, involving money and
drugs."

"No, God damn it, this isn't about a rich kid getting
gunned down 'cause he won't pay his drug bills! That's what
everybody thought at first but we've already talked to his
fraternity brothers and they swear he's as clean as cellophane. It wasn't him they wanted anyway. It was the girl."

"What girl?" Cully said.

"Dead kid's girlfriend. Name's Victoria Lopez. They
killed Pendleton 'cause he was trying to protect her. What
they wanted was her."

"Why?"

"If I knew that I wouldn't need my goddamn detectives!
Now would I!" When Quang resumed his scribbling again,

61

Bellflower's eyes bulged. He wiped his face with a huge palm and said, "Obviously, I still don't have one."

He glared down at the body of Chaz Pendleton. "What nobody can figure out is why the body looks this way!" he said. "The witnesses say he was shot with a pistol! But with all that blood splattered everywhere, he looks exactly like he fell off a twelve-story building! What the hell happened? Did they hit him with a shotgun nobody saw? Did they run over him with their van?"

Cully looked up from the huge puddle coagulating in the sunlight and said, "What happened was, about ten thousand students on this campus know CPR. Half of them worked on this one, and pumped his blood right out of the bullet holes. Your witnesses didn't mention that because they thought it was obvious, and your patrolmen didn't think to ask."

Bellflower looked sideways at her.

Cully said, "And you, Commander, are dressed in your street clothes because you rushed down here in a panic as soon as you heard a boy had been killed and his girlfriend kidnapped at U.C.L.A. I'd say from your actions you have a kid enrolled at this campus." She paused. "How am I doing?"

"What was your name again?" Bellflower said.

"McCullers," Cully said. "And this is Quang."

"I remember you now, McCullers. Number one in your class at the academy. I requested you in my command."

"We're your detectives, Commander," Cully said. "We may not be all you want, but we're all you've got."

Cully walked away, toward the officers who had been questioning the witness. Quang, with a glance at Bellflower, snapped his notebook shut with a flourish, and followed her.

CHAPTER NINETEEN

There is a grim joke known to all homicide detectives. It is told in various forms, but mostly it is known as Smooth-

Talkin' Leroy. Cully's father used to tell it from time to time. It's an old joke and most people have heard it, but for those who haven't it goes like this:

A bunch of guys are in a pool hall shooting a few racks, and they get to screwing around and Willy Brown gets shoved backwards and hits his head on the edge of the cue rack and dies, right on the spot. The guys in the hall have all done time, so they figure they better break the news easylike to Willy's wife, or she'll report them to the cops and open up manslaughter charges.

The problem is, nobody wants to be the one to tell her. So one of the guys says, "Hey, I know this dude, over to the service station, Smooth-Talkin' Leroy, he know how to say anything so nobody get his feelin's hurt." So they go across the street to the service station and explain it all to Leroy, and he says, "Sure, I break it to the lady jus' right, won't be no problem." So they give Leroy the address and a six-pack for his trouble, and he wanders over to Willy Brown's house and knocks. His wife comes to the door. And Smooth-Talkin' Leroy says, "Uh, is you the Widda Brown?" And she says, "I'm not a widow!" And Smooth-Talkin' Leroy says, "The hell you ain't!"

It's a dumb joke and a racist joke and that's why homicide detectives like to tell it—but it's only partly why. The other reason is that there's nothing on earth they dread more than having to tell a victim's family that someone they love has been murdered. You get used to the sight of bodies rotting on a floor, and the smell of the room where they've been shut up for days, and the buzz of the coroner's saw as he slices through their skulls on the way to autopsy their brains. But you never learn to tolerate the sight of the live face of the victim's loved one who opens the door with the wary fear of the innocent and watches blankly as you say what you have to say; you never get used to watching the expression on that face fall like a screaming bomb and explode in panic and pain.

And yet the visit cannot be avoided. To solve a murder, the detective of homicide looks to complete the iron triangle of method, motive, and opportunity, and for the latter two it is often family members themselves who provide the best information, and they are most apt to be helpful when their emotions have just been stripped raw.

Chaz Pendleton's parents—according to Bellflower's assistant, who filled Cully in as she and Quang were checking the preliminary reports before leaving the scene—were in Europe, and would be notified by the commander himself. Victoria Lopez's family lived in Encino; the job of informing them belonged to the detectives working the case. "Smooth-Talkin' McCullers," Cully mumbled as she slid behind the steering wheel of their unmarked sedan.

"Excuse me?" Quang said.

"Nothing," she said, and started the engine.

CHAPTER TWENTY

They drove north on the San Diego Freeway, up through the Sepulveda Pass and down into the San Fernando Valley, to the home of Victoria Lopez.

They found a winding street where the homes sprawled among groves of tortured oak and eucalyptus. The Lopez house lay beyond an iron gate flanked by brick pillars, guarding a bridge over the creek bed that cut like a moat across the front of the property. Cully pressed the button set into a wrought iron palm tree beside the pavement, and, after a long pause, a voice answered: "Yes?"

"Detectives Quang and McCullers, from the Los Angeles Police Department," Cully announced. The gate swung slowly open. She cruised the car up the drive, past the tennis court to an expanse of pebble-embedded concrete in front of the open garage. The garage had three stalls. One was empty. In the other two were a pickup truck and a Porsche.

"Lots of money," Quang said, as they moved along the winding walk to the front doorway.

"Lots and lots," Cully agreed. Before she could knock a man opened the door. He was on the short side of medium, and was slender, but had the straight spine of a soldier. His hair was black and glossy, his skin like cocoa, his teeth straight. His eyes, deep brown, were red rimmed.

"Esteban Lopez?" Cully said, emphasizing the second syllable of the first name, in the proper Spanish way.

The man nodded, and only afterwards said, "Yes."

"You've already been told about your daughter," Cully said. Not a question.

"One of her sorority sisters called," Lopez said. When Cully did not ask anything right away, Lopez added, "She said the police were there and . . . would surely be coming soon." Lopez spoke with a heavy Spanish accent, though he enunciated his words carefully and precisely. "Would you care to sit down?"

Lopez led them to a living room carpeted in blush pink, with Laura Ashley wallpaper and track lights. Cully and Quang took seats on the floral-print sofa; Lopez sat in one of the matching wing chairs. "May I get you something to drink?" he asked.

Cully was silent for so long that Quang grew uncomfortable. "Thank you, no," he said.

Cully sat motionless, studying Lopez's face. Lopez stared back, lowering the lids of his reddened eyes until they looked hooded. Growing impatient, Quang said, "Have you received any other communication about your daughter?"

Lopez looked at him. "What do you mean?"

"A ransom demand. Has anyone else called about her?"

"No."

"What about your wife? Has she had any calls?"

"She is in church," Lopez said. "We just got back from Mass when Vicky's friend called, and . . . my wife went back to church."

The living room was full of crucifixes—on the wall, above the doorway into the dining room, and on a devotional table in the corner, where a candle burned above a dozen framed pictures of Victoria and an equal number of a young man who must have been her brother.

"Can you give us a description of your daughter?" Cully asked the father.

"Don't you already have that?" Esteban Lopez said.

"Sure, from her friends at school, but different people see in different ways."

Lopez took a breath; it was an effort for him to talk about his daughter. "She is . . . eighteen. About . . . two inches taller than her mother, that would be five foot . . . three. She has black hair and . . . and brown eyes and she is . . . to me . . . very . . ." He could not say the word "beautiful." He stopped and chewed his lip; he refused to cry.

Cully became preoccupied again, staring at the pictures and the devotional table, so Quang asked, "Can you think of any reason why anyone would want to abduct your daughter?"

Lopez shrugged. "You tell me."

"Is that your son?" Cully said abruptly, and nodded across to the photographs on the table.

"Uh . . . yes," Lopez said, taken off guard by the question.

"He's older than Victoria." It sounded to Lopez as if this pretty young female detective was trying to make small talk, just to be polite.

"Yes," Lopez said. "Edwardo. Edward. He's a junior at Pomona College. He's going to be a lawyer."

Cully nodded. Then she asked if they could take a picture of Victoria, any one that might look more casual than the yearbook photo they already had. Lopez pulled an eight-by-ten from its frame and handed the picture to Quang, who promised to take care of it, and stood.

"By the way," Cully said, pulling out her notebook. "The girl who called you, what was her name?"

"Jennifer. Or Janet or something," Lopez said. "I was confused at that time."

"Of course," Cully said. "Thank you. You'll be hearing from us."

CHAPTER TWENTY-ONE

Ricardo had no trouble at the border. The van was properly registered and titled; Ricardo had all the right papers, and the Americans didn't bother to stop him, and on his side of the border the Mexican customs officer just waved him through.

Victoria Lopez did not scream. Ricardo had told her that if she made a sound he would tell the border officers that he was bringing his sister back from El Norte, where she had been working as a whore, and they would not believe anything she said after that, and afterwards, he promised, he would rape her, and make her a whore.

What a ridiculous lie! And she had believed him. Ricardo was pleased with himself. He could make people believe whatever he wanted them to.

Ricardo drove the rest of the way to Mexico City, and thought of his talents.

"He's lying," Cully said, as they drove away from the Lopez house. "Nobody called him—nobody in Victoria's sorority, anyway."

"Just because he bobbled the girl's name a little?" Quang said. "The man's distraught! His child has been kidnapped, he's entitled to a little confusion."

"He wasn't worried about the brother. If you had one child kidnapped, wouldn't your first thought be that the rest of your family was in danger too? I gave him every chance to tell me he was worried about his son, and had called him and reassured him. But Lopez knew what the kidnappers wanted, and knew it had nothing to do with Edward."

Quang had missed that, and added anger with himself to the awful pity he felt for the Lopez family.

"I hate being lied to," Cully said.

CHAPTER TWENTY-TWO

When the hammer drops, as they say in the murder trade—when the meat hits the street—the detective of homicide feels an internal clock begin to run. He has, he figures, seventy-two hours to solve the crime. That number reflects several realities. One is the convenience of finding suspects in the easily solvable kind of murder, where the victim knew the killer. Another is state of mind of the perpetrator; during the first three days after taking a human life, the bats flutter and the death dog howls inside the killer's mind, and confession looms like a compulsion, promising relief; but after surviving the worst of that, the instinct for self-preservation overcomes all guilt; the mind rationalizes, justifies; and without a confession, murders may be solved but never resolved.

The last reason is even more practical. In Los Angeles there are two official homicides every day, and fewer than a hundred detectives to work them. To solve as many as possible detectives and their supervisors have to move on.

So the rule becomes: once the hammer drops, you run till you can't run no more. You chase down every lead, trying to close the gap between you and the killer, before the clock runs out and the next corpse hits the slab, and its paperwork hits your desk.

Cully and Quang started their race, a contest made more frustrating because they could not pick up a trail. Back at their desks at the Van Nuys station, Cully first sent a memo to Brando Michaels, head of the division's antigang CRASH, asking if he had any idea why a street gang would be kidnapping a college girl. They sent out a description of the van, notifying the California Highway Patrol and the Border Patrol as well as all the traffic sections of the L.A.A.D. They sent teletypes through a communications network that spread throughout the country, and arranged with the Communications Division for a broadcast every hour. Finally they notified Missing Persons, in case any corpse resembling Victoria Lopez should turn up.

Then Cully and Quang began the mind-numbing task of reading all the reports Bellflower's men on the scene had gathered, and calling every witness for follow-up. These chores consumed four hours and turned up nothing. Then they contacted every available sorority sister of Victoria Lopez and fraternity brother of Chaz Pendleton. All of them were anxious to tell everything they knew, and like most people with such willingness, everything turned out to be what Ragg Wilson would call "Zip-Oh-Dee-Doo-Doo."

Cully and Quang found themselves at midnight, blurry and blank, staring at each other across a desolate acre of desktop, without a clue in sight. "Why don't you go home," she said through a dry mouth. "I think we've hit a wall."

Quang put down the pencil he had been poking at his blotter, and said, "Yeah. I didn't get much studying done."

"Maybe you can get in a couple of hours before you go to sleep," Cully said.

Quang nodded, not realizing she had meant it as a joke. "Maybe tomorrow morning we'll have a lead on the van."

"Yeah."

He picked up his coat. "You coming?"

"You go ahead," she said. "I need to visit the ladies' room before I leave."

Quang left her and headed for the parking lot.

Cully sat alone at her desk and thought of Esteban Lopez, and Leonard Bellflower, and her own father.

CHAPTER TWENTY-THREE

She could not have said what drew her back to the Lopez house that night.

All of her training, from the formal lectures of the psychologists at the Police Academy to the jokes like the one about Smooth-Talkin' Leroy that the veterans used to distance themselves from the human emotion of the job, told her never to break the wall between a victim's private life and her own.

Maybe it was because she knew Victoria Lopez was alone and vulnerable and afraid, and those were the feelings that Cully McCullers most hid from the world, that now she felt compelled to touch Victoria through her family.

Maybe it was because of Cully's own father, an Irish cop who differed from Esteban Lopez in every particular except one, and that was the fiercely private yet bottomless way he loved his daughter to the last days of his life, that drew

Cully now to Victoria's father, as if to comfort him now in the way that she could not comfort her own.

Whatever it was that pulled her against the logic of her mind, she knew she could not go home and sleep until she had at least driven by to see if the house was dark; and, seeing a light in the living room, and discovering the front gate open, she found herself standing on the front porch of the Lopez home, knocking softly on the door.

She heard a shuffle behind the door, and voices—female voices; and then the door opened, revealing two women. They were dressed identically, as if in mourning, in black dresses that stretched to the floor. The younger woman's once-black hair was streaked in silver, like a frozen raven; the older woman's hair was all frost. Victoria's mother and grandmother, Cully knew immediately. Both held pale white rosaries. The only color was the red at the rims of their eyes; even now the grandmother wept. Light from a grove of candles burning on the votive table in the living room washed over the left side of their faces, and the old lady's fingers still worked the beads, as the younger Mrs. Lopez said, "Yes?"

"I'm Detective McCullers," Cully said. As she saw the terror start into their faces, she added quickly, "I just came by to see that you were all right, to . . . tell you we're working and doing everything we can to . . . get Victoria back home safely."

The realization that Cully had not come to inform them of Victoria's death left the mother weak; she hugged Cully in relief, clinging to her, and when the grandmother pleaded in Spanish, Mrs. Lopez translated what Cully had said, and then both women were hugging her.

"Please," Mrs. Lopez said. "Please! Come sit down! Please! I will get you something to eat!"

"No, no thank you," Cully said, but she let herself be drawn into the living room. Mrs. Lopez kept insisting that Cully must be hungry; the grandmother's fingers kept rolling down the beads.

"Is there any news, any at all?" Mrs. Lopez said.

Cully hesitated, wanting to give them hope and needing

not to deceive them. "We're investigating everything," Cully said. "We won't give up. I promise you."

The sight of this woman at their door in the middle of the night was like an angel to them; the old woman said so, in Spanish.

Cully ignored the remark, though she understood it. "How is Mr. Lopez?" she asked.

Mrs. Lopez looked up, toward the room above, concern mangling her face. "Trying to rest," she said.

"Well, I . . . didn't want to intrude," Cully said. "I just wanted to say, if there's anything I can do . . ."

They both hugged her again. Mrs. Lopez's grip was strong. But the old lady shuddered, and then she asked something.

Cully was not sure she had understood. The grandmother tugged at her arm, and Cully realized they wanted her to kneel with them at the table, in front of the candles and the pictures of Victoria.

Cully McCullers did not believe in God—or at least not in One who required the pleading of His creations before He would deliver them from evil. But with Victoria's mother holding her right arm and her grandmother tugging at her left, Cully sank to her knees between the two terrified, tearful women.

And she prayed.

CHAPTER TWENTY-FOUR

Ricardo took Victoria to the place they had prepared. Guillermo would not want to see her—not until she was tucked away so that no one could ever reach her without his approval. Ricardo saw to the accomodations and the guards and then went up to Guillermo's office.

As Ricardo entered, Guillermo was looking out over the mountains and Mexico, the great city in the swamp. He always became reflective when he took a bold step. "You have a good flight back?" Ricardo asked.

"Mmm," Guillermo mumbled, without looking at him.

"We have her," Ricardo announced.

"Any problems?"

"The little cockroaches popped a guy—her boyfriend they think. They got away okay, but I guess I'll have to go back soon and make sure they don't start scratching too loud. Right now they're beginning to wonder why they got no supply."

The questions of the Chicano street gang were no threat to Montoya; even the easy possession of Victoria Lopez he took for granted. He had something else on his mind.

"I talked with de la Puente," Guillermo said. "I told him about Alejandro."

"You told him your brother was killed?" Ricardo said, surprised.

"Of course he knows that, doesn't he, Ricardo? Isn't he the minister in charge of drug control, in the cabinet of the President of this whole country? Wouldn't the gringo police tell him they had just killed two Mexican citizens who had gotten off a plane from Mexico carrying drugs?" Guillermo liked to go on and on like that with Ricardo. They had both been hungry boys in the same village, and Guillermo liked to remind him that he was now the leader because he was smarter.

"So there is no need to try to save embarrassment, is there, Ricardo? He knows I did not prevent my own brother from being killed!" Guillermo's anger flared then—but the sudden passion was not for Ricardo's stupidity. It was for revenge, and Ricardo had seen the same flat look come into Guillermo's eyes before, whenever he had set himself to take a life. "What there is a need to do," Guillermo went on quietly, "is to show de la Puente what happens when we are hurt. How we make others hurt."

Ricardo sat wondering who Guillermo meant. Would he go after the police in Los Angeles? That did not seem wise to Ricardo, but Guillermo's violence was never predictable. Ricardo had sometimes thought that if he could ever learn to think like Guillermo—

"I have a suspicion about Alejandro's murder," Guillermo

said. "It may not have been simple bad luck that put the Los Angeles police on him. De la Puente told me about a man who is an agent of the American Drug Enforcement Agency. They call this man El Rojo—he has red hair and a red beard. He speaks Spanish like a Mexican, de la Puente says, and he lives here in Mexico, watching the young men who buy the big houses and the fast cars."

Guillermo paused just long enough to run his tongue around the inside of his cheek. "Alejandro . . . liked the luxuries of our riches. The cars, the parties, the women. As you know." Ricardo knew that Alejandro had more than liked to party; he had lived for it—and died for it. He had been content to take orders from his younger brother because he so enjoyed the money and cars and women he got in return. Guillermo, on the other hand, had more Puritanical tastes. "This Rojo visits the expensive clubs in our city. He sees Alejandro. He has heard the rumor that the Montoyas have eliminated El Negro, and he has Alejandro watched. When Alejandro flies to America, the DEA man makes a phone call to the L.A. police. 'As long as you're watching the airport, watch for this guy too.' Not enough to bring attention to El Rojo; just enough for my brother to end up murdered."

"What do you want me to do?" Ricardo asked.

"Go kill El Rojo," Guillermo said.

CHAPTER TWENTY-FIVE

Only a few people in the DEA knew his real name. Since drug dealers had begun murdering their agents, the United States Drug Enforcement Agency had been keeping the true identities of their people secret. But even before that, the man who sat in the lavender leather booth at the Club 2000 had learned how to be discreet, and that was why he was still alive.

His fellow hotdogs in the DEA called him El Rojo, or simply Rojo, for red. His true hair color was the flame shade of a Texas sunset. His mother was Apache, mostly, or at least that's what she said. His father, she told him, was a cop, but Rojo didn't know if that was true either.

What he did know—what he had learned growing up in El Paso with an alcoholic prostitute for a mother and a question mark for a father—was that nothing in the world could make him quit.

Rojo had joined the agency when he was twenty-two, just out of the Marine Corps. He was a fierce-looking man, an inch under six feet, a wiry hundred-sixty-five pounds, with wild amber eyes under the flaming hair. He made friends easily, he was afraid of nothing, and he spoke Spanish so well he could put on different dialects. All he had ever told anyone at the expensive nightclub in Mexico City was that he "had done very well" in the real estate business in Phoenix. They assumed that was a lie. He was brash with his jokes and daring with his eyes, and the way he fearlessly stared at the women of drug dealers convinced them that he must be a dealer himself. When they shared drinks with him, and casually spoke of fringe issues in their business such as the cost of new light planes or the arrangement of portable landing lights for the construction of temporary runways in the desert, he listened with interest and spoke with great knowledge. And the more they saw through the one lie about the real estate business, the more they believed the other unspoken lie that he was one of them.

He moved about the city without escort, and this added to his mystique. Young bucks in the drug trade sought his friendship, and Rojo gave it to them. Four weeks in Mexico City, he had already netted Alejandro Montoya, and in another four weeks—who knew what he might accomplish?

Ricardo Flores sat on the other side of the neon-lit dance floor and watched Rojo. Ricardo could see himself in the mirrored wall behind Rojo's back. Ricardo watched himself as much as he watched Rojo, and he thought, *Do you have it, Ricardo? Do you have the head and the* cojónes *that Guillermo has?*

Ricardo sat there drinking for two hours, until the weight of the .357 Magnum with the mercury-tipped bullets began to cramp his shoulder. Damn heavy gun, but it left almost nothing of a skull. You kill somebody with this and it takes the Federales two weeks just to figure out who the victim was.

At one in the morning Rojo yawned, as only a man who is confident with women can do. He kissed the two on either side of him, and shook hands with the men who had brought them. The couple on his right stood to let him out of the booth. Rojo threw a few thousand pesos on the table, said something, and they all laughed.

Out in the parking lot, Rojo walked to his white BMW. Just as he put the key into the door he heard a voice say behind him, "Leave the key exactly where it is. Do not take your fingers off it."

"Fuck you," Rojo said; but he did not move his fingers.

"If I want to shoot you," Ricardo said, "I do it right now. But what I want is you let me in the car. The passenger side." Ricardo laughed. He was amazed at how easy this was. "I don't want to steal your car either."

Ricardo walked into the light on the opposite side of the BMW, and smiled across the top of the car at Rojo. He felt Rojo sizing him up. Rojo opened the driver's side door, slid in behind the wheel, and closed the door. He could have driven away; the glass in his car was bulletproof. But he touched the car's central locking system and let Ricardo in.

As Ricardo settled onto the stiff leather he saw that Rojo had a gun in his left hand, pointed at him from beneath his right elbow; he could punch a bullet squarely into Ricardo's gut.

"That's not nice," Ricardo said. "I show you all this friendship and still you don't trust me."

"Say what you came to say," Rojo told him, keeping the gun so steady it was frightening.

"I was sent here to kill you," Ricardo said.

Rojo looked doubtful, so Ricardo held up both hands and very slowly opened his jacket with his left, and with the tips of the thumb and forefinger of his right he lifted out the Magnum and laid it like a stiff fish on the console between them. "Exploding bullets," Ricardo explained. "Just a nick and your head pops like a watermelon, so I could be shit for a shot and still leave you dead. I'm really pretty good though."

Rojo looked from the gun to Ricardo, and said, "You always talk this much, without saying anything?"

"What do you want me to say?"

"Who sent you to kill me?"

"Oh. Guillermo Montoya."

"So why didn't you?"

"I thought you and I might make a different deal," Ricardo said.

THE FOURTH DAY

CHAPTER TWENTY-SIX

Cully's phone rang. She groped for it through her sleep, and picked it up. Red numbers blared 5:29 from her digital clock and stung her eyes as she said, "Hello?"

"McCullers! This is Dugan!"

"Rosie!" she said quickly, and sat up. "What's happening? You found Victoria Lopez?"

"Get down here!"

"You found her? Victoria Lopez?" Cully said.

"Who's Victoria Lopez?" Dugan said. "Get down here. Now!"

Cully reached the station just after six A.M. The mobile video trucks from the three network affiliates and one cable news service were jammed along the curb, and the battered station wagons of newspaper photographers knotted the early morning traffic. She saw the cluster of reporters held at bay by the main doors of the station; the captain had locked them out for some reason.

She turned a block early and took the back streets to the rear of the station. She hurried into the building, looking for the first person she could grab to tell her what was going on, but the halls were as empty and still as the coroner's body room on a Sunday morning.

She punched at the elevator button, and when the doors didn't open immediately she bounded up the stairs. She barged through the doorway on the detectives' floor and found everybody strangely still at their desks, indulging in none of the chatter that keeps the boredom away. Then she spotted Dugan. "Rosie!" she said. "What's—"

Before she could finish her question she saw the full loom

of Commander Bellflower, barreling down the corridor. "In here!" he barked, and all the detectives, some unshaven, some still damp from their morning showers, and all without their first cups of coffee, gathered into the homicide cubicle after him.

Captain Dick Fresco was at Bellflower's shoulder. Fresco looked liked death.

"We got us a problem," Bellflower said, his voice bending the glass walls. "Some of you know it, some don't, so here's what happened. Nelson and Cooper were freed yesterday. The charges of police brutality were dropped by the grand jury. Hoo-ray, hoo-rah, right? So you dickheads decide to go out celebrating! You all head down to the Fuzzy Taco."

Bellflower stopped. His enormous head gave off waves of heat. "You have a few drinks. Then you have a few more. Your friend and mine, Ragg Wilson, is one of the guys there. About midnight, after seven straight hours of drinking, most of the cops leave and drive home." As Bellflower said the last words he looked at Fresco; cops driving while intoxicated threw them both into rage, but that was a fury that would have to come later. "Ragg, however, has forgotten to eat, and as much as the others have had to drink, he's had even more.

"And then . . . there was a woman, at the bar." Bellflower paused and shook his head, as if he could not believe this was happening now. "You know the story. At first the guys started joking around with her. She was by herself, and a bunch of boozy cops around a stray woman . . . And of course she was wild for their attention. She was . . ." Bellflower stopped again, stared at the linoleum floor he had been wearing a path across, and said, ". . . a very fat woman. And apparently she didn't have a face like Elizabeth Taylor. I say apparently because now she doesn't have a face at all."

Cully's heart started pounding.

"At first their flirting was a joke," Bellflower went on. "But sometime just before or just after the other cops left, Ragg decided he was in love. He took the woman out to his car. He was too drunk to drive, but that didn't matter, because our two lovebirds couldn't wait to get to a motel.

They started going at it right in the front seat of Ragg's Plymouth."

His black-and-white. Cully, and the other detectives in the room, saw it all now. The image of every cop in the city of Los Angeles being turned as foul as the body odor of a detective and a murder victim humping in the front seat of an unmarked police car.

"But Ragg was not only too drunk to drive, he was too drunk to fuck too. Or so he says. Because he doesn't remember a lot. He does remember that after about twenty minutes his pecker was still limp. He says it was like trying to fuck a bucket with a rubber band."

Frazier, behind Cully, moaned in sympathy.

"So just to keep the lady from being too disappointed, he goes down on her."

"Attaboy," Frazier whispered, as if watching it all from the sidelines.

"Slobbers all over, in fact," Bellflower went on. "A half hour of this and the lady isn't getting anywhere either. She pulls her pants up and her dress down and she goes home. That's Ragg's story, anyway."

"Where did they find her?" Cully said, her voice flat and low, and Bellflower sought her with his eyes. He began talking directly to her.

"Beside her apartment," Bellflower said. "She lived in a thirty-unit apartment complex they call Wild Horse Acres, about five minutes from the bar. She coulda walked to it, I guess that's possible, though Roger says she had enough alcohol in her to make two cows drunk. It was past midnight, on a quiet road, but somebody shoulda noticed a woman staggering home—if she did walk home."

Bellflower pressed his palms to his eyes, and took a deep breath before he ended his story. "This morning, about four-thirty, the boy that throws the papers in the apartment complex found her body. It was lying ten feet from her front door. She had been beaten so badly that . . . Her whole body was one big bruise, but mostly he—whoever killed her—went at her head. Her skull was so broken up the pieces just moved around, and as the final pièce de résistance the killer picked up a fifty-pound rock from this stone-lined walkway and dropped it on her head. Her skull caved in so quickly her brain exploded out her eye sockets and slapped up against the picket fence."

The room was silent. Everybody was sweating, and everybody felt chilly.

"All anybody saw was that she and Ragg left the bar together. Ragg says he woke up in his car about two in the morning, and drove home. Nobody remembers his car in the parking lot, nobody at his apartment building saw him enter his place."

Bellflower heaved a sigh, and looked around the room. "Brutality charges dismissed against two cops, and twenty more go out to celebrate and a woman ends up murdered like that! Tons of people—hell, our own guys—saw the victim with Ragg, barely an hour before she died! Her fingerprints are in his squad car! His hair is on her underwear, for Christ's sake! Now most of us in this room don't believe Ragg Wilson did that. I mean the part about killing her. But tell that to them!" He pointed toward the front of the building, where the reporters waited.

"Any other suspects?" somebody said.

"One," Bellflower said. "One very good one. The woman's ex-boyfriend. Lived with her until about four weeks ago. Perfect psych profile too—institutionalized twice for psychopathic behavior. But he's got an alibi. He says he was bowling, and nobody can testify different." He paused. "Ragg Wilson can go to the gas chamber on this one, folks. You know it and I know it. And he knows it. So far the boyfriend won't budge, and to most of the people in this city, who think Nelson and Cooper were guilty anyway, he's a scapegoat for one more fucked-up cop. Ragg's gonna sniff the big glue, and the rest of us are gonna wish we were in the gas chamber with him, before this one is over."

Captain Fresco stepped forward. "Every other investigation is suspended until we get this one put to bed. We've got assignments for every detective." He started handing out the team sheets he'd scrawled, and the detectives moved forward.

"One more thing!" Bellflower called. "I've known Ragg

Wilson a long time. I know in my bones he didn't do this. But if my bones are wrong . . . Well, then we've gotta prove that too. 'Cause we're cops. Okay. Let's go."

CHAPTER TWENTY-SEVEN

Reuben and Jesus had hidden out in Los Angeles for twelve hours, each in the apartments where their families lived. They had expected to feel loose and safe, just as soon as they had turned the girl over to Ricardo Flores and had watched him drive off to Mexico; yet that night they found themselves jumping at every noise. But with the dawn of a new morning they felt brave enough to venture out and sniff the air to see what trouble might be following them.

They met at nine A.M. at their familiar corner. They had not planned the rendezvous; they both just went to the same place at the same time, as they always did. *"Qué paso?"* Reuben said.

"Nada," said Jesus. They both grinned and slapped hands back and forth. On such a fine morning, with the night sweats behind them both and everything back to normal, they decided to head over to Long Boulevard, to see how business was going.

Long Boulevard runs perpendicular to Sepulveda Boulevard in north Van Nuys, where the big auto assembly plant lies; the plant is visible at the end of the street. The plant belonged to General Motors but Long Boulevard belonged to Los Malos.

It was Reuben's theory that Long Boulevard was such a good place to sell drugs because the workers on their way to clock in could look up and see what they were facing— a whole day standing on the assembly line in the massive gray building, doing the same rote task hour after hour— and that made a few lines of powder or a couple of rocks to smoke at lunchtime an irresistible lure.

The day shift at the plant clocked in at eight-thirty. There were always some stragglers, and some buyers who worked in offices and didn't get into work until nine. Reuben and

Jesus arrived at what they figured would be the perfect time to check receipts on the morning's coke traffic.

They found an angry knot of Hispanics, all wearing checked flannel shirts buttoned to the neck and Bermuda shorts—the uniform of Los Malos. Reuben and Jesus did not even get to ask what was happening; the members of their gang were waiting for leadership, and when it showed up, they jumped at it.

"We gotta stop this shit!" one of them said.

"We gotta stop it right now!" another agreed.

"They gotta know it, man! They gotta know this is our place, man!"

Reuben and Jesus looked down the street. At the far end, toward the plant, were two big young blacks, leaning over and handing single-hit packets of cocaine into cars, right in the middle of the drug supermarket that was the exclusive and eternal franchise of Los Malos, the glorious and bad Chicanos of Van Nuys, California.

CHAPTER TWENTY-EIGHT

It was seven A.M. when the detectives broke. They agreed to hit the field for three hours and reconvene at ten to pool their leads and hunches and redirect their efforts.

They came back full of facts and empty of evidence. One team had studied the victim: her habits, her apartment, the preliminary autopsy findings. They had a well-preserved crime scene, with no indication of any tampering by the perpetrator or blundering by the first civilians and investigators to arrive, but so far the victim team had discovered nothing they hadn't known already.

Another team had covered the Fuzzy Taco and all those who had been there. Part of this was easy, since half of the bar's occupants on the fatal night were cops in the Van Nuys Division. The investigative team interviewed these men and everyone else they could find who had been to the bar that night, and no one remembered anything unusual— except for a bunch of unusually drunk cops.

Cully's team took the boyfriend, and their job was the most intriguing and frustrating of all. The closer they looked at the guy, the more convinced they were of his guilt. His medical history was readily available to them—he had been committed to institutions not twice but three times, with physical violence a component of every incident. As a child he had been grotesquely abused; as an adult he had returned the favor on a daughter, ultimately taken by the state. He had a history of arrests for violence stemming from traffic incidents; judges had dismissed the convictions because no one had been permanently hurt and the jails were crowded anyway.

Cully's team had microscoped his alibi. They had sweated him personally. And, like the others, they had nothing.

There was one last team. It was made up of Bellflower and Fresco. They had gone down to the interrogation room where they had mothballed Ragg, and asked him how he was doing. Neither of them had the heart to ask if he had anything to tell them. But Ragg volunteered all he knew; he said, "I'm hung over, I'm tired, I don't remember a damn thing, and I wanna go home."

On the way back upstairs, Bellflower stopped and made a phone call. Then he and Fresco went up and listened to what the detectives had to say. Everybody chattered, and nobody said anything. Finally Bellflower said, "From where I'm standing this all sounds like a bunch of nothing. Anybody else hearing it different?"

Nobody answered.

"Anybody got any ideas?"

Again nothing. Bellflower's deflated gaze fell on Cully. "McCullers!" he said. "You sure this boyfriend's alibi can't be broken?"

"I said it was holding, sir, but it might leak a little."

"Yeah? How?"

"The guy claims he was bowling all night, and the clerk at the Parkview Lanes just down the road from the apartment complex remembers him coming in, but he doesn't know whether he was actually there the whole time."

"Why not?"

"Because he went to sleep at his desk. Any guy sleepy

enough to doze through the crash of bowling pins would be a worthless alibi in a full trial. The pin reset counters at the desk said the boyfriend had rolled enough frames to have been there for several hours, but he could have bowled fast, slipped out for as long as an hour, done the crime and come back to pick up his ball, and nobody would have noticed."

Bellflower's face had brightened briefly, but his hope faded as quickly. "We can run the route and time it," he said. "We can prove it's possible, and even probable that he killed her. But without a witness or a confession, we've got exactly zero. But if the prosecutor follows the Ragg theory, he's got lots of witnesses." He looked at his detectives. "You guys! And he's even got Ragg, to admit it's his saliva on the dead girl's snatch."

A low murmur rose from the back of the room. "Doubting Thomas," somebody said, and they all turned to see Tom Ridge walking slowly up the corridor. Cully heard Fresco say to Bellflower, "That's who you called?"

"You got a problem with that?" Bellflower shot back.

"It just . . . makes us look a little helpless is all," Fresco said.

"Want me to send him back?" Bellflower said.

Fresco shook his head.

CHAPTER TWENTY-NINE

Ridge stopped outside the open door of the bullpen. He was clearly embarrassed by the situation, and reluctant to come in. Bellflower stepped out to him.

"Thanks for coming," Bellflower said.

Cully was standing right by the door. She saw Ridge nod in the direction of the front entrance, where all the press was gathered, and she heard him mutter, "Kind of a big party you've got here."

"Don't worry about them," Bellflower said. "I'll keep 'em off you. I swear."

Ridge stared at Bellflower. It was clear Ridge would take

that promise seriously. Finally he said, "Okay, what have you got?"

In two minutes Bellflower retold the facts of the murder. The thirty detectives in the bullpen listened to the rumble of voices, and watched without making a sound.

"Okay," Ridge said when Bellflower was finished. "Let's see what we can do."

Ridge, Fresco, and Bellflower started for the parking lot. Bellflower turned back and barked, "McCullers! You come with us. On the way out you can fill Ridge in on the boyfriend. The rest of you guys stay here. We'll let you know what we come up with."

The detectives stood frozen for a moment. Then Frazier said, "Bullshit!" and they all ran for their cars.

CHAPTER THIRTY

They drove in an unmarked car—Captain Fresco at the wheel, Bellflower beside him, Ridge and Cully on opposite ends of the back seat—to the Wild Horse Acres apartments. A loose motorcade of eleven other sedans followed them, pursued by a battalion of minicams and mobile satellite units. Seeing Ridge glancing back at this entourage, Bellflower said, "Don't worry, we've got containment at the sight. And with all those other guys, nobody's gonna target you for a story."

Ridge said nothing.

Bellflower nodded to Cully, and she told Ridge about the psycho, former mental patient ex-boyfriend of the murdered woman, and the alibi nobody could fracture. Ridge glanced at her occasionally, but mostly he kept his eyes down.

Bellflower broke in and said to Ridge, "You know how it is. We know the guy's mental record, we know his priors, we know his motive of jealousy, and we know the vicious nature of the crime fits his past. All that is empty dookey. You gotta find a way to get me a confession."

Ridge just nodded, and rode.

When they reached the apartment complex, Fresco waved to the uniforms who had set up the perimeter to protect the crime scene, and they stepped aside for the sedan to pass. The photographers camped at the perimeter were used to the constant comings and goings of detectives, and paid them no attention.

At the unit where the woman had died, Ridge got out of the car and looked at the crime scene. They all did—Bellflower, Fresco, and the squad of other detectives including Cully McCullers—but Ridge stood so motionless and silent as he stared at the spot of the murder that no one else wanted to move or ask a question. The body had been removed hours before for forensic examination, but the enormous imprint of its bloody demise still marked the pavement, and Cully, pushing herself close enough to watch Ridge, thought: *He's seeing it all in his mind, imagining every detail Bellflower told him.*

And recalling those details was not hard. The heavy stone that flattened the large woman's skull still lay on the asphalt, and the bloody gray splatter of her brain matter still stained the fence beside her.

Ridge looked for barely a minute. "What day of the month is it?" he asked. "The sixth?" He turned and looked at one of the detectives standing at the door of the apartment. "You found her checkbook?" Bellflower and Fresco frowned at each other. Personal records, especially financial ones, are routine targets in a murder investigation, but a detective will go to them only when stumped, or to check a theory. What had Ridge seen in one minute, that thirty other detectives had not noticed all morning long?

The detective at the apartment door shrugged and pointed to a cardboard box on the folding table they had set up to catalogue everything they were carting away. Ridge fished the checkbook from the box, flipped back through the stubs, and said, "Where's the manager of this place?"

"In his apartment, two doors down," another detective said. "Little guy. Owns the place. He's scared to death this ain't gonna help business."

Ridge strolled down to the owner/manager's unit and

knocked on the plastic-coated aluminum door. He had to knock again before a thin bald man answered. His scalp was sunburned and freckled, and his eyes looked large and too blue behind gold glasses. Poking his head out the door he said, "I'm sorry, I'm upset. Who would do such a thing to such a sweet, sweet . . ."

The man's name was Ned Walt; it said so on his door, along with the manager nameplate. "Mr. Walt," Ridge said, "could you come down to the station? I'd like to talk."

The whole entourage of cops who had followed Ridge down to the manager's unit had stood back from the door when Ridge knocked and said nothing when Ridge led the landlord past them and put him into a police cruiser and asked the uniform in it to drive Mr. Walt over to the Van Nuys station. But as soon as the cruiser pulled away they surged at Ridge.

"Van Nuys?" Bellflower demanded of Ridge. "Why not Devonshire?"

"Devonshire's his local station. He'll be less comfortable at Van Nuys. It'll be his first hint," Ridge said.

"Hint?" Fresco said. "You think this guy did it?"

Bellflower grabbed Ridge's arm. "Ridge! You been here five fuckin' minutes, you think you got the guy?"

"We'll see," said Doubting Thomas.

CHAPTER THIRTY-ONE

When they got back into their car, Ridge held up his hand to cut off Fresco's first question, and they rode back to the station in silence, Ridge thinking with closed eyes as he rubbed and pinched the bone between his eyebrows and composed what he was going to say to Ned Walt.

Bellflower had stepped away from them and made a quick phone call from a phone booth before they started, and when they reached the Van Nuys station and walked in the detective's entrance, they found out why. A reporter was waiting for them. His name was Charlie Gulker. He was thirty-eight years old. He wore a tweed sports coat, corduroy pants, and thosg over-the-ankle Hush Puppies they call desert boots. His granny glasses were the only giveaway of his hippie past. Every cop that knew him trusted him; Ridge was one of the few who truly liked him; but Ridge, the instant he saw Gulker, wheeled on Bellflower.

"I promised I'd keep 'em off you," Bellflower snapped, before Ridge could speak. "But somebody's gotta watch this. We come up with an alternative to Ragg, the whole city's gonna say we're reaching. We come up with a confession, they're gonna say we beat it out of a guy."

"You promised me," Ridge said.

"He'll keep you out of it," Bellflower said. "He swears. In exchange for the exclusive, he won't mention your name unless he buries it with the whole team."

Ridge stared at Gulker a minute and then nodded. "No offense, Charlie," Ridge said.

"None taken, Tom," Gulker said.

Rose Nose Dugan barreled up. "We got your guy in Interrogation One!" he said to Ridge. "You need anything?"

"A blackboard," Ridge said.

"A blackboard?" Dugan said, his eyes lightening up. "Sea of Life?"

Ridge nodded. Maybe he smiled a little. Maybe he didn't. Nobody was sure, afterward.

CHAPTER THIRTY-TWO

Bellflower, Fresco, the reporter Charlie Gulker, Dugan, Cully, and six other Van Nuys detectives had squeezed their way into the tiny observation room, so that it was hot and stank of sweat, but no one seemed to mind. They shifted and turned until everybody had a view through the one-way mirror into the smaller interrogation room on the other side of the glass. A video camera through the mirror made their room even smaller but nobody complained. A small speaker, connected through a recording system, hung in the top corner of the room and linked them to the otherwise soundproof cubicle next door. Ned Walt sat alone on the other side of the glass. Behind him was a blackboard. He sat calmly, looking a little sad. He kept checking his watch; time had dragged by slowly for him, during the hour that he had been the guest of the Los Angeles Police Department.

Ridge entered the cubicle. He sat down across from Walt and looked at him for a long time. Walt's face began to change. The mournfulness in his eyes suddenly turned to surprise, then to fright; then he looked away. Ridge stood slowly, moved to the blackboard, and chalked a line across its width, four inches from the top. "Mr. Walt," Ridge said, "this is the Sea of Life."

Rose Nose Dugan clinched both fists in front of him and shook them in celebration. "Shh!" Bellflower hissed sharply, though their room was completely soundproof. Rosie stiffened, suddenly afraid he had jinxed Ridge.

"And down here," Ridge said, drawing a minute circle in the lower left corner of the board, "this little piece of whale turd lying at the bottom of the Sea of Life, is you. And way over here—" Ridge drew a flat oval in the upper right corner, above his first chalk line, and even added the suggestion of a palm tree, "—is the Island of Freedom. Between you and this island are man-eating sharks." Ridge tossed his chalk onto the wooden lip of the board, and faced Walt. "And the only chance you have, the only tiny, miniscule hope you have of ever reaching the Island of Freedom, is to tell me everything."

Ned Walt sat motionless for a moment; and then his face quivered like a mountain of snow before an avalanche, and fell suddenly into a river of tears.

Excitement jolted through the observation room. No one even whispered.

The little landlord, even broken as he was, did not want to say anything; but Ridge droned what he had figured out, which was everything. "Ned," he said sympathetically, as one might speak to an old friend, "I understand why you did it. That scum-ball boyfriend of hers moved out and left her without any money, and you felt sorry for her. You let her slide on her rent. It was just a gift you made her, I understand that, you weren't buying sex from her, she gave you that because she appreciated the mercy you showed her. And the sex with her was good, too, you didn't have to try, she just enjoyed everything you did and appreciated it too. But that unfaithful bitch . . . She knew you really loved her, and the more she knew that, the more demanding she got—the more she took you for granted. She would dress up and go out. And you followed her. Down the road to that bar. You saw her drinking with those men. You saw her out in the parking lot—what she did in the front seat of that car. . . ."

Walt blubbered, "The other cops . . . think it was her boyfriend."

"The other cops," Ridge said, nodding. "Yeah. They were so busy thinking about him they never thought about you. Trouble is, I came along, Ned." Ridge sounded as if he truly regretted it.

"How did you know it was me?" Ned Walt said, and sniffled. The cops watching from the tiny room grew tense; they knew the question was not an admission but a challenge. In another instant their suspect could stiffen and deny everything.

Ridge smiled like an indulgent priest. "Well, come on, Ned! The guy that beat her to death was good with a hammer—it's hard to swing one that many times. Of course you did all the work around that nice little apartment complex you own. Nobody could afford to hire somebody else to keep it that neat, and you're a handy guy. The boyfriend, heck, he never used a tool in his life.

"But the obvious thing, Ned, the obvious thing was the walkway stone. The guy that beat her to death knew how heavy those stones were, and what they'd do to her head, since he'd laid every one of those stones with his own hands."

Cully's eyes darted for an instant at Bellflower, and he felt her look but did not return it. In the other room Ridge went on sharply, "And Ned, look at me. Look at me, I gotta tell you something. One of two things is gonna happen to you in this Sea of Life. The sharks in the legal system can have you. You'll get a lawyer, a judge, a prosecutor, and all the cops out there are gonna go through your life with a vacuum cleaner. They'll find your fingerprints all over her apartment, but you were her landlord, you can explain that."

Ridge paused, giving Walt time to calculate his odds of beating a charge of murder. "But," Ridge said, "how are you gonna explain us finding her pubic hair in your sheets, Ned? 'Cause we're gonna get a search warrant and go back to your place right now. If we put together a case, and take it to a jury, and show them what you did to that girl, they're gonna scream for your blood. The women on the jury will get sick at the sight of you, and the men will want to pull you to pieces. They're going to want you to die in the gas chamber. They're going to insist on it.

"Or," Ridge said, pausing for a heartbeat, "you can climb into my boat, Ned. You can let me row you. For a crime of passion, a jury would feel pity, and in short time, you might make it to the Island of Freedom. But the only way, the only way you get into my boat, Ned, is with a confession."

In the observation room, the detectives grabbed at each other's arms, and stopped breathing.

Ned Walt bowed his head, nodded, and began to sob.

Rose Nose Dugan, in the observation cubicle, shook his head in awe and whispered, "The winner, and still fuckin' champion!"

CHAPTER THIRTY-THREE

The confession process took two hours. First Walt told his story to Ridge, and then he repeated it after being Mirandized. The other cops in the observation room had scrambled out the moment the landlord finally, ultimately broke, and word of what was happening in Interrogation One in Van Nuys spread to every police division in the city; but Cully, Fresco, and Bellflower stayed in the stuffy little booth to watch, with only the reporter Charlie Gulker remaining with them, scribbling notes.

During the drone of Walt's repeating his confession,

Cully pulled Bellflower aside, and whispered to him. "Commander," she said, "what is it with Ridge and reporters? What is it with him and publicity?"

Bellflower studied her face for a moment. "It's a private thing," he said.

But her ego had just been stripped away, along with that of every detective in the division; she had earned the right to be admiring, and curious. "Something about it scares him," she pressed. "What is it about publicity that scares him?"

"You'd better ask him that yourself," Bellflower said.

Ten minutes later the door to Interrogation One opened, and Ned Walt was led out in handcuffs by two uniformed cops, who took him to the elevator for his trip to the holding cells downstairs. Then Ridge appeared. The cops cheered. Ridge nodded, smiled faintly, and walked down the hallway like a gunfighter into the sunset.

CHAPTER THIRTY-FOUR

With Ridge vanished into legend, and the reporters to other stories, and Ragg Wilson sent home to sleep and shower and suffer a flare-up of his hemorrhoids, Cully McCullers went back to the task of finding Victoria Lopez.

While Quang telephoned the various police divisions of the city, starting near the U.C.L.A. campus and working outward in hopes of discovering something about the van used in the abduction, Cully called the Lopez house. Victoria's mother answered the phone and told her that her husband had gone to work. Her voice sounded formal, as if she was reading a prepared statement.

Cully hung up, looked across at Quang, and said, "They don't trust us."

"Who?" Quang was usually not this obtuse; but he was preoccupied with the certain promotion he had missed by not being the first to solve what some now called the Fat Lady Affair.

"The Lopez family," Cully said. "They're waiting to

be contacted, or they already have been. And they don't trust us."

"We need surveillance."

"Sure, but Dugan's not going to give it to us. And the F.B.I. won't get involved. To them it's a gang abduction, not a real kidnapping, and since Lopez says there's no ransom demand I've got no room to argue." She rubbed her hand through her hair. "Okay, look, what've we got? We've got a girl, we've got gangs. Gangs mean drugs, but everybody says Victoria and Chaz weren't into drugs. But some local Hispanic gang wants her for some reason."

She stood up and went down the hallway to the CRASH Unit cubicle. CRASH was the acronym for Community Reaction Against Street Hoodlums; it was the antigang task force. Its leader was Brando Michaels, a jovial guy with a soft round face who led Himalayan trail hikes on his vacation time and ran ten marathons a year. For a man who spent nearly every night gathering the remains of dead teenagers from the streets he was remarkably happy, especially around pretty women, and his smile was bright as he looked up and said, "Detective McCullers! What can I do you for?"

"You see my memo? I've got a girl abducted at U.C.L.A. Seems to have been by a local Hispanic gang."

"Kidnapping's not a gang crime!" Michaels said. "Especially a gang of beaners! They might abduct a chevy and give it a new shag carpet dashboard, but that's about it for Mexicans and kidnapping!"

"So did you never see my memo, or did you just throw it away because you thought it was stupid?"

"Ease up, Detective." The truth was that Michaels hadn't read the paperwork in his in basket; but he didn't need a rookie detective climbing up his back about it.

"Look, Michaels, I'm sorry. I've got a case I'm working on and it's going no place and I'm happy Ragg's off the hook but all that did for me was put me further behind. So I'm sorry, okay?"

"It happens. So what do you need from me?"

"There's a piece of this missing somewhere. And it's got to do with what the gang wants from the girl's father. If it was money I think he would have tried to pay them already.

Whatever it is, the family's not talking, so I figure they know the ransom demand and intend to go along with it to get their daughter back. The last thing I want is for the girl to get hurt. But the kidnappers killed the girl's boyfriend in making the abduction. And—"

"And that means the girl is a witness to a capital murder crime."

"Yeah," Cully said.

"So even if the father pays the ransom, they're not going to let somebody who can put them in the gas chamber go walking back home."

Cully nodded. She had it figured this way all along, and Michael's appraisal reassured her that she wasn't just letting fear lead her judgment; but instead of reassurance she now felt sick fear in her stomach.

"I'm going to keep trying, though I don't think I'll get anywhere with the family," Cully said. "But if we could get a line on the gang, we might bust this open from that end."

"Anything I get happening the least bit out of the ordinary, I'll call you," Michaels said.

Cully nodded her thanks and went back to her cubicle. Michaels reached into his internal mail basket, and started trying to catch up with his paperwork.

CHAPTER THIRTY-FIVE

Cully and Quang spent the next hour trying to communicate with other police agencies, all of whom had their own jobs to do—mostly involving trying to communicate with other police agencies. Descriptions had gone out—of the kidnapped girl, the van, the abductors—but to be sure that the agencies had paid attention to their paper blizzard, Cully and Quang had to follow up with a call, and the detectives, like everyone else, had trouble getting other cops on the telephone.

But then, just after lunch, Cully's phone rang. On the other end was Michaels. "Detective McCullers!" he said brightly. "You might want to get out here on the Hollywood Freeway south, at Cahuenga. It may not be anything, but hey, it's freeway-close!"

They drove to the Cahuenga Pass, where the Hollywood Freeway dumps traffic out into the San Fernando Valley. At the Barham exit they found traffic mired in a solid wall. The incident had occurred on the other side of the freeway, on the inbound lanes, but the rubberneckers had slowed enough to stop everything behind them. So Quang, who was driving, used his flashers and took the shoulder to the exit. The whole side of the freeway was closed off. Quang looked smug and natural, driving the wrong way up an off-ramp.

They rolled to a stop at the yellow ribbon stretched across the road surface. The Highway Patrol had sealed off the inbound lanes of the freeway a mile behind them, diverting traffic onto the surface streets, thereby creating a nightmare for the motorcycle patrols, but the California Highway Patrol guys stood quietly by their Moto Guzzis as the LAPD worked. Highway patrol officers see plenty of gore, but murder is an unusual sight for them and creates its own dark reverence. The five southbound lanes of the freeway lay empty now, a mile of vacant concrete bleaching in the sun. In the center of this openness were three LAPD cars, surrounding an orange lacquered '72 Pontiac.

Trigger Frazier and Micro Morris were already there with Michaels. Frazier, standing at the rear window of the orange car, leered at Cully as she and Quang walked up, and said loudly to Michaels, "Hey, our resident lady brain is here! Now we'll get some real help! Detective! Come on over and analyze this for us!" He beckoned them so broadly his belly shook.

Quang started to step toward the car, but Cully stopped him with the back of her hand against his chest, and stepped over to face off with Frazier. Frazier raised his eyebrows at the acceptance of his challenge, put his hand against the top of the Pontiac, where it had already been dusted for fingerprints, and leaned down to the open back window. "Come on, Bull Barrel, what do you think of this?"

She leaned down, coming face to face with the corpse of

a Chicano boy. The bullet hole at the center of the bridge of his nose still oozed red and gray froth down his left cheek. He was slumped toward the driver's side. Frazier leaned down beside her, gave a low whistle and said, "Pretty, huh?"

She straightened and sucked in a deep breath to try to clear the smell. She said, "It's an execution. Somebody, maybe in his own gang, walked up and shot him."

Frazier raised his eyebrows again and pursed his lips. "Wow. That's brilliant. Isn't that brilliant, guys?" He grinned. "How do you know this?"

"I've shot a pistol," Cully said. "This boy knew whoever killed him well enough to let him get close, because nobody hits a target like that without being right on top of it."

"Well, honey," Frazier said, grinning, "don't underestimate the Mexicans. They'd win a lotta gold medals if the Olympics had a contest for drive-by shooting!"

"Yeah!" Morris said behind him. "Or a track event called spray-and-run!"

The police photographer snickered into his viewfinder. The uniformed patrol officers who had nothing else to do because the freeway was already blocked off anyway looked toward Frazier and grinned.

Frazier continued, "No, sugar, this Paco bought his taco at sixty miles an hour. Him and his *pachuco* friends were lowriding along the freeway when they came up on a car with markings of the Two-Tone Bloods. So our buddy with the third eye here yells out, 'Hey, *puta* you pussies, we Los Malos, *numero uno!*' And so the brother in the other car reaches into the glove compartment, hauls out a thirty-eight, and *boom!* Right in the snot locker! Second round clipped the side of his skull and spun him back around. But, uh—" Frazier closed his eyes, and nodded, "—nice guess anyway." Morris and the two uniform officers with him were chuckling. Even Michaels was swallowing back a snicker.

Cully wondered if her face was as red as it was hot. "How do you know all this?" she said to Frazier.

"That's what the other Malos told us. Spatter a Mexican kid with his amigo's brains and he'll fill you in pretty quick on all the details. But maybe they don't teach girls that in college." Frazier stretched and pretended to yawn. To the uniforms he said, "I guess we've seen enough here. You boys finish up!"

"You know," Cully said, "you're mighty smart when you've got a witness to tell you the story. The boys in this car must have been pretty spooked, so I guess they told you the truth, but on the other hand maybe they were so shaken up they didn't. And this was no great shot. It was blind luck, and bad luck. A bullet fired from one car to another, on the freeway, with a crosswind between them of sixty miles an hour, minimum—how much deflection would you get out of that? The guy with the gun could have meant to shoot out the windshield, or just put a round through the car. If he hit the guy between the eyes on the first shot, the macho thing would have been to blow the smoke off the barrel and drive on, but he must have freaked out to shoot again. That's for starters. To lock this case for more than manslaughter, you're going to have to nail the intent, so you've got to show what the shooter meant to hit. Was the wind between the cars significant? Do you know how far apart the cars were at the moment of the shots? Were there any skid marks? You might check that, before you have Willard and Millard there call out the tow truck and open up the freeway again."

She walked toward her car again, stopped again, and called back, "But most of all, you better ask yourself why two gangs are fighting outside their home turf. Michaels wonders that—that's why he called me."

She stalked away again. Her anger was like a chronic itch; having barely scratched its surface she felt it breaking out all over. She was furious with Frazier, with every smug pig she had to work with.

"Great ass, huh?" Frazier said, ignoring his humiliation. "How could you ride next to her, and not go crazy wantin' to put your hands all over her?"

Michaels wondered that too. Then he thought he'd better take a vacation, if he was asking the same questions as Trigger.

CHAPTER THIRTY-SIX

Quang was still silent when they fell in with the traffic on the open part of the freeway; high speed usually made him talkative. Cully wished again that they could talk and be the kind of partners cops were supposed to be. Maybe he just doesn't like me, she thought. Or maybe, unlike the other cops surrounding her, he was simply a gentleman.

Quang glanced over and said, "They really don't mean to antagonize you, you know."

Cully looked at him. "Frazier? Morris? Those guys?"

"Yes."

"Yeah. Right."

Quang grinned, trying to look inscrutable. He casually cruised along, nearly running an old woman in a Datsun off the road. "Are you aware of the pool they have started?"

"Who?" Cully said, frowning.

"The detectives, at the station. Uniforms may enter as well. Tuition is twenty dollars, and the first gentleman to achieve amorous intimacy with you may claim the total investment."

"Amorous intimacy?"

"Physical conquest."

"You mean sex."

"I believe 'drill her' is the precise description of the requisite."

"Are you in this pot?"

Quang hesitated. "I joined my brother officers in this speculative venture, yes."

Cully was silent for a half mile. Quang worried that he had overplayed his hand. He was about to apologize when Cully said softly, "Do you think you've got a chance to win?"

Quang's eyes flicked over at her. "Well now. Perhaps. Perhaps I do. You are obviously an open-minded lady of refinement who might welcome the opportunity to experience the French method of—" He stopped when he felt the barrel of her pistol against his temple. "Hey," he said. "Hey."

"Tell me something, Quang. Did you see *The Deer Hunter*?"

"Officer. Detective McCullers—"

"Maybe I should drill you."

"Hey. Scarlet. Cully. Hey!"

She cocked the hammer. He tried to turn to look at her but she jammed the metal to his head. She said, "Ever since I got out of uniform and put on a skirt I've been getting leers, and every time I walk through the station my brother detectives smack their lips behind my back. I may have to put up with that from them but I sure don't have to take it from my partner."

"Cully," Quang said gravely, his fingers white on the steering wheel. "That weapon could go off!"

"Go off?"

She pulled the trigger.

The hammer snapped but nothing else happened. Quang, when he heard the metallic impact beside his ear, sagged down toward the wheel, then sat bolt upright and rocked the car across three lanes of freeway traffic.

Cully gave a low, vicious chuckle, as she tucked away the gun. "My dad's thirty-eight," she said. "I keep a couple of chambers empty. A full load is too tempting when you work around assholes."

"You—you are authentically insane! To-to-to-to threaten me! Your partner! With a gun!"

"God damn you, Quang! God damn all of you! Here, I'll put my gun away! Pull the car over!"

"What?"

"Pull the fucking car over! I'll beat the shit out of you with my bare hands!"

Quang drove straight down the middle of the road, all the way to the station. It was the best driving he had ever done.

CHAPTER THIRTY-SEVEN

Cully knew he would report her. At least he ought to. A cop who shows a reckless disregard for the danger of firearms needs help—that's what they told them at the academy.

Cully needed help all right; but the help she needed wasn't to control her emotions, it was to get the job done. Victoria Lopez was out there somewhere, with people who killed without remorse, and her father was lying to the police. He didn't trust them. It wasn't that he found them corrupt, he just found them ineffective. And wasn't he right? Who could have confidence in men like Frazier?

But in her own car as she drove away from the Van Nuys station, without even bothering to go upstairs and check in, Cully thought, *And look at you! Why should he trust you? What have you done to save his daughter?*

Cully felt stupid, useless, unworthy. But she drove out to Esteban Lopez's house anyway, and switched off her headlights and waited, watching the house from the dark because she did not know what else to do.

CHAPTER THIRTY-EIGHT

Early in his career, Guillermo Montoya had learned the power of mutilation.

He was only five and a half feet tall, so it was hard for him to look fierce. And he had fine features: a straight nose, narrow chin, and smooth, walnut brown skin.

Guillermo Montoya had grown up in a village two miles on the Mexican side of the Guatemalan border. He had never been afraid to move back and forth on either side of the border; he had never been afraid of anything. When he was ten years old the man in his village who owned the store where they sold canned peaches and whiskey asked him to pick up a package from another man on the other side, and Guillermo did what he was told. For his trouble—a five-hour trek—the storekeeper gave him two sticks of licorice. Guillermo thanked the man, and left his store, but only to slip back from the shadows and listen outside the window as the owner made a call on his telephone. Guillermo watched the strangers—two men in an American car—who came and picked up the package an hour later.

The next time the storekeeper asked Guillermo to make another trip, the boy did not negotiate for a higher fee. He simply made the trip again, carrying down one package and bringing back another. He accepted the candy. He went outside, and hid while the storekeeper made his call. Then he went back into the store and asked to buy some condoms, which he knew were under the counter. The storekeeper smiled, and leaned down to fetch them. Guillermo hit him on the back of the neck with the hatchet he had picked up in back of the store, the one the storekeeper used to hack open crates of tequila.

When the men in the Oldsmobile came they found the storekeeper's head staring at them from on top of the counter. They drew pistols and backed out of the store. A boy was sitting on the hood of their car; the boy was Guillermo Montoya. The boy told them that something terrible had happened. A fat man, very tall, had entered the store, not half an hour ago, when Guillermo was there buying salt for his mother. The fat man, Guillermo told them, had not minded Guillermo's audience; he lifted the storekeeper by the hair and severed his head with a machete. "Then he turn to me," Guillermo told them, "and gave me a message. He say I am to wait here, and hide, until I see two men come. They will ask for a package, a small package wrapped in brown paper and string, that weigh about as much as a dead chicken. I should say to these men that they can have the package, if they give El Gordo ten thousand dollars."

Guillermo tried to sound scared; and he worried that he was doing a bad job of it. But the two men from the Oldsmobile were too frightened themselves, with their eyes darting all about, to notice that Guillermo's whine was phoney and theatrical. "Where is this Gordo?" they asked him.

"Watching," Guillermo said.

The men ducked and twisted all around, peering at the shadows of the jungle.

"He told me," Guillermo said, "the place where I am to take the money, a spot far in the mountains, that only locals know. He said that there he will give me the package he took from the storekeeper, and I will bring it back here, to the gringos who gave me the money."

"How much money?" the men with the Oldsmobile asked.

"Ten thousand dollars, not pesos," Guillermo said.

The men looked at each other, and backed up, away from Guillermo, and whispered. They moved toward him again and handed him money. They still had money in their wallets; Guillermo had underestimated the price. Guillermo took the money and slid off the hood of the car. "Oh," he said, "by the way; El Gordo says if you try to follow me he will know it because he is watching now. He will kill me, and whoever follows. Then he will have both the package and the money."

With that Guillermo moved up the trail that wound toward the misty tops of the mountains. He walked a short distance, then slipped into the vegetation, so thick a man could not see ten meters ahead of him, and through which Guillermo could move as quickly and silently as a lizard.

The two Americans waited in the store, drinking beer from the cooler of the man whose head still rested on the counter. They laughed, argued with each other, laughed again, argued again. Once a woman from a farm outside the village came in to buy sugar and saw the head still on the counter, and she screamed and rushed away and the men with the Oldsmobile howled with laughter and drank more beer and pissed into the bean bins. At sundown their laughter stopped. They knew they had been cheated, and now they grew afraid; they were no longer so sure of the strength of their pistols, now that it was so dark they could not see anyone slipping in from the trees. The head still stared at them from on top of the counter, and it was no longer so funny. The gringos moved out of the store to their car, and found the paper-and-string package lying in the middle of the front seat.

When they started to drive away their headlights lit up Guillermo Montoya, standing spraddle-legged in the road. They stopped, and Guillermo moved to the driver. "El Gordo gives me another message," Guillermo told the men. "He says there is no reason for deliveries to stop; next week there can be another package, exchanged the same way. El Gordo says his prices will be reasonable; not as good as this time, when he had to prove he was a man of sincerity, but good nevertheless; dependable, and better than the store-keeper's rates."

The men in the car, who were feeling very smart now that they had their ten pounds of *coca* paste on the seat between them, said for Guillermo to tell the fat man they would be back.

The store sat vacant for a day, with the head still on the counter and flies buzzing all around it. But during the second night Guillermo's brother Alejandro visited the store, and the next morning the head was gone but Alejandro wasn't. He became the new storekeeper. And a week later the Americans came back, and Guillermo made another exchange. He had visited the man across the border, had told him plans had changed with the storekeeper and the new deal was slightly different.

Now Guillermo Montoya was twenty-three, and he knew that all of his wealth was due to his willingness to butcher. He thought of that as he walked from his apartment, on his way to see Victoria Lopez.

CHAPTER THIRTY-NINE

Guillermo owned the building that housed his apartment and his office. He had built the high-rise with government-subsidized financing, just after the great earthquake. He also owned the pile of rubble next door, a two-story mass of broken concrete and twisted steel. There were many such piles throughout Mexico City, remnants of the wreckage. But this pile of rubble was different.

In the center elevator of his high-rise, Guillermo used a special key to descend all the way to the subbasement. When he reached it, he stepped out and nodded to the young man who sat in the semidarkness beside the elevator door. The young man sat upright and saluted with the hand that held a walkie-talkie, connected by special transceiver relays to watchmen outside the building.

Guillermo passed through a steel door, into a long utilities tunnel lined with water pipes and electrical conduit and illuminated by a single light bulb hung in the center of its hundred-foot length. At the far end was another steel door. It came open as Montoya reached it, and Ricardo Flores smiled at him.

"Welcome to paradise," Ricardo said.

"How did your date go?"

"The redhead will never be found," Ricardo said. "Not even by the coyotes."

Guillermo nodded, and smiled.

The two of them wound their way through a series of rooms in what had once been the foundation of a massive building. Most of the rooms—actually just structural compartments in the former foundation—were intact, but here and there the ruptured concrete jutted out, and they had to step around or crawl through. A ventilation duct, originating in the new building next door, snaked its way along beside them, and was accompanied by smaller pipes for water and electricity. They reached the real room, a five-meter-square compartment with white walls, a mattress with flowered sheets, a toilet, a sink, a refrigerator, a hot plate, and Victoria Lopez.

She was standing in the corner, holding herself as if cold, though the room was pleasant, to Guillermo's thinking. Another of his soldiers was in the room with her, but he kept a respectful distance. Victoria spun away as Guillermo entered, and kept her face toward the corner.

"What's this for?" Guillermo said in Spanish.

The girl hesitated, her breath shaky. "I am an American," she said in English.

"Oooo," Guillermo sang, "I am impressed! But is that why you tell me this—to impress me?" When Victoria did not answer or even turn around he said, "Or . . . is it something else? I know! It is to make me afraid!" He walked up and tickled the nape of her neck with the back of his fingernail. "And I am very afraid."

"The police will find me!"

"So you keep telling my friends who stay here with you. I must pay them extra because they have to listen to you so much! But why do you refuse to look at me?"

Victoria drew another unsteady breath. "Because . . . I don't want to see your face."

"Ah. I see. You think we will kill you if you have seen our faces!" Guillermo laughed, so loudly she was startled. That was just what he wanted; he liked seeing her jump, liked seeing her flesh quiver. "I don't know what they teach Mexicans in the North, but either the Americans who live there are very smart or the Mexicans who go there are very stupid, huh? I don't want to kill you. I don't have to kill you. Look at me. Look at me!" He snatched at her arm and spun her around so that her body was toward his; still she kept her face away and he grabbed her chin to pull her straight. When he had held her this way for a few seconds her eyes finally snapped around to his. "I am not the enemy of your country. I make an enormous fortune there, a huge, enormous fortune for a poor stupid Mexican like myself. I do not force one person to give me a penny. The people in the North who buy what I sell want what I sell, it is very easy. To you, a college girl, I may be no better than a prostitute. Have it your way, if you really believe you know how the world works. You would be agreeing with your government, which makes speeches about how badly it wants to stop men like me. But I sell drugs openly on the streets of America. Anybody who wants what I sell can find it easily, anywhere. Why doesn't your government punish the people who buy what I sell? Because they too are Americans. They, Señorita Lopez, do not want me stopped."

Before he finished, Victoria Lopez was crying. He took her in his arms. She kept her elbows tucked between his chest and hers, and pushed at him, but there was no strength in her arms. "Why me?" she shrieked. "What do you want with me?"

"Not you," Guillermo said. "Your father. I want him to do me a favor. He refused the first time I asked with money, so now I ask him a different way."

Montoya watched the eyes of the terrified girl as she seized on this sudden hope; if her fate depended on her father's willingness to save her, then she had nothing to worry about. He watched the relief flood into her face, then savored her surprise when he said to the men watching there in the concrete room, "Strip off her clothes and tie her up."

Victoria tried to struggle but two of the men grabbed her arms and stretched them out so tight she couldn't twist. Guillermo stood back as Ricardo unbuttoned her shirt, pulled off her jeans, yanked off her bra, and stripped down her panties. They pushed the nude girl into a wooden chair in the center of the room and tied her ankles to the chair legs and her upper arms and wrists to the chair backs, using strips of cotton cloth so the bindings would not mark her. She was screaming.

Guillermo withdrew a length of jeweled mother-of-pearl from his pocket and held it in front of her eyes until she stopped screaming. Then he pushed the button on the knife and the blade jumped out before her face. Her mouth was open but no sound could come from her throat. Very slowly he lowered the knife; her eyes followed the movement of the blade. With the fingertips of his free hand he pinched the nipple of her left breast, and pulled it out, stretching it taut. He brought the edge of the knife up against the tight skin. The other men around her were breathing hard; Victoria could not breathe at all.

But Guillermo was completely relaxed. He smiled. Victoria, when she saw him smile, thought he was only trying to frighten her, and she relaxed.

That was what Guillermo wanted. He jerked the blade.

THE FIFTH DAY

CHAPTER FORTY

The new morning was a milky haze, the sky too bright to look at and too dull to see.

Cully droned through her exercises and showered without a conscious thought. She dressed in jeans and Dingo cowboy boots; today she felt like an urban commando.

She drove downtown, to the warehouse of the Lopez Produce Company. On the loading dock she grabbed one of the workers by the ropey arm as he carried a crate of cantaloupe from a roller conveyor to a delivery truck and asked him, "Where can I find Mr. Lopez?" The worker nodded toward a door halfway down the dock, and Cully strode to it, and entered without knocking.

Esteban Lopez sat at a battered metal desk, covered with invoices and bills of lading. The desks of two secretaries, working on similar stacks of paper, jammed up the rest of the floor space in the little room. Lopez looked up as Cully entered; first his face showed surprise, and then it became a mask.

"Aren't you going to ask me if I have any news?" Cully said.

Lopez stared at her, then said, "Juanita. Francesca." The two secretaries looked at him, at Cully, at each other, and then left.

"Mr. Lopez," Cully said, "I went to U.C.L.A. last night, and talked with Victoria's sorority sisters."

Lopez said nothing.

"Every one of them," Cully added. "I asked them who telephoned you on the day Victoria was kidnapped, to tell you what happened."

Lopez's eyelids began to quiver; he pushed back from

111

his desk as if he meant to jump to his feet and leave, but he did not stand.

"None of them called you," Cully said. "You said they had. You even tried to remember a name—Janet, Jennifer or something. But none of them called."

Lopez stared at the bookshelves lining his wall. "Everyone was shocked," he said. "It would be hard to remember every detail."

"It would be impossible to forget that detail," Cully said. "Every one, Mr. Lopez. I talked with every single one of Victoria's sorority sisters. They had hashed and rehashed all the details of Victoria's abduction, until it all blended together in their minds, so that the ones who hadn't seen anything still had as strong a mental picture as the ones who had. But nobody remembered calling you. None of them had."

Lopez lowered his head. Cully could not see his face, but she thought at first he might be crying. She stepped up to his shoulder and saw that he was not crying; he was fingering a toothpick in a silver cup on his desk. The cup, barely the size of a magnetic paper clip holder, contained only the toothpick; the toothpick was one of those festive kind that caterers put out at a party for skewering meatballs or boiled shrimp. It had green cellophane curlicues glued to the top end, and the curls were bent and old; the toothpick was a souvenir of some kind, and sat in the tiny goblet like a bouquet in a miniature vase.

Cully said, "Mr. Lopez. You lied when you told us one of Victoria's sorority sisters had called you. You knew already she had been kidnapped. So you know the reason. The kidnappers called you, before or after, or they got to you some other way, but you know who took her and what they want." Lopez answered nothing; he took the toothpick from the goblet, felt the prick of its still-sharp point upon his finger, and rolled it gently around his blotter. "I understand your being afraid," Cully said. "But you're going to have to trust me. If you're going to get Victoria back, the way you want her back, you've got to trust me. Trust me," she said again, and finally Lopez looked at her.

But his eyes did not focus. They were far away. "Victoria

. . ." he said, and smiled. "Victoria listened to all my stories. About Mexico. When I was young." He spoke in phrases. "My son Edward was too busy to listen. My stories bored him, I knew that. But Victoria always listened.

"I told her many times about how poor we were. How we had so little, and no room at all in our house, since twelve of us lived there. I told her how I could keep no toys, even marbles I had made myself, because I had no place to keep anything safe, and my little brothers and sisters would find and play with anything. I was not selfish," Lopez said quickly, looking at Cully as if she had judged him. "It was just . . . that children like to have their own domain, and I had none. So I would choose a common object, like a toothpick, and say to my mother or my father, 'This toothpick is a gun.' Or a magic wand. Or a flute— anything I wanted it to be. 'But please don't tell my brothers or sisters. They think it is a toothpick.' "

Lopez looked back down at his desk, at the toothpick with the green cellophane. "I told Victoria that one day when we were in a restaurant. An expensive restaurant. I guess I was trying to tell her that everything in life costs money. I was trying to prepare her more for life.

"So then she pulls this toothpick out of her sandwich, and reaches it across to me, and says, 'Poppy, this toothpick means . . . I love you.' "

He paused for a moment, steadied himself, and smiled as if he had just thought of something very funny. "You know, when she started going with that Pendleton boy, she didn't tell us about him at first. That was okay, girls don't like to talk to their fathers about the boys they date; they think they're women already, you know? But I always insisted on knowing everybody she went out with—you know, when she was in high school—and I told her, 'Hey, I want to meet this guy.' And . . . Well, you know, she brought him down one day, to the warehouse, to meet me. And then I knew they were serious. So I said, 'Hey, Victoria, invite your boyfriend's parents to come down and meet all of us.' And then I saw that she was afraid to do that. It hurt me, you know, and I screamed at her and said she was ashamed of us for not being as rich as the Pendletons. And I told her that if she was ashamed of us, then I was ashamed of her!"

He looked down at his hands. "That was two weeks ago. We haven't talked since then."

His eyes suddenly filled with tears. He would say nothing else, but only stared at the festive toothpick.

CHAPTER FORTY-ONE

Cully drove to the station. She found her cubicle half empty; Quang's desk was deserted and picked clean of everything, even the blotter. She paused at the door and stared at the naked desktop, now showing the scars and ink stains of three generations of careless detectives. Rose Nose Dugan moved up behind her. "Captain wants to see you," he said.

She walked to the office of Captain Fresco, knocked, and went in. He looked up from his paperwork, then looked back down. "I understand you're packing a spare pistol now," he said.

Quang. He had reported her.

Fresco kicked back from his desk and stood. Anger flushed his face. "You take a pistol . . . when you've just faced an official inquiry into the biggest individual shooting of the year . . . and threaten your partner with it? You put the barrel of that pistol against your partner's head? And pull the trigger? Jesus fucking Christ!"

Cully saw it was no act. Fresco was outraged, and he could flush her whole career. He paced, back and forth in front of her, but his eyes stayed glued to hers. "I'm trying to protect this police force, lady, and you're making that a tough job. We live by our reputation, that's all a police force is, and don't look at me like you think that's shallow! When I was a street cop, everybody out there was a man, six feet or better, and we looked tough because we were tough! Veterans! Of wars and street fights! Nobody fucked with us on the street because they could tell by looking it was a bad idea!"

He jabbed a finger an inch from Cully's nose. "Now they make us hire women! And little tattletale runts like Quang! When I was a street cop, somebody pulled some shit like you just did and we wouldn't go crying to the captain about it, we'd wait till the guy put the gun down and then we'd kick some sense into him. I'm talking man to man!"

He stopped himself. "Okay, so you don't have to be a blue-eyed Irishman to be a cop anymore, but you fucking well better start minding the rules! You go into a shooting review board and come out with a bouquet. Well, don't come back here and shove it up my ass! You got anything to say? Anything at all?"

"Yeah, Captain, as a matter of fact, I do."

Fresco was interested in her tone. It annoyed him, but he liked it too. "Yeah?" he said. "What's that?"

"The department, in its firearms guidelines, recognizes the legitimacy of carrying a second pistol for the purposes of self-defense."

"From your own partner?"

"That's point number two. You want to talk about big cops, big male cops, in the old days when nobody dared give them any trouble? Well, you know what my fellow cops want from me?" She waited, forcing him to answer.

"No. What do they want?" he said at last.

"They want to know that I can back them up. They want to know whether I take any shit. So I've got news for them. I don't."

She looked at him. He looked at her.

She said, "Anything else you want to say to me, Captain?"

"You're being reassigned."

"That's fine with me."

"I want you to work with Thomas Ridge," Fresco said.

"Ridge?" she said. "Why him?"

"Because he's the best there is. And before you get the idea that you belong in that league, let me tell you I didn't have much choice. I couldn't throw you out of the department, since your shoot-out gave the Policy Board a chance to brag about the success of their hiring policy. And I couldn't leave you with a partner you'd threatened with a gun. Part of Ridge's job is to train other detectives, and you need training. Now. *You* got any questions?" He moved back to his desk and sat down. "Good," he said.

She started out the door, and he called, "McCullers?"

She turned back. "Sir?"

"Did you really threaten to put your pistol away and beat him to death with your bare hands?"

"No comment, sir."

He nodded. When she closed the door, he smiled.

CHAPTER FORTY-TWO

Cully walked back to her cubicle, sat down at her desk, and tried to stop her emotions from bouncing around. She was just telling herself that her life was her own and her destiny hers to control, when she heard a deep male voice say, "McCullers?"

She looked up. Tom Ridge stood in the doorway.

"Yeah," she said, and stood too quickly.

"Tom Ridge," he said, and stuck out his hand.

"Scarlet McCullers. Cully," she said, and accepted the handshake. Up close this way, face to face in the office, he seemed even taller, and she could see the sinew about him. He had the wiry strength of a farmer. There was a kind of country freshness about him, something pristine. But his eyes were the kicker, blue and soft, yet so tightly focused that if you looked just at the eyes, he seemed angry.

Ridge looked down at Quang's empty desk. He paused, and then said, deliberately, "The last person to have this desk was a man." Ridge's eyes took in the whole desk top in one wide stare, and flicked toward the chair. "He was Asian, probably . . . Vietnamese." Ridge touched the dark spot on the chair's headrest, rubbed his fingers together, sniffed them and continued, "He used oil on his hair, most likely Vitalis. He was . . . about five six, a hundred thirty-five pounds. He spoke English without an accent and he had a mole right . . . here." Ridge tapped a fingertip to the right side of his nose.

Cully sat slowly in her own chair, looking at him in blank awe. But then she got it. "You walked past him in the parking lot," she said.

Ridge smiled. "He was carrying a boxful of desk stuff." He took off his sport coat, and hung it on the back of his chair. He sat down and looked at her again. "Why do they call you Bull Barrel?" he said.

"Everybody's heard that story," she said tightly.

"Everybody's heard it. But you're the only one who *knows* it. And if we're going to be partners, I'd like to know why the person who's supposed to be watching my back from now on has a macho nickname."

She looked down at the desktop, and held a brief argument with herself, then looked up and said, "If I tell you this story, you've got to swear—I mean swear—you won't laugh."

"What happens if I laugh? You gonna shoot me?"

She stared at him. He stared back at her.

"I was a rookie," she began, through a clenched jaw. "On my first patrol . . ." Ridge propped his elbows on the top of his desk and gripped his chin with both hands as he listened. "Ragg Wilson and me. We got a call about a convenience store robbery. Black suspect, green station wagon. Just then we saw one. Had to be him, how many green station wagons are there, right? We stop him, Ragg covers him, I search him." She stopped and licked the inside of her teeth before she began again. "I get to his pants. I feel something . . . something . . . well, hard."

Ridge snickered.

Cully glared at him. Then something amazing happened: she snickered too.

"How hard was it?" Ridge asked.

"Oh, come on!"

"No, I mean, you're a professional officer of the law, trained to observe; how hard was it?"

"You trying to embarrass me?" If he was, he was succeeding; she felt herself blushing.

"Come on! Tell me the story!"

"Well, it was . . . well, yeah, it was . . . hard! But the thing was, how big it was."

"Well, how big was it?" Ridge looked seriously concerned. "We're talking a matter of male pride here."

"Well, it was . . . I thought it was a pistol, okay?"

"A pistol, but not like a shotgun. I just want to get this straight, because I don't want to be perpetrating any racist myths here."

Cully was grinning. She couldn't help herself. She said, "So I just . . . I thought it was a pistol. So I jump back screaming, 'He's got a gun! And it's a bull barrel!' And Ragg covers him, and the guy yells, 'That ain't no gun! That's my johnson!'"

"That's my johnson," Ridge repeated.

"That's my johnson," she said again.

At the same moment, they both burst into laughter.

"You do have a sense of humor, don't you," Ridge said.

Cully stopped laughing. "Maybe."

"No, you do!" Ridge said. "Everybody thinks you don't."

She said nothing; Ridge studied her. "You know how it looks to them?" he asked. "They think you're a beautiful woman who gets furious when somebody notices she's beautiful."

"That's their problem."

"That's your problem. Some poor guy in a green station wagon nearly got his head blown off because he couldn't have you raking your fingertips around his body without getting excited. Your partner tries to flirt with you and you scare the piss out of him. Literally. Some people around here think a woman with that kind of attitude can't be a cop."

"So what do you think, Detective Ridge?"

"I think they're right. But I don't think that's your attitude."

"You don't. So why don't you tell me what my attitude is."

"You're here to prove something. I don't know what that is, but I don't care, either—I like people with drive. The point is, you can't prove anything if all they see, when they look at you, is their own erection."

"I may come to like you, Ridge," she said at last.

"I hope so," he said.

They stared at each other again. He seemed conscious of it, and looked away, before he said casually, "Why don't you tell me about the case you're working on right now?"

CHAPTER FORTY-THREE

She laid out all the particulars.

"You call this the Lopez case," Ridge said. "Not the Pendleton case."

"That's right," Cully said.

"Why do you think she was kidnapped?"

"It's just a theory," Cully said.

"I'd like to hear it."

"Her father owns a produce company. They bring tons of stuff across the border from Mexico, every day. And they're just one company. Produce shipping, that's a nightmare for Customs. They've got to get to know who's clean, who they can trust. They're not going to check every melon, every day."

Ridge nodded. His eyes seemed to smile.

"And Lopez, he's clean," Cully went on. "So maybe somebody suggested he carry a load through, and maybe he refused. And then, maybe, somebody grabbed his daughter and said, 'I don't believe you heard me the first time.' "

She watched Ridge nod. He was thinking. She liked that. As much as she wanted to get Victoria back, part of her was afraid that Ridge would listen for a few minutes and then give her the solution as easily as he had solved the Fat Lady Affair, as that affair was destined to be called. Cully wanted help; but she didn't want to feel like a fool.

"You think Lopez figures he can get her back on his own," Ridge said.

"I figure he's going to try. The way it looks to him, he doesn't have any choice. He doesn't trust us. Maybe he shouldn't. But he sure ain't talking."

"So let's watch him."

"We can't get approval for that. Fresco won't give us surveillance, for a victim who won't cooperate."

"I've got somebody who might do us a favor. You want to try him?"

CHAPTER FORTY-FOUR

They took Ridge's car, a department Dodge. He drove the freeways to Santa Monica Boulevard—not to the Hollywood section, where the male prostitutes troll, but to the west, where Century City gleams. They talked about traffic and the weather. She wanted to tell him about Esteban Lopez's toothpick, but that seemed too personal.

Ridge turned south into Beverly Hills and pulled up the in-ramp of one of the city's free public lots. Cully said, "Where're we going?"

"The restaurant across the street," Ridge said.

"There's a no-parking zone right in front," she said. Any self-respecting detective would stash his sedan there.

But Ridge said, "Naw. Too much attention."

"This guy can't be seen talking with cops?"

"Let's just say it wouldn't help him."

"We're gonna meet him in the restaurant?" she said.

"In his car. He never goes anywhere except in a chauffeur-driven limo. There it is." He led her over to a stretch Mercedes parked among rows of exotic cars in the restaurant's lot. A Hispanic, with raven hair slicked back from his forehead and mirrored sunglasses balanced on an arched Aztec nose, sat at the wheel. He was the only one visible in the car; the passenger compartment's windows were tinted. Ridge glanced around, opened a back door, and nodded for Cully to slide inside.

She found the passenger compartment empty. She sat on the beige leather of the rear-facing middle seat. Ridge came in after her and sat beside her.

"Where is he?" Cully said, fingering the creamy aromatic leather upholstery.

"He's right here," Ridge said, and the black panel behind them hummed down. "Hey, Louie! How's it going?"

"Mr. Detective Ridge!" the driver said, with the crisp emphasis on every syllable that makes you think Hispanics are enjoying speaking English. He reached a big, powerful hand back through the opening and Ridge twisted in the seat to slap palms with him.

"This is my new partner," Ridge said, "Cully McCullers."

Louie released Ridge's hand and pressed Cully's fingertips in a courtly gesture; at the same time with his free left hand he lifted the mirrored sunglasses for a better look at her. His eyes were a tobacco brown, his cheekbones like baseballs and the skin misjoined beneath one eye in a knife-fighting scar. He grinned and said, "Partner! You always needed a partner, Mister Ridge!"

"How's the family, Louie?" Ridge said, and turned to Cully. "He's got six kids. But that's four different wives. Louie doesn't believe in wearing a woman out."

Louie laughed. "They're fine, Mr. Ridge."

"The kids or the women?" Ridge said, and Louie laughed again, from his belly.

"When does he get here?" Cully said.

"Who?" Louie asked.

"Your boss."

Louie grinned. "Not for two hours, unless the chick he's with figures all his promises are bullshit! He's told four blondes already they're getting the starring part in his picture! But if their brains was as big as their boobs, they'd be building rockets, huh, Mr. Ridge?"

Ridge laughed.

"So what you need?" Louie said.

Cully realized suddenly that Ridge was there to talk to Louie—not to Louie's boss. She felt her face grow warm with embarrassment; she didn't like looking dumb in front of Ridge. Ridge pretended not to notice her blush, but she knew he had; he noticed everything. He said to Louie, "I need to know about a man named Esteban Lopez. The Lopez Produce Company, you know him?"

"Sure, I know the guy! I mean, I don't know him, but I know him," Louie said.

"Is he clean?"

"Who knows, man?" Louie bobbed his head around as if trying to work a crick from his neck. Cully would later come to know such a gesture as a kind of stall that hard guys will use in coming to terms with themselves for helping out the police. It was obvious that Louie liked and trusted Ridge; it was also obvious that Louie had been on the bad end of a nightstick a few dozen times in his career. Louie looked straight out through the windshield and said, "If he's dirty, he's too smart to let anybody hear about it."

"Right," Ridge said. "And if you didn't hear about it, Louie, it didn't happen."

"I can tell you this much," Louie said. "Esteban Lopez, man, he's tough."

"How tough?"

Louie grinned, warming to the story. "Some guys tried to move in on him a few years ago. I mean some *guys*, man, the kind with names like Rocco and Pepperoni. They started a little produce business, nothing much happening, just a couple of trucks, a front for something, who knows what, but they wanted to be in the produce business so they can do some other business, you know? Probably loan sharks, that's what I heard. So anyway, they go to Lopez and say they want to buy him out. Lopez says he ain't selling. So they bang him around some. Real quiet, so none of the guys out in the warehouse hear. They leave him with a few ribs broken, and they walk out, see, where they got their car parked by the loading dock? Well, old Lopez, he—" Here Louie had to stop, to laugh. "These guys hear something behind them and turn around to see this big fucking forklift coming right at them! And they're jumping out of the way, man! And Lopez, he don't stop, he just runs that forklift right off the dock, right on top of these guys' car! And it was a nice car too, man, a Lincoln, real sharp."

Louie and Ridge both chuckled, and Cully found herself laughing in spite of herself. She said, "What did they do to him then?"

"What you mean, those guys?" Louie said. "They didn't do nothing."

"Why didn't they break his neck? Or shoot him?" she pressed.

Louie chuckled, and looked at Ridge, to share his amusement at Cully's question. "What they gonna do, with fifty Chicanos standing there, looking at a squashed Lincoln? Pepperoni and Sausage, they don't say shit, they just walk backwards for about thirty feet and take off! Left the car there, too! Guy that worked for Lopez, he told me the story, when he sold me the car! I used the engine of that Lincoln in a Ford Bronco I was rebuilding. I take my kids fishing in it now!"

Ridge stared out the smoked windows. Short round men and tall blond women moved along the sidewalk outside, but Ridge's eyes did not follow them. Louie winked at Cully. "Thinking!" Louie whispered loudly, and nodded confidentially to her.

Ridge ignored the comment, if he heard it at all. Finally he looked back at Louie and said, "I need a favor."

"Anything you want, Chief!" Louie said, with another grin at Cully.

"I want you to go to work at the Lopez warehouse. A day, maybe two."

"I don't know, Mister Detective Ridge, sir. That's a lot of vacation time."

"Yeah. Right," Ridge said.

"So what am I looking for?" Louie said.

"Guys getting nervous," Ridge told him. "Doing what they don't normally do. I'll square it with your boss, while you're away."

"Just tell him I'm working undercover for the police," Louie said, and grinned at Cully. "He's a television producer. He loves that bullshit."

CHAPTER FORTY-FIVE

Ridge led Cully into the restaurant, where men in sport coats and argyle socks ate eggs Benedict beneath palm fronds. "Should I wait here?" she said, as they scanned the room.

"Yeah," Ridge said. "If they know you're a cop, they'll sign you to a three-picture deal."

She watched him as he moved across the room to a man who could not have been more than thirty. The young man looked up and his eyes grew wide in excitement when he saw Ridge coming, and Ridge gave him a nod. The young man held up a hand, silencing the conversation of the three others at the table with him as Ridge leaned down and whispered into his ear.

Cully watched Ridge play the scene, working the kid like a master. She knew what he was saying, something like: "You're doing us a big favor here, a bigger favor than you know. I can't tell you what it involves but it's important, and it's a serious favor to me and to the department."

Everybody loves to have cops owe them favors, and the young producer was no exception. As Ridge stood up, he glanced sullenly around the table—to great effect—and stalked away. The producer glowed.

Back in Ridge's car, they took the San Diego Freeway, and cut over to the Santa Monica. Ridge was lost in thought, and Cully did not want to disturb him.

Fifteen minutes later Ridge stopped at a massive stone cathedral. Cully looked at the sign: The Church of the Blessed Sacrament. "We gonna make a donation?" Cully said.

"Uh, no," Ridge said. "I'm sorry, this is about . . . something else. It won't take long. Why don't you come with me?"

He said it casually, but his eyes were hard and cold.

CHAPTER FORTY-SIX

This time the monsignor was in his vestments in his panelled office. And this time the monsignor was ready for Ridge's sly contempt. "Hello, Captain," he said, smiling as he met them at the door.

"It's Detective," Ridge corrected him.

"Oh, yes," said the man in the purple robes.

"And this is Detective McCullers. My partner."

Another priest sat on the green leather sofa beneath the monsignor's framed landscapes of the University of Notre Dame. His thin white hair lay limply above the fair Irish blush of his face. He had crowded to one side of the sofa, as if he deserved to take up no more room than that. "This is Father McKenna," the monsignor said.

"Father," Ridge said.

"Father," Cully said.

The monsignor stretched his hand toward the two velvet chairs in front of his desk, and Ridge and Cully sat. The monsignor then sat in the wing-back leather chair behind his desk, leaned back, and said, "I must tell you honestly that I am relieved. The girl whose picture you brought . . . Let me rephrase that: The girl whose body was the one in the picture, is not, was not, a Catholic."

Cully watched Ridge lean forward. His eyes were dead still, his breathing shallow. He was hungry. "Yes," he said, not a question.

"She had been a Catholic, however. And that is why Father McKenna knows her." The monsignor spoke formally, without contractions, as if making a statement. "My relief that she renounced her Catholicism is unquestionably a sin. When Father McKenna telephoned me and said he recognized the picture and then described his encounter with her, I tried to justify my relief. I told myself my relief was because she was no longer Catholic and I hoped that whatever new faith she adopted—or even lack of faith— was not so severely violated by her suicide as our faith would be. But I see now that this was one of Satan's lies. One of the lies we tell ourselves—that I told myself—to try and escape the sense of failure."

Ridge nodded. Cully looked from the monsignor to Ridge and back again. Whatever was going on, she was not in this conversation, and possibly not even on the same planet where it was being held.

The monsignor stood up and walked slowly from the room.

Ridge turned and looked at the old priest on the sofa, who raised his eyes and smiled sadly. Cully thought the priest's eyes showed a kind of resignation. He pushed himself to his feet.

Father McKenna was slender, and probably no more than sixty, but he had the shallow half breath of emphysema. His index and middle fingers were stained yellow from smoke, and his hands fidgeted now as if he would love a cigarette. When he spoke he had to push the words out, so they arrived all sandpapered around the edges of his baritone. "I am instructed to tell you everythin'," he said, emphasizing the word "instructed" in that Irish way, with a smile, that mocks authority and loves it at the same time. "Everythin' I know about the girl in the picture the monsignor sent me. Everythin' I can tell you . . . without violatin' my oath . . . as a priest."

"I understand the girl wasn't Catholic," Ridge said. "I didn't know your oath as a priest extended to non-Catholics."

Father McKenna smiled at Ridge with pale lips and darkened teeth and light blue eyes surrounded in faint yellow. "The monsignor told me you'd be this way," he said. "You don't have to be. I'm not unwillin' to talk to you." ·

Ridge nodded. "Then talk, Father."

"She came to me, one mornin' seven months ago. It was a Tuesday. I remember because I was plannin' my speech for the Knights 'a Columbus meetin'." He paused and interrupted himself. "That makes you smile."

Ridge stopped smiling, but Father McKenna would not let him go. "Yes, Detective. Priests write speeches. And we get on the telephone and call carnival managers and say, 'Can ya send us a Tilt-A-Whirl and a Mad Elephant and a bigger Ferris wheel this year?' We plan Bingo Nights. And once in a while we baptize a baby. And hear a confession." The priest was running out of air as he finished, and the effort sent his lungs into spasms.

Ridge waited for the coughing to subside. "And that's what the girl wanted?" he asked. "To confess?"

"Yes," Father McKenna wheezed. "Only she was not a

Catholic anymore. She'd been newly baptized a Protestant. She said so."

"So you took her out into the sanctuary, where the sun came through the stained glass and the devotional candles made splotches of red light."

McKenna looked at Ridge, "How did ya know that?"

"Because you're a good man, Father," Ridge said. "And an Irishman. You couldn't hear her confession, but you wouldn't turn her away cold. And you wouldn't stay in your office to talk to her, you'd take her out into the church where it was beautiful and spiritual and poetic, as any true Irishman, even a priest—especially a priest—would do with a beautiful young redheaded girl. That's where you'd take her, when you wanted her to open up her heart."

Father McKenna gazed with awe at Ridge. "Yes," he said.

Ridge sat without moving, without acknowledging the priest's surprise or his admiration. Father McKenna looked down at his lap, where the black robes hung on his bony thighs.

"And you were kind to her, Father," Ridge said. "You saw she had a problem, and needed to talk or else she would never have come to you, and so you sat down with her."

The priest nodded heavily, as if the guilt was black iron, weighting the back of his neck. He rasped, "I said, 'How may I help you, child?' And she told me a story. I will not tell you all the details—that is where my oath as a priest enters in. But I can tell you this much. She had sinned and she wished not to deal with the consequences of her sin. I told her . . . what any priest would have told her: that forgiveness lay in the determination to sin no more."

The father stopped there. Cully saw that he wanted to tell them more, but that was all he was going to say about the nature of the dead girl's sin.

"So what did she do, when you gave her this advice?" Ridge said.

"This was not advice!" Father McKenna said quickly.

"This was what I had to tell her. Listen. A girl comes to me and says she is not a Catholic but please, Father, please, could she talk with me for a moment, only a moment? I see she is in a spiritual agony. She describes her plight. And I give her the discipline and solace of Christ's love through the Church. That is what my Church expects of me."

Ridge suddenly turned angry and his face went red. "So what did you tell her to do?" he demanded.

"It was more . . . what I told her not to do," McKenna said. And stopped talking.

"Do you know her name?" Ridge asked.

"She said it was Mary. That's all I know. But she did tell me what church she belonged to."

"Which one was that?" Ridge said, suddenly excited.

The priest told them. It was the First Church of a mainline Protestant denomination, in the San Fernando Valley. Ridge wrote down the name, and stood. Cully stood too, but Father McKenna did not move. He remained on the edge of the couch, again staring down at his lap.

Ridge walked to the door, stopped, and looked back to Father McKenna. "Sometimes," Ridge said slowly, "I'm convinced the original sin, the one in the Garden of Eden, was the belief that what we do matters. That any bit of life is in our own hands."

Father McKenna looked up. His face was calm.

The calmness at first relieved and then troubled Ridge. "Go to your confession, Father," Ridge said.

"I already have," Father McKenna said.

Ridge trembled. Cully could almost feel it through the air. The old priest smiled. "It's like boxers know other boxers, by the scar tissue around the eyes," he said. "You were once a seminarian."

"You better go reread your tea leaves, Father," Ridge said. "I couldn't be a priest. I never could stand to play bingo."

CHAPTER FORTY-SEVEN

Cully could barely wait until they were outside in the hallway. As soon as Ridge had closed the door to the monsignor's office, she said, "What is it with you?"

Ridge glanced at her, and rubbed his nose to stall. "What do you mean?"

"I mean, do you hate this man or something?"

"Hate him? No, of course not. Why would I hate him?"

"I don't mean hate him, but you sure had an edge for somebody who's trying to help you."

"I guess I was a little impatient," Ridge said.

"It's hard for a priest to tell you that a girl wanted an abortion."

Ridge stopped, and smiled slowly. "You're really very good," he said.

"Thanks for the compliment, but it's pretty obvious, isn't it? An agonizing decision? The consequence of her sin? Not something she had done, but something he hoped she wouldn't do?"

But Ridge wasn't listening; he was staring blankly down. "Seven months ago," he said. "The autopsy showed she had been pregnant, but Roger couldn't tell us if it was a full-term birth or a late abortion. I wonder what she did about the pregnancy."

Cully barely heard the question. "What's going on here, Ridge?" she insisted. "I need your help! It's something I'm not seeing. You're furious with these people. And you're getting personally involved with this case of yours about the . . . Lady of the Lake."

Ridge looked around. "Come on," he said, and led her down another hallway, away from the door where they had come in. They found the entrance to the sanctuary, and went into an enormous cathedral where pillars wide as a squad car held up a peaked ceiling and stained glass windows broke streams of daylight into thousands of colored shapes upon the pews.

He ushered her to a seat on the purple cushions of one of the back pews. He did not sit beside her, but turned his back to the cross and faced her, leaning against the next pew. "Look," she said, cutting off whatever he was about to say, "I know I'm getting emotional. But Victoria is a real girl, a real live girl, and the Lady of the Lake, whoever she was, is a dead one. I'm sorry, but she is. And, and I'm sorry, but I don't see why you're even interested in a suicide."

"She wasn't a suicide," Ridge said.

Cully was about to say something else, but stopped. "How do you know that?" she said.

Ridge looked up at the sunlight filtering in through the stained glass. "First it was her knees."

"Her knees?"

"They were perfect. No bruises. And I just thought: Wouldn't somebody despondent enough to commit suicide, but devout enough, or desperate enough, to wear a cross like hers, spend a lot of time in prayer? Wouldn't her knees have some bruises, from all the kneeling? Even if you gave up on God before you took the plunge or pulled the trigger, wouldn't you try a lot of prayer first, if you were that kind of person?"

Cully sat in the echoing silence. Then she said, "Okay, but—"

"That isn't all," Ridge said. "There are other marks on her body—scratches on the insides of her forearms, and a faint bruise on the back of her neck. I can't figure out how they got there."

"Ridge," she said slowly, "I want to help you. But I don't understand you. I don't see why you think what you think, and why we came to this church, and why you're furious with these priests, and—"

"Do you know about this church?" he said, a little sharply.

"Huh?"

"Do you remember, sometime around your sophomore year in high school, reading in history class about the Teapot Dome Scandal?"

"Yeah, but—"

"I don't remember what it was about either, except that it had to do with a businessman bribing a member of the president's cabinet, in the early twenties. Well, the secretary of state was convicted. The businessman, on exactly the same evidence, was acquitted. That businessman gave the money to build this cathedral."

Cully paused as this sank in. "So . . . what?" she said. "You think the Church should have refused the money?"

"You think *he* would have taken it?" Ridge said, and pointed toward the wall above the altar, where the sixteen-foot Jesus hung in crucified golden agony.

"I don't know," Cully said.

"I don't know either," Ridge said, and walked away from the sanctuary.

CHAPTER FORTY-EIGHT

Ridge drove straight to the San Fernando Valley. Forget Victoria Lopez, Cully thought, we're on the trail of a dead girl, a girl who can't be helped.

The church Father McKenna had told them about was in an upper-middle-class bedroom community. Ridge had to call the station to get the dispatcher to look up the address. At the address they found a small sanctuary, covered in new stucco and sporting a round stained-glass window. On the front lawn stood a metal sign, fashioned with a gothic arch and posted with individual letters, a small version of what a theater might use to post the title of a movie. The sign said simply, "Services led by the Reverend John Crowell." On their way to the church office Ridge and Cully passed through a sunny courtyard, where a banner hung: "Try our new Contemporary Worship Service, 'Let the Son Shine.'"

The church secretary, a buxom, friendly woman, told them the Reverend Crowell was off that day, it being a Friday. He would be working on his house, which he was remodeling himself, but he was always happy to have visitors drop by. She gave them the address; it was up the hill, toward Mulholland Drive.

They found a one-man building sight, hanging on a hill-side. Half the house was gutted to the rafters; the rest had already been redone in brick and half-timbering. A man in jeans and a ripped T-shirt was carrying a load of lumber up a ladder. When he saw the car pull up he shoved the wood up onto the rafters and climbed back down, slapping his hands together to knock off the dust.

He was large—over six feet and well over two hundred pounds—and in his mid-thirties. His sandy blond hair was thinning a little but that made him look more masculine; with a bushy mane he might have looked boyish. He smiled, walked over to Ridge and Cully as they got out of the car, and said, "I'm John Crowell. My secretary called and said you were coming."

He shook hands with Cully first, then with Ridge. "Sorry I'm so dirty," he said. "I have to stay so clean six days a week that I try extra hard to get filthy on my day off."

"We're Detectives Ridge and McCullers, from the LAPD," Ridge said. "She's McCullers."

Crowell nodded, but looked concerned, as all people do when paid an unexpected visit by the police. "Is something wrong?" he said.

"Is there a place we can sit down?" Ridge said.

"Sure, I . . . Come on in!" He led them into the finished half of the house. The furniture was old and simple, but tasteful: solid oak chairs, old couches upholstered in forest green. "I'm sorry it's a bit eclectic," Crowell said, laughing at the word. "I lost my wife before we had a chance to collect much furniture, and I'm afraid I chose badly at some of the church's rummage sales."

They sat down in his home study, a small room with a large desk and bookshelves lining the walls. He waved a big hand toward a tweed sofa, and took a seat himself on the edge of his sturdy old desk. "How can I help you?" he asked.

"We were wondering if you knew this girl," Ridge said, and leaned forward to hand Crowell the picture he had folded in his coat pocket.

Crowell leaned forward to meet Ridge's hand, then sat back on the edge of his desk and unfolded the sheet. His eyes—blue, and bright as china—froze on the picture of the dead Lady of the Lake. Slowly he lowered the photograph, till it rested on his knees. He stood suddenly, circled the desk, and studied the blank green space of his blotter before he looked up and said gently, "It's Mary. Mary Ann McCready." He looked back to the blotter. He clinched his front teeth. "What happened to her?"

"She drowned herself in Lake Hollywood."

Crowell took a deep, deep breath, a long loud inhale through his nose, and put both palms on either side of his nose. He blew out slowly, making an audible *pheewwww*. Then he uncovered his face and made his hands into fists.

"Can you give us the name of her next of kin?" Ridge asked.

"She was raised in a Catholic orphanage," Crowell said. "She once told me she never felt like she had a family, until she joined this congregation."

"Did you know her well?" Ridge said.

"She was a new member," Crowell replied. She started coming about a year ago. At first just every Sunday, then every time we opened the doors. Both Sunday services— we've started a contemporary service early on Sunday morning—and she would come to that and stay for Adult Bible Study and then attend the traditional Sunday service after that."

Crowell paused, and, since Ridge wasn't saying anything, Cully asked, "Do you have a lot of members who are that dedicated?"

Crowell smiled. "No," he said. "I'm afraid not."

Ridge said, "So she started coming all the time . . ."

"Oh, yes, right. She started coming all the time, and I . . . sensed she had a need. Counseling is a large part of my role here as copastor. It was one of my specialties in doctoral studies."

Ridge said, "So you lingered at the door after a service, as you always do, and when she passed you shook her hand and asked how she was doing."

Crowell studied Ridge a moment and said, "Yes, that's what I did."

"That would be the gentle way of approaching someone with a problem," Ridge said.

Crowell sat back in his chair, nodded, and took another

of his long, meditative breaths. "Are you asking me to tell you what those problems were?" he said.

"That would help," Ridge said.

Crowell hesitated.

"We have to clear every death like this," Ridge said. "If it was suicide, we have to put it to rest."

"I'm sorry, I didn't ask if you wanted anything to drink. Would you like some tea?"

Crowell stood, but both Ridge and Cully shook their heads and he sat down again. "We really need some help here," Ridge said. "You obviously knew her . . . ."

"It's just . . . I'm sorry, it's so difficult. I'm shocked by the news, and I'm torn. I want to help, but whatever she told me in confidence was . . . in confidence." Crowell frowned. "She was . . . deeply torn. She had some . . . serious personal dilemmas, that I tried to help her through . . . ."

"We're not asking you to tell us the specifics of her problems," Ridge said. "We don't want to invade her privacy, or yours." Cully shot a glance at Ridge. There is nothing a homicide detective wants to do more than invade privacy; it is the only way cases get resolved. The law itself recognizes no rights of privacy for a person who had been murdered, and its legal agents systematically destroy any semblance of personal sanctum. They strip the body naked, rip it apart, slice it, saw it, puree it in a blender, peek up every orifice and then mangle it some more. They may go through a victim's home and poke into every drawer, look at every picture, vacuum the sheets, peruse the medicine cabinet, read the love letters. Ridge was the best homicide investigator anybody in the LAPD had ever seen, and here he was telling this minister that they wanted to respect everybody's privacy in this small matter of a girl found floating dead in Lake Hollywood.

But Crowell bought the bull. He nodded, relieved, and it was clear to Cully that he did not want to talk about what Mary Ann McCready had told him any more than the priest had.

"If you could just tell us a little about the girl herself," Ridge prompted.

Crowell rubbed his face, wiping off sweat, wiping on dirt. "Mary Ann . . . was a wonderful girl. Easy to like. I know that sounds like somebody trying to speak well of the dead, but it's not that. She had so many good qualities. She was an actress, and she was beautiful, but the longer you knew her the more beautiful she became.

"She was raised a Catholic but her father's family had been members of our church. When Mary Ann started attending, it was because she was researching a role she was up for, a part in a TV movie of a woman who was a churchgoer. She kept attending, I think, because she liked my sermons. At least I flattered myself with that thought. And . . ."

Tears swelled into Crowell's eyes; he stopped and squeezed them away. "I'm sorry," he said, sniffing to steady himself. "She was an easy person to care about."

"She was an actress," Ridge said gently. "Was she successful at that? I don't remember seeing her in anything."

"She wasn't in anything," Crowell said, smiling fondly at the memory. "She never got down about that. When people met her, she never said, 'I'm an out-of-work actress,' or, 'I'm trying to be an actress.' She always said, 'I'm an actress.' I hear a lot of complaining in my job, and it was refreshing to know somebody who was so positive."

"She sure made an abrupt turn, didn't she?" Ridge said.

Crowell rubbed his fingers on the desk he had made with his own hands, and looked out the leaded glass window. "You don't need to hear any clichés from me," he said. "You know how people keep secrets, even from themselves. The person with the biggest smile might be dying inside."

"We understand she'd had an abortion, about seven months ago," Ridge said.

Cully had been wondering when Ridge was going to say that. An interrogator keeps that sort of knowledge like a rat in a box, and lets it go at just the right moment to see who jumps onto a chair, and who knew the little ugly monster was there all along.

Crowell was surprised, Ridge saw, but did not recoil. He looked at both detectives sadly, and nodded.

"It would help us if we could talk to her doctor," Ridge said.

"I don't know who that is," Crowell said. "I knew her agonies over the decision. But once she made up her mind, I kept out of it."

"Do you know where she lived?"

"Oh, yes. She was in one of our women's groups, and even had organizing committee meetings at her apartment." He took a slip of paper from his desk and wrote down an address, and handed it to Ridge.

Ridge took the note and stood. "Thanks," he said, "you've been a big help."

"Should I make arrangements for claiming the body?" Crowell asked.

"It's thoughtful of you to ask," Ridge said, "but the state has some red tape to go through, if someone dies without relatives. You could go down to the morgue and identify the body, if you would."

"I . . . would try," Crowell said, his lips turning gray.

"It's an awful chore, I know," Ridge said. "Especially on deaths by drowning. A body that's been floating all night looks . . ." Ridge trailed off, and his silence was worse than any description he might have given.

Cully saw then that Ridge's gentleness had all been an act. Whatever Ridge's problem with clergymen was, she didn't know; but he never seemed to miss a chance to make one uncomfortable.

The address Crowell gave them was not far away. They drove to it without speaking.

They found a stucco apartment house, with a rounded arch plastered in the center of the front wall and paint in sea blue and salmon, to make the building look deco. But in one corner was a charred blotch. Workmen were there now, hammering on new studs, framing a new corner of the building.

They didn't have to go in. "Fire," Ridge said. "In her apartment. Everything's gone."

CHAPTER FORTY-NINE

They did not speak on the way back to the station.

Upstairs, in their cubicle, Cully said, "I'll go check the computer, and see if anything's turned up on that all-points I sent out."

Blinking, Ridge frowned at her.

She gave him a clue, with her eyebrows raised. "Victoria Lopez?"

"Oh. Yeah," he said. "Do that."

When she returned, having found nothing, he was looking at pictures spread across his desk, pictures of the Lady of the Lake.

Cully sat down and stared at him. He either ignored her or did not notice her. She picked up a ballpoint pen and began to tap it against her desktop, as steady and loud as rainwater dripping on a concrete floor. After a full minute of this he glared at her.

"What," he snapped.

"Come on, Ridge! Here I am, feeling dumb and childish because I'm taking something personally, and you come up with this thing about the Lady of the Lake!"

"What do you mean by that?"

"Talk about being obsessive! You've got a suicide there! I don't care how sad it was, she did kill herself! And I've got a live girl I want to save! Can't you get obsessive about that for a few minutes?"

Ridge stared at her. "She didn't kill herself," he said tightly. "It wasn't suicide."

"What, just because she didn't have bruises on her knees? Come on! She prayed on a pad, okay? Or she didn't pray at all."

"She was murdered."

"Right."

He stood up. His lips were pale with anger. "You got something you have to do right now?"

"In fact I'm waiting for a call."

"From who?"

"Computers. The FBI. CRASH. Anybody that can get me a lead on Victoria Lopez!"

"They'll find you in the car, if they want you. Come with me. And that's an order."

CHAPTER FIFTY

Out in the parking lot he slammed the key into the ignition, wrenched the engine on, and jerked the car into gear.

He drove to Lake Hollywood. He stopped at the barrier, pulled the metal posts from their sleeves, and drove along the perimeter, forcing angry joggers out of the way until they reached the spot along the fence where he had found the button. He got out of the car. "Come on," he snapped.

She got out and followed him to the fence, an unbroken perimeter of eight-foot chain link topped with a triple strand of barbed wire. "Climb it," he said.

She looked at the fence, at him, at the fence and then back at him. "Fuck you," she said.

"Climb it," he said.

She stared at him. She sneered, turned to the fence, curled her fingers into the open diamonds of the chain link, and went straight up, kicking the toes of her boots into the fence for support. She made it look easy—until she reached the top. There the strands of barbed wire made it dicey. But the wire was loose and she was able to pull it down enough to swing a leg over.

"Stop right there," Ridge said. She was straddling the fence, her toes pigeoned in to lock her in place.

"Like this?" she said. "What in the—"

"How do you get down from there?" Ridge demanded.

"How do I—"

"How do you get down from there?"

"I kick my right leg over to the lake side, and jump."

"Exactly," Ridge said. "Now come on back."

She kicked her left leg back to the road side of the fence, and landed on her feet. He looked at her and waited, to see if she had gotten it.

"The scratches on the insides of her forearms," Cully said.

"Right. There's no way she got them climbing this fence. Or picked up the faint bruise on the back of her neck."

"So how did she get them," Cully said.

"I don't know. If I know that, I know how she died. I know exactly how she died, and I know who killed her."

Cully looked out at the lake. "Okay," she said. "Okay. Maybe Mary Ann McCready was murdered. But one way or the other, Ridge, she's dead. And Victoria Lopez is alive. Don't you think that maybe our priorities ought to be—"

"Don't," he said sharply. "Don't ever accuse me of not caring. We're gonna find Victoria Lopez, I personally guarantee it. But with or without your help, I'm gonna find who murdered Mary Ann McCready."

CHAPTER FIFTY-ONE

They were driving back to the station in steaming silence when the radio squawked. Ridge picked up the receiver and answered: "Yeah."

"Ridge?" the dispatcher said. "Michaels called for McCullers. He's got some action down in Watts that he thinks she might want to see."

Night was already falling as they reached Watts, with its small, stucco houses surrounded by parched grass and broken toys. They turned a corner and saw a whole circus of lights—light bars on police cruisers flashing in blue, ambulances blaring red, even a fire truck that had rolled out to join the fun. Ridge drove almost to the action, then pulled down a side street, to park in the dark. "You're leaving it here?" Cully said.

"Sure. Hey, with all the excitement out here, and the residents crowding around, we may get a riot, and I want to be far enough from the action to run."

"But the car'll get stolen! . . . Won't it?"

"Not tonight. Everybody with felonious inclinations is in his bed right now pretending to be an angel. The ones out on the street—the ones who might start throwing rocks at us if the mood hits them—are the citizens who want to know why we let full-scale wars happen every few days in front of their houses."

Ridge was right; the folks were all out, talking in abnormally loud and high-pitched voices, burning off the adrenaline from having crouched behind their beds as a gun battle had raged on the street in front of their houses. They milled around the cops now on the scene. There were twenty officers in uniform, and at least that many more in the street clothes they had been wearing as they prepared to go home at end of shift; and the cops, with the uniformed officers feeling conspicuous and the plainclothes officers wearing their badges clipped outside on their belts and their guns displayed in shoulder holsters, moved around trying to look calm.

The street was littered with brass shell casings. In every direction was evidence of blood—a dark splatter here, a smear there where a wounded victim had dragged his own body away. And everybody was pissed off.

"Hey!" a man in an undershirt screamed from the edge of the cordon. "You let this happen in your neighborhood? This ain't no pigpen! This here's a residential district!"

"Where are the bodies?" an ambulance attendant said to a uniformed cop. Ridge and Cully, overhearing the question, turned to catch the answer, but the uniformed cop only shrugged.

Cully hung next to Ridge's shoulder—not for protection, but for the way he flowed purposefully through a crowd that seemed to jumble up everybody else. Ridge shouldered his way in, honing in on Michaels, who stood in the middle of the action, barking out instructions to the uniforms. They reached him and Ridge said, "Looks like a war zone."

"It is," Michaels said. "You know the freeway shooting yesterday, a kid from Los Malos killed by some guys from the Two-Tone Bloods. So today, broad daylight, the beaners come down here with Uzis and shoot up the Bloods. Course the Bloods ain't all that stupid. They were waiting for 'em.

Which of course means they were the ones who shot the Los Malos kid on the freeway."

Michaels stopped. He seemed to want to be sure that Ridge appreciated his deduction. Ridge nodded.

"It was just a fucking pitched battle," Michaels went on. "We figure at least a thousand rounds fired. We'll never know because everybody's been picking up the spent casings for souvenirs. We got six trails of blood but no bodies at the end. They've crawled off into garages, under houses, everywhere. We've found three other guys hurt, two black, one Hispanic, and all of 'em claim to have been innocent bystanders caught in the crossfire."

"Even the Latin guy?" Ridge said.

Michaels chuckled. "Right. A beaner out for a stroll at dinnertime in Watts." He looked at Cully. "Ever seen one of these shoot-outs before?"

"I've seen plenty of crime scenes," she said.

"Yeah, but in Watts, I mean. We had one last year, guy got his jaw shot off. We had the victim all packed up and off to the hospital, and we were marking out the crime scene, circling the spots where we found the shotgun shells and the casings, photographing everything, where his jaw was lying, all of it, and we thought we had the situation under control, with the crowd back so they wouldn't steal the evidence for souvenirs. Then damn if a dog didn't run up and grab that jawbone and take off with it! Har har har!"

"Come on, Michaels, where's the dead one?" a detective said, and Ridge and Cully turned to see Benson, a Detective Three from Rampart Division. Benson was surly; he'd been hauled down to Watts at end of shift because Michaels was sure he had a homicide. But now Michaels couldn't produce a dead body, and all the overtime Benson expected to cash in on was vanishing.

"Hang with me, Benny, I'll get you a dead one."

"Bullshit," Benson said.

Michaels said, "Hey, look, we got gore all over the place here."

"Yeah," Benson said, "and not a one of 'em's anywheres close to dyin'. Shot all over the place, and every one of 'em's gonna live."

"Not Blinky," Michaels said.

"Who?"

"Blinky," Michaels repeated, playing to Cully and Ridge. "Shot right through the temple. They took him to County USC. He's probably dead already. So quit worrying, you're gonna get your overtime." Benson huffed away and Michaels said, "Man, I hope Blinky's as serious as they say. I don't give 'em some dead meat, Homicide's gonna be pissed."

Michael's radio crackled. "Hey," a voice said.

"Yeah," he said back into it.

"You see me?" said the voice.

"Where?" Michaels said into the radio.

"Behind you," came the voice.

Michaels, Ridge, and Cully all looked far up the street, to where a detective in a sweatshirt was waving his free hand. In his other he held a radio. "Yeah," Michaels said into his unit.

"Woman up here was shot too."

Michaels looked hopeful. "Ah," he said to Ridge and Cully. "Success at last."

They walked up the street to where Michael's partner stood, with a couple of teenage black girls, who said as soon as they arrived, "Yeah, Miss Mary Jefferson, Miss Mary Jefferson. She been shot!" The girls pointed to a white frame house. The detectives, all four of them now, walked up to her door.

Michaels, still hoping to impress Cully, said, "Detective McCullers, why don't you take this one?"

Cully looked at Ridge, who gave a shrug. Cully stepped forward and knocked on the door.

Mary Jefferson swung the door open on the first knock. She was slender, maybe fifty, with a straight, proud spine. She said, "Uh huh?"

Cully showed her badge and said, "We had a report that someone in this house had been shot?"

"That's right, that's right, I got shot! Got shot right here, right here!"

"Where?" Cully said, looking at the obviously strong and animated woman.

"Right here!" Mary Jefferson repeated. "In my own house! With the doors locked!"

"But where did you get shot?" Cully said.

Mary Jefferson put her hands on her hips, like Cully wasn't listening.

"I mean where did the bullet hit you," Cully said.

"Right here! Right in my face!"

She bent at the waist, thrust her head toward them, and pointed to her left cheek. It was unmarked. Cully looked at Ridge and Michaels, who both seemed as baffled as she was. Cully said, "Uh, ma'am, I'd give anything if I could have a complexion as pretty as yours."

Mary Jefferson was not impressed by the flattery. In exasperation she grabbed Cully by the arm. "Here!" she said, and tugged her into the kitchen. The other detectives followed.

Against a side wall stood a washer and dryer. The dryer was humming. Mary Jefferson shouted, louder than she had to. "I was standing right here! Doing my laundry!" She pointed to the floor, where the plastic trash bags that were her laundry sacks lay. "I be puttin' my socks in the washer, when *bap!* Somethin' slap me right upside the face!" She put her finger into a hole in the wall. "The thing that done it be right there on the flo'!" She pointed down to the linoleum, where a nine-millimeter bullet from an Uzi lay.

They left Michael's partner to bag the bullet and take her report. Outside again, Michaels said, "Do you believe these people? Bullets bounce off 'em!" He walked to his car and grabbed the radio. "What's the status on Blinky?"

"Who?" came back, through the crackle.

"That gang kid we sent to County USC! Shot through the temple! What happened to him?" Michaels demanded. "Dead, right?"

A voice came back, "He's been moved."

"Moved?" Michaels shouted into the radio. "You don't move a guy who's dying!"

Whoever was manning the radio base unit knew Michaels and understood his predicament; he laughed. "He's not dying. Doctor's report says the bullet passed through both temples but missed his brain. Sounds like it screwed up his optic nerves a little, but that's all—except from now on he'll *always* be Blinky."

"Do you believe these people?" Michaels said, tossing down the radio mike and turning on Ridge and Cully. "Everybody says they're dumb, but they ain't dumb! They just got a big brain and a little brain, and when they go outside they take the big one out and put the little one in, so nothin' gets hurt!" Michaels stopped his tirade, and stared down the street, where the red and blue lights still revolved, and photographers took pictures of the blood smears on the street, and ambulance attendants still collected the wounded boys the cops kept finding, hiding in garages and cellars. "I tell you," Michaels said softly. "We're just here to keep 'em from eating the bodies."

<h2 style="text-align:center">CHAPTER FIFTY-TWO</h2>

"I've got an idea," Cully said, when they were back in the Ford.

"About what?"

Cully didn't say. All she told him was, "Let's drive back to the lot at the station. We've got to take my car."

Back at the Van Nuys station they parked and she led him to her BMW. She tossed Ridge the keys, and got into the passenger seat. He slid behind the wheel. "Where we going?" he said.

"Long Boulevard."

It had been several years since Ridge worked vice, but he recognized the street. It was Drugville, Cocaine Lane, Treat Street. Every so often the department would stage a big bust there, complete with helicopter floodlights and film crews from the local television stations. They'd haul in a few dozen sidewalk drug dealers. The trouble was, the publicity gave the street a greater reputation, increasing the demand, and the local dealers seeped unstoppably from the neighborhood, like maggots from the residue in a garbage can.

In five minutes Ridge was at the head of the street, up

near the auto plant. "Cruise down once, not too fast," Cully told him, and he obeyed. The street looked deserted. "They're all laying low," she said. "They've heard about it, already heard about the shooting in Watts. But maybe this is better. Yeah. This is perfect! Right. Right. Okay." She looked at him. "Undo your tie. Right. We look perfect, the car makes it. We're just a couple of yuppies, out to score some crack, maybe for the first time. Okay, turn around. Cruise back, real slow this time." As Ridge obeyed she pulled her Beretta automatic from her purse, jacked a round into the chamber, and tucked it between the seat and the door.

"You got a cherry light for this car?" Ridge said.

"No. Why?"

"If we're gonna need guns, we're gonna need a cherry light."

"I don't have one. I was afraid it would scratch the paint."

Ridge looked at her. She looked back at him.

When they glanced back to the street they saw a black kid, no more than fourteen, wearing a T-shirt and designer jeans and a five-pound gold chain, step into the street.

The kid waited in the middle of the block, as if he was going to catch a bus. Ridge stopped the BMW. The kid leaned down to Cully. "Rock, baby, all the bes'."

"How much?"

"Fifty," the kid said.

Cully already held her purse in her lap. She opened it and handed some bills out the window. As the kid reached for the money Cully grabbed him by the wrist and dragged him half into the car window. "Now!" she yelled at Ridge, and he flipped on the overhead light and held his badge up to it. All over the street there was movement; a dozen kids standing in the shadows turned and ran.

Cully had all of the kid's arm and most of his head through the open window. "What the fuck!" the kid yelled.

"Fifty, for one rock?" Cully said.

"Shit, baby, okay! Forty!"

Cully grinned like a wolf. "It's not the price, asshole! I'm the law! And what I want to know is, why the fuck is it so expensive?"

"The street clean, it clean!" the kid yelled. He was terrified; it was his first bust.

"Why are they shooting at each other in Watts?" Cully said. "You know about that? Huh?"

"I don't know nothin' 'bout—"

Cully jerked her automatic up and jammed the barrel into the boneless flesh below the kid's chin. The kid froze; only his eyes snapped to Cully.

"The beans been havin' the only stuff, man!" the kid said. "They been comin' over on our side, gettin' the price. The Bloods hadda pop 'em!"

Cully let the kid go. He stepped back and froze for an instant as if he thought he was about to take a bullet. Then as quickly as he knew he was not even being arrested, he regained a cheery mood, and even smiled at Cully.

"You the *man*?" he said to her.

Cully glanced slowly at Ridge. "I ain't the man, I'm the law," she said, mocking Clint Eastwood. "Anybody asks you, you tell 'em you been hassled by Bull Barrel McCullers."

Ridge hit the accelerator and laid a track of rubber on the street, and they were away. Inside the car, their laughter was louder than the engine.

Back in the parking lot of the Van Nuys station, Ridge turned off the engine of Cully's car and they sat in silence. "We've got a gang war," he said. "No supply on the street."

"What if all this gang stuff has to do with Victoria. Am I being paranoid here? Am I taking my own problem and seeing it in everything I look at?"

"I don't know," he said. "Maybe. And maybe not."

Encouraged, she talked faster. "Kidnapping a girl, that's a big move. A one-time move—isn't it? Something you'd do if you wanted to bring in a big shipment."

Ridge nodded.

"Whoever's got Victoria doesn't want to bring in a *melon*ful. He wants to bring in a *truck*ful," Cully said.

"Our only track is Michaels," Ridge said. "We've got to grab some of those gang guys. They might lead us back to whoever's pulling their strings."

Cully nodded.

"Maybe tomorrow we can pick up another trail on the Lady of the Lake," she said.

Ridge looked away from her. "You're right about something," he said. "Victoria's alive. She would have to be, and Lopez would have to know that, he'd have to have some proof, before he'd do whatever the mastermind south of the border is ordering him to do."

Neither one of them wanted to discuss just what that proof might be.

He slid out of the car and left the driver's side door open. She got out too and walked around. For a moment they faced each other.

"Good night," he said.

"Good night," she said. She got behind the wheel. He closed the door for her, and walked back into the building. She wondered if he was going, one more time, to look at the photos of the bruises and scratches on the dead limbs of the Lady of the Lake.

THE SIXTH DAY

CHAPTER FIFTY-THREE

Cully was twenty minutes late getting to the station. On the way to work she had stopped at a Jack in the Box for an egg sandwich, and she felt lousy.

Ridge was already at his desk when she walked in, and it didn't help her mood any when he looked up and said, "You look tired."

"I'm okay," she said.

He studied her face. She didn't want to tell him that she had been parked on Rancho Avenue, outside the Lopez's house, until one that morning. She was afraid Ridge could read that if she looked at him, so she didn't. "What's up?" she said.

"Michaels called. He says he has a little party lined up for us."

Eleven of them. All in white T-shirts and low-top black Converse basketball shoes with the laces loose. Boys, not one of them over nineteen and half of them not old enough to drive. Scorpions tattooed on hands, on cheeks, and below the eye, tattooed teardrops—the mark of hard time in prison—juvenile detention for an adult crime. Three of the young Hispanics in this group already had convictions for murder.

Michaels led them into the lineup room and arranged them in two rows. One half were lined up in back on the risers and the others were in front just a few feet from where Cully and Ridge sat. Michaels chuckled; "Kinda like a glee club, ain't it," he said.

The gang members' lips were tight and pressed to one side in a tide of disgust, and they moved in the slow, shoulder-swaying motions of the *pachuco*. Their eyelids were rolled back, their glances were twitchy. Because the gang outnumbered the cops in the room, Cully, Ridge, Michaels, and the uniformed officers at either end of the lineup had left their pistols outside to prevent themselves being overpowered and held hostage.

"All right!" Michaels snapped at them, smiling. "We want to know why your gang got into a shoot-out with the Two-Tone Bloods. Now who wants to tell us?" He paused, and reacted to the silence in mock surprise. "Gosh, nobody, huh? Man, I guess you guys are tough, I guess nobody's gonna talk. Okay, you, you, and you. The rest of you go back to your cells."

Michaels was playing a game called Fast and Drowsy; you talk as if you want to hurry before you fall asleep with boredom. It made the legal process seem relentless and inevitable. The uniforms led the bulk of the gang away, leaving only the three members Michaels had chosen. Michaels was laughing, chuckling half under his breath. The remaining three boys drifted together. They didn't like the way the cop was laughing. They were hoping the tall guy and the woman with the tits were wimps from Juvenile Authority. But if they were, why did this fat cop with the freckles and the big knuckles just keep grinning?

The uniforms came back. "Interrogation," Michaels said. "Separate rooms."

They led the boys away. Michaels turned to Ridge and Cully, and was still smiling; the enjoyment was no act. "Come on," he said. "You're gonna like this."

The boy in the first room sat slouched down, with one arm stretched out across the table in front of him, the other arm hooked on the back of his chair. The pose looked practiced. Michaels was talking before he closed the door. "We want to know why you hit the Two-Tone Bloods last night, José," Michaels said.

The boy, whose name was Rodolfo, looked up and tried to sneer. Cully was surprised at how small these boys in the gangs looked when they were under the fluorescent lights of a police interrogation room.

As if to Ridge and Cully, Michaels said, "Aw, hey, this

one's too tough to talk, we might as well give up on him, huh?" But he sat down anyway, across from the boy, and grinned into his face. "We got an attempted murder charge going. So here's what we're gonna do. We know you're illegal. So's your whole family. So we're just gonna deport them." Michaels sat back and chuckled. Cully wondered how many times he had said things like this. She wondered how many times he had done what he said he'd do.

"But you, José, you we're gonna send to prison. Not the juvey stuff this time. This time you're gonna do serious time."

"Joo can't covick me for notheen, man!" Rodolfo said.

"The fuck I can't," Michaels said. "You shot up a buncha niggers, José! I had 'em coming up to me and swearing they saw all kinds of stuff, out there on the street last night. Shit, I can get niggers to swear to anything I want. And what I know is, they all said it was your gang. So you wanna be macho and not talk to me, that's okay, but you're gonna go to prison anyway, 'cause you got lucky and I picked you out."

Michaels gave the kid a few seconds to let this sink in. Then he leaned forward and whispered. "You know what happens to a little beaner like you in the state penitentiary? Especially to one who's killed a black man? Forget what you heard from your buddies out on the street, your alumni buddies who come back from San Quentin and tell you all the shit about how tough they were. How tough you think you're gonna be, five feet tall and a hundred ten pounds, in a cell with two big buck niggers who can bench-press the weight of your whole fucking gang? First thing that happens, they decide which one of 'em gets you for the night, and then they decide both of 'em can have you. Hell, all of 'em can have you! And then they say, 'Hey, little spic! Shave your legs, sweetheart, 'cause for the next seven years you're gonna be my woman.'"

Rodolfo's eyes were wide and wild. Michaels wasn't finished. "Hey, José, you make the choice, man, it's all up to you. I'm just trying to tell you the truth here. You're gonna get butt-fucked every night. That's on a good night. On a bad night, maybe one of those big bucks wants to pull his dick out of some other nigger's butt and stick it straight into your mouth. Hey, José, I don't know, maybe that sounds like fun to you! Anyway, it won't last long. Oh yeah, I know what you're thinking, that even on a murder conviction you'll only get five years. But it won't go on that long. With a hundred guys fucking you up the ass, all the time? Man, the shit you can die of when that happens, it'll kill you in less than a year.

"Or," Michaels said, "or . . . you can talk to me, and maybe I can help you."

By the time Michaels finished, Rodolfo was trembling. He struggled to control himself, and began to say something in English, too garbled to be intelligible, then switched to Spanish. "I didn't do anything," he was saying. "I didn't do it."

"I don't give a shit," Michaels said in English. "It was your gang, so as far as I'm concerned it was you. Hey, I don't care who kills niggers and I don't care who kills you! I just gotta send somebody away, okay, and any little beaner'll do."

Rodolfo began speaking rapidly in Spanish. "Whoa, José," Michaels said, "English, man, English! What was that again?"

Cully piped up, "He's saying they had to do it; they didn't have any choice."

Rodolfo looked at her hopefully, and kept spouting. Michaels, with a tape recorder running, was content to let the boy talk. "The Negroes—the blacks—were moving into the valley, where they didn't belong," Cully translated, following Rodolfo's bursts of words. "They chased them, and one of their brothers was killed."

"Does he mean the guy on the freeway, the one in the Buick?" Michaels asked, and when Cully translated the question the boy nodded, and launched another torrent of Spanish.

"Some black guy named Two-Tone came over to their turf a couple of days ago and had a meeting with Reuben. Reuben's their leader. The black guy says the Mexicans are getting moved out, they're having their supply cut off, but he's going to have plenty of cocaine and he can deal through them, if they're willing to trade through him and pay his price. Reuben says fuck you. He sends some of his gang after the blacks, and one of his guys gets killed on the freeway, so they decide to hit the blacks on their own street. And they did."

"Walked into an ambush is what they did. Where's Reuben?" Michaels asked Rodolfo.

Rodolfo looked back at him. He was willing to go to the cell with the blacks before he would tell the cop that. Michaels shrugged. "Ah well," he said. "I hope you like wearing panty hose."

They left the kid in the interrogation room and walked out into the corridor. Ridge said to Michaels, "Two-Tone?"

"Yeah, there is a guy named Two-Tone, he writes it with the number instead of the letters. We've busted him a few times for possession, but never could make a dealing charge stick."

"Can you find him?" Ridge said. "Fast?"

"I can find him, I don't know how fast."

"Find him. Quick as you can, I'd really appreciate it."

"Okay."

"And let me know when you do. I'd like to be there when you arrest him."

Michaels and Ridge exchanged a knowing look that Cully didn't understand.

CHAPTER FIFTY-FOUR

There was a note on Ridge's desk when they got back to the cubicle. It said "Call Louie," and gave a number. Ridge dialed it immediately.

It rang six times before a man answered, "Yo!"

"Louie Sanchez," Ridge said.

"Who?"

"Is this the Lopez Produce Company?"

"This is the pay phone in the warehouse, *pendejo*."

"Louie's a new guy. Big hands, big knuckles, big laugh, big scar on his cheek."

"Oh, *that* Louie Sanchez," the voice said, and the phone clattered against the wall. Ridge heard Louie's name shouted in the background, and then Louie came to the phone.

"Yo," he said.

"Louie?"

"Hey! Mr. Romeo!"

"Louie! How's it going?"

"Not so good, Mr. Ridge, you going to have to give me overtime on this job, man. Those dudes down here, they hump, man, they really work!"

"Don't let it give you a rash, Louie," Ridge said, and he heard Louie laugh. "Find out anything? Hang on a second, I'm gonna put you on the speaker phone, so Detective McCullers can hear."

Ridge punched up the speaker button, and Cully said, "Hi, Louie."

"Oooo, Miss Detective, I love yooooooouuu," Louie sang.

"Down to business, Louie," Ridge said.

"Well, hey, this Lopez is a real Lee Iococcoanut, Mr. Ridge. I mean, tote that barge, lift that bale! But he's soft, too, he's always giving his guys money when they got sick kids and shit. They all love him."

"Yeah," Ridge said. He already knew that. Disappointment sounded in Ridge's voice, and it was what Louie wanted; he liked to surprise. "I found out one other little thing. You didn't tell me there already was a cop down here."

Ridge hesitated. "No, I didn't tell you that."

But his pause had been too long to fool Louie. "I knew you didn't know," Louie said, and laughed. "Ridge ain't gonna send me in someplace and not tell me there's cops already undercover there."

Louie was right about that; Ridge lived by the cop's code of loyalty to his true friends, and Louie was one. But Ridge was not worried about Louie getting caught up in somebody else's undercover work: Louie had been in jails both in America and in Mexico, and he could tell a snitch and he could smell a cop, no matter what shit pile they had rolled in. What did worry Ridge was that there were cops sneaking through his own investigation. "Who is the guy?" he said.

"Some dude out in a piece-a-shit pickup, man, actin' like he was trying to fix the transmission. Worked on it all day and came in and asked for a drink of water, and then asked if he could use the bathroom. Then he asked the foreman if they needed any day labor, and the foreman had seen him working all day on that truck so he says yeah, we got some trucks that need unloading. Put the guy on the same dock as me, man."

"So how'd you know he was a cop?"

"He had everything right, man, the haircut, the undershirt, the shoes. Even had the right accent—for east L.A. But then—get this—the dude, instead of sitting down for coffee break, he squats like he's a Mexican peasant, just come across the border, like they taught him to do that in undercover cop school or someplace. But illegals, man, they don't talk like they come from east L.A."

"What was he looking for?"

"I don't know. He was just hanging around, unloading trucks like me."

"Okay, Louie. Well . . . work another day, okay?"

"Aw man, do I get a pension for this or something? Hey, Mr. Ridge, I tell you about my new bumper sticker? It says, 'How am I driving? Call one-eight-hundred-E-A-T S-H-I-T.' "

Ridge laughed.

"Oh, and one other thing, Mr. Ridge. Did I mention my one other thing?"

"Which one other thing is that, Louie?"

"They brought an empty truck in this morning."

"What do you mean?"

"I mean from Mexico. All the way down and all the way back, empty."

"You're sure."

"I saw it. They parked it by itself, not at the dock, but a few hours later when we opened it, it was empty."

"Thanks, Louie," Ridge said.

"See you later, Mr. Ridge," Louie said.

Ridge punched off the speaker phone to hang up, and looked at Cully.

"You sure Louie's right about another cop being down there, undercover?"

"Louie's never wrong about things like who's a cop and who isn't."

"What would another cop be doing down there?"

"The same thing Louie is, watching and waiting for something to happen, without knowing exactly what that something is?"

"Who else would be there?" she said. "Vice? Who?"

"Maybe it's not one of ours, maybe it's FBI or somebody, I don't know. Speaking of which, did you ever get any response on the John Does we sent out?"

"You mean the four guys I . . . No, nothing. I mean, all the agencies returned negative reports, they couldn't make the two unknowns."

"I'll call them to double-check, and see if anybody might be working a separate case, totally apart from the kidnapping. We don't want to step on our own . . ."

"Dicks?" she said.

Ridge blushed.

"Why would anybody send a truck empty to and from Mexico?" Cully said.

"Maybe that was a dry run. Maybe it ran the same route they'll use to smuggle the drugs, and they wanted to send over a clay pigeon to see if anybody shot at it."

"We need to watch them," Cully said.

"It'll happen at night," Ridge said. "Tonight, tomorrow, the night after. Why don't you go home and get some sleep? I'll stay here and run the cross-checks with the other agencies."

She nodded, and stood.

"Thanks," she said.

"For what?"

She held his eyes for a moment with her own, then smiled softly and walked out.

CHAPTER FIFTY-FIVE

Reuben Morales and Jesus Sanchez met in the spray room of the auto body shop where Jesus's cousin worked. The "room" had plastic walls and was empty except for a few hundred layers of dried paint on the concrete floor and the plastic itself, but this was the only place they knew where they felt screened from the rest of the world.

They were almost twenty years old. They had survived long enough to smell trouble—not just the everyday danger of instinctive street violence, but the more complex threat of secret alliances—and the stench of that kind of trouble was big right now. They had been told to kidnap a girl; it would smooth out a new arrangement that would make them rich. But they'd had no deliveries from Montoya. The blacks were coming into their territory, and when they tried to chase them out the blacks shot back like they weren't even trespassing.

"We gotta talk to Montoya," Reuben said.

"I don't know," Jesus said, staring at the paint-speckled floor beneath his highly polished oxfords.

"The chocolates, they're still coming in. We hit them, they still coming, man."

Jesus knew that; it was why they were talking. But the idea of confronting Montoya scared him. "Montoya wouldn't deal to them behind our backs," Jesus said, wanting badly to believe it.

"Then why are the chocolates coming?" Reuben demanded, showing Jesus the anger he was afraid to show Montoya. "They got supply, man, and we don't got nothing to sell."

Jesus thought hard for a moment. "Then tell him that way."

"Huh?" Reuben said.

"Tell Montoya that way. Don't be mad, don't accuse him. Tell him the way you just said it to me. The chocolates got supply, man, and we don't. So they come in and sell on our streets, and pretty soon all the other Chicano gangs that buy from us, they won't buy from us no more. They'll buy from the chocolates."

Reuben thought about what Jesus had said. He knew it was the wise course. But it made him think of something else too, something that was almost unthinkable. "What if he's doing it on purpose, man? What if Montoya wants to deal with the blacks? So he says to them, 'Let me be your new supplier. You buy from me, I give you supply and I cut off Reuben and Jesus.'"

"He wouldn't do that, man."

"I would, I was him," Reuben said. "They move more stuff, they distribute to other cities. We just move in Los Angeles. A small part of Los Angeles, man."

Jesus had had such a suspicion before, but it was so unsettling that he had pushed it from his mind. But now, hearing Reuben say it, he felt it was not just possible but certain. "We grabbed the Lopez girl for him," Jesus said.

"For a big shipment," Reuben said. "But where is that shipment? We don't got no shipment, we don't see no shipment, we don't know nothing about no shipment."

They went to the pay phone and dialed the number Jesus had memorized. When the voice in Mexico City answered, Reuben spoke English. He thought it was safer and more private.

He asked Montoya why the blacks had supply and were so bold. Montoya laughed, and said he would send Ricardo Flores to explain it all to them.

Reuben hung up and told Jesus what Montoya had said. Both boys were afraid, and both, at the age of nineteen, believed the best way to deal with fear was to act as if nothing could scare or hurt them. "You know what we gonna do, man?" Reuben said. "We gonna send six guys down and watch that Lopez house."

"Out in Encino? Why, man?"

"Montoya don't tell us what he's doing, he don't say when the shipment's coming, or how! He's making deals with Lopez, man, and they ain't gonna do business at the warehouse, where everybody is, they gonna do business out on Easy Street. Maybe the chocolates go out there, maybe some other dealers we don't know about. But we get some guys out there, watch his house. And we tell 'em, we tell our guys, man, if they see anything, if they see any way we're getting fucked, then we fuck them back, man."

Death, like all things human, has its fashion. Pit bull terriers, Uzis, and assault rifles come in and out of vogue, and the choice is a matter of personal style, whether the individual's taste runs to following, or bucking, a trend.

Reuben and Jesus had their own way. They liked shotguns and they gave three of them to the boys they sent to check out the action at the house of Esteban Lopez.

CHAPTER FIFTY-SIX

Guillermo Montoya entered the concrete room. The girl lay on the cot with her face to the wall. She no longer whimpered; she no longer made any sound at all. Montoya looked to his soldier, sitting at the table on the other side of the room and holding a magazine with pictures of fast cars. The soldier moved one side of his mouth in a little shrug to say the girl has been like this for hours, and it is very boring.

Montoya motioned slightly with his head. The soldier stood, lingered a moment to be sure he understood what Montoya wanted, and left him alone with Victoria Lopez.

Montoya walked slowly to the side of the cot, his footsteps scratchy and resonant on the concrete. She did not move but he knew her eyes were open wide as she listened and waited for him to speak.

He spoke with his hands, touching her softly on the spine, as one might stroke a kitten. She twitched, and would have pressed herself further against the wall; but she had decided that hysteria was irrational and she was struggling to stay rational.

Montoya's hand hung in the air for only a moment after her reaction, and then began to stroke again, his middle fingertip lightly tracing down the bumps of her backbone. "It isn't in me to hurt people," Montoya said. "It's something outside of me." He kept stroking. "I am sorry about the knife. It won't happen anymore. I want to be good to you."

She wanted badly to believe it. Without looking away from the wall she said, "Why won't you let me go?"

He laughed.

"If all you want is money," she said, "why do you have to keep me so long? My father will pay."

"Things take time," Montoya said. "Everything takes time. Even love."

She heard this with horror, then jerked onto her stomach and buried her face in the pillow.

Montoya looked at her back for a moment. He walked from the room.

Ricardo Flores met him outside the door. Montoya greeted him brightly. "Cardo! *Qué paso?*"

"More came in an hour ago," Flores said. "It's almost all here."

"Let's go see."

They walked through the debris of the fallen building, but instead of going into the apartment next door they headed through another tunnel, that came up in a modern warehouse. Montoya looked at the small crates.

"Three thousand kilos," Montoya said, rubbing his fingertips over the boxes in the same way he had rubbed Victoria's spine. "Three billion American dollars. Va-voom!"

"Va-voom!" Ricardo agreed.

CHAPTER FIFTY-SEVEN

There is no night in Los Angeles. There is a time when the sun goes down and a big moon rises, but there is no real night. In the hours when the sun is gone, the smog, or the fog, or just the plain moisture in the air, becomes luminescent from the sea of lights blanketing the earth, and a figure two hundred yards down an unlit street is still visible from the diffuse glow of the atmosphere.

But though there is no night, there is a darkness, even

during the day, when the sun burns but cannot penetrate the smog and out of frustration turns liquid and spreads itself across the whole sky, so that there are no lines of light and shadow but one squint-making, relentless burning that blends everything together, that blinds men to their distinctions, making everything and everyone look alike after awhile—this is real darkness.

When the light is darkness, the darkness is black indeed. Cully McCullers thought this as she sat in her BMW along the rolling road in Encino, where the trees reached overhead and screened out even the night glow of the air. The thought sounded Biblical to her. Ridge is doing that, she figured, Ridge is making me think in terms of sin and redemption.

Down the road, high in a second-story window of Esteban Lopez's Tudor house, a light burned, like a candle placed in the window for a sailor long missing at sea. As if to say, Victoria Lopez, we have not forgotten you.

A car rounded the bend far down the road, and slid up the twisty lane, its lights slowly silvering the undersides of the oak leaves as it came on. Cully ducked down against the leather of her passenger seat and the car rolled past and moved away, its exhaust blowing loudly in the stillness. Cully sat back upright. She watched the house. Sometimes she thought she saw movement by the light, as if someone paced. But by the time she raised the binoculars to her eyes, the window always looked bright but lifeless.

Why won't this man talk to us? she wondered. *Why does Esteban Lopez lose his daughter and not turn into the frantic, furious, terrified sap that any other father would become?*

Why won't this man talk to me? she wondered. Only now she wasn't thinking of Lopez, she was thinking of Ridge. Images blurred like that in Los Angeles, in nights that bring no darkness and days that bring no light.

A breeze, powered by the swirling air above the ocean but driven in from the direction of the desert, trembled the leaves in the trees above her, and made a loud whisper. She had locked her doors—what woman, alone in a car on an unlit road at one in the morning, would not lock the doors?—but had rolled the windows down a couple of inches, and the breeze freshened the air inside the car and brought in the scent of orange blossoms which mingled with the smell of the leather upholstery. Sitting alone, she thought of her own life and its broken expectations.

Everything blurs!

Ridge, Ridge, Ridge.

And Esteban Lopez. Somebody has you by the cojónes. *What has Ridge by the heart?*

Something tapped on the window, not eighteen inches from her head. She whirled. There was a man in the blackness, standing just outside her car.

"Ridge!" she whispered. "What the—"

He walked around the front of the car and waited at the passenger side. When she did nothing he pulled at the door handle. "Let me in, would you?"

With a shaky hand she unlocked the door. But he just stood there.

"Is your overhead light off?"

She couldn't figure out what he was saying.

He whispered again. "Your overhead light? Will it come on when I open the door?"

She hadn't thought of that. She fiddled with the switches on the light, swore, and finally positioned the control so that it wouldn't automatically light up. Ridge opened the door and slid in beside her. He shut the door softly, making a soft whump that was barely louder than the breeze in the oaks.

He turned to her. She could see his face, but could make out no expression in the darkness; maybe there was nothing there to read. He turned away again, toward the house, and said, "You couldn't sleep either, huh?"

"Nah," she said, casually. "You knew I'd come out here to stare at Esteban Lopez's house."

"Lopez is going to be personally involved with satisfying this ransom demand; it's too big for him to trust to anybody else. To save his daughter, he's gonna do something personally. I knew you'd have that figured out."

"You're a hell of a partner, Ridge."

He laughed. "I always wanted a partner like you," he said.

They found themselves looking at each other, and then looked away quickly.

Cully swallowed. Her mouth was dry. Here she was, on a quiet dark road with a man who made her pulse quicken, and a full moon rising above the oak trees like an orange peacock strutting across the sky.

She tried to think of some small talk, but Ridge beat her to it. "Your father was a cop," he said.

"Right," she said. "How'd you know, you read my file?"

"No. Dugan told me, when he asked me to take you as a trainee."

"Yeah? What'd he say about me?"

"He said your father was a cop!" Ridge smiled at the way she had bristled.

She was growing to like the way he saw through her. And she was coming to know him too.

"My father was a street cop," she said. "A good one, the kind that wanted to save the world. There's no dramatic story about him; it's just that it seems like there should've been."

"In L.A.?" he asked.

"Yeah. He seemed happy, when we were little. But the city changed, or he changed, or something. He and my mom had a good marriage, I guess, but things started happening. He would call from work and say, 'Where are the kids?' And she'd say they were out in the front yard playing, and he'd go nuts. 'Get them the fuck inside the house, you stupid bitch!' You could hear him yelling right through the phone in my mother's ear. I didn't know till I became a cop myself that what he was seeing was dead children—abused, mangled, or just randomly murdered. He became an alcoholic, they divorced, and he died a . . . a drunk."

Cully didn't want to cry, and talking about her father would make her, so she stopped.

"And you became a cop," Ridge said.

"Yeah." She took a deep breath, smelling the orange blossoms and the night-blooming jasmine.

"Ridge?"

"Yeah?"

"There's something I want to ask you."

"Let's see if I've got anything on my schedule for right now. No, all clear."

"What is it . . . why is it . . . that you don't want any publicity? I mean that you stay away from it so . . . hard."

"Why do you think?"

"I don't know, that's why I'm asking."

"You're the smartest cop I ever ran across. Maybe the smartest person I ever ran across. I'd like to know what you think, before I tell you."

She glanced at him, across the moonlit mile between them. She said, "I don't want to pry."

"I don't mind," he said.

"Okay. I think it's got something to do with your personal life. You're divorced, aren't you?"

"Yeah. What, does it show? I mean, do I look like someone . . . damaged?"

"No. Well, yes. I mean no. I mean, we've all had our romances that didn't work out. I'm just trying to get a fix on . . ." *Yeah, Cully,* she told herself, *just what is it you are trying to get a fix on?* "I mean, it's just that a guy who looks like you is either divorced or gay, and you're not gay."

He smiled. "How do you know?"

The way you look at me, she wanted to say. Instead she just smiled.

"I had a short, sad marriage," he said. "It didn't have anything to do with why I don't want reporters asking questions about me."

They talked slowly, as if they had all the time in the world. Out in the darkness, three wild-eyed young Hispanics who believed they were expected to shoot anything they did not understand at the home of Esteban Lopez maneuvered around the car.

"Asking questions about *you,*" Cully said. "So it's some secret you have, that you don't want discovered."

"That I don't want to talk about, yeah. But I'll talk about it with you."

Another glance lit the air between their eyes.

"Okay," she said, "is it something religious? I mean, something that has to do with whatever boils up inside you when we're inside a church, or around priests or preachers?"

"Damn," he said, "you're scary."

"Look who's talkin'," she said.

Ridge wanted to kiss her. He couldn't get himself to close the distance between them. Thomas Ridge was a throwback, a relic of a lost age, a romantic; to him a kiss was like telling the most intimate secret: You have the power to shatter my heart. That was not a secret Ridge was ready to tell, so he tried to tell Cully another secret about himself. "I don't want publicity because . . . I don't know if I can make this clear. It's like the reason you don't want to talk about your father."

"What do you mean? About my father?"

"Somebody you love. Somebody whose life has to do with yours, even though they're dead. Because to you they're not dead, and they never will be. And if you open it up, and let other people start deciding they know what it all means—"

They heard a noise. Or maybe it wasn't a noise at all, maybe it was the reflection they both caught at the same moment, or the way a shadow moved on the asphalt outside the car. Ridge's hand went beneath his sweater and suddenly he was holding his pistol. Cully grabbed her purse, where her own gun slept.

"Start the car!" Ridge whispered. As she twisted the key she saw the other shadows, huge forms of men, and when the BMW buzzed to life she saw them freeze. "Take off!" Ridge shouted.

Before she could obey him the back window shattered from the blast of a shotgun. Then everything happened at once.

Ridge twisted and fired three times, *boom! boom! boom!* through the empty gash of the back window.

Cully hit the accelerator, and the car took another round, this one in the windshield.

Ridge turned again and fired through the now open windshield. He shouted, "The lights! Turn on the lights!"

She twisted the light stalk, and the headlights flared on. Three men stood in the sudden gush of illumination. Two turned and ran, but the third raised his arm, his gun barking, the muzzle flashing.

Ridge put two rounds into his gut.

The man in the road stopped shooting and then Cully ran over him with the car.

She blasted up the road with her foot flooring the accelerator, until she hit the first turn. She made the turn but oversteered, then slammed on her brakes, and the little BMW began to swap ends, first sliding clockwise and then counterclockwise as she overcorrected. The car came to rest facing back down the road, where everything was quiet and peaceful now, except for the body that lay in the beam of the headlights and leaked blood onto the asphalt.

CHAPTER FIFTY-EIGHT

After the first shooting in the drug dealers' driveway, Cully hadn't wanted them to see her come apart. This time she didn't care what the cops surrounding her saw. She sat in the interrogation room and shook so hard she had to hug herself to keep her teeth from breaking.

One of the station lieutenants—Shelby, a twenty-five-year man—was sitting directly across from her at the green metal table. To her right was Dugan, and to her left a sergeant who did nothing but operate a tape recorder.

"Detective McCullers," Shelby said, "you are unwounded, is that correct?"

Cully dimly realized he was saying this for the sake of the tape recording, but she didn't yet see the implications of that. She nodded her head because she wasn't sure she could control her voice.

Shelby was a thick man. He spent two hours a day exercising—lifting weights and running. He knew everything there was to know about the track and the weight room, but he hadn't been out on the street in twelve years. "We just need to ask a few questions," he said.

"Yes, sir," Cully said, stammering a little. "Thank you, sir."

"How long have you known your partner, Detective Third Grade Thomas Ridge?"

"Sir?"

"How long have you known Ridge," he repeated.

She looked at each of the men around the table. "Since the department made us partners," she said.

Her inquisitors looked at each other after she answered. The first time she had been debriefed at a shooting incident, they had not done that. The first time, with the four dead drug dealers, they had slapped her on the back and looked at her with envy. Cops who kill bad guys get nicknames like Boom Boom. The guys who talked with her after the first shooting wanted names like that for themselves. These guys wanted something else. "You never met him before that day?" Shelby said.

"Well, sure, I met him, or just saw him really, at the autopsy, when they were examining the men I shot the first time. Ridge was at the morgue, looking at a . . . you know, a drowning victim. The Lady of the Lake. That's what we —what Ridge—called her . . . ."

"When you met that other time, what did you talk about?"

For thirty seconds, Cully did not speak. Then she asked, "Where is Ridge now?" The first cops at the scene of the shooting had driven her and Ridge back to the station in separate cars.

"He's in another room, answering these same questions," Shelby said.

"I see. So now I'm supposed to be sure of every little detail because any lies will stand out if our stories don't match."

"Who said you'd want to lie to us?"

"Who do you think you're talking to?" Cully said.

"Detective—" Dugan began.

"Come on, Rosie! I understand you guys asking questions, but don't insult me by thinking I'm too stupid to see through them!"

"So tell us what we're thinking, Detective," Shelby said.

He was good, no doubt about it. Cully had painted herself into a box. "You guys wonder if we were screwing around. If we went out to that dark road, not because we were working on a case, but because we were working on each other."

Shelby shrugged, raised his eyebrows, and waited for her to answer her own accusation.

"Fuck you," Cully said.

They took her from the interrogation room and led her into Fresco's office. Bellflower was there, along with the captain. Cully took a seat and a couple of Internal Affairs men led Ridge in. Bellflower stepped into the corridor to mumble for a moment with the I.A. detectives, then stepped back into Fresco's office and closed the door.

Ridge looked at Cully only once, just long enough to tell her that he'd received the same treatment. Then he leveled his stare at Bellflower.

"Quit looking at me like that, Ridge," Bellflower said.

Ridge was about to say something, but Fresco stood suddenly from his desk and walked into the center of the room saying, "Let's get something straight. Before you two start measuring dicks and *Ms.* McCullers here starts telling us to stick 'em in each other, I want it clear this is my division." He turned, paused, and spoke directly to Bellflower. "You're the commander, but these are my people. Internal Affairs has some jurisdiction, and you have authority. But if somebody's gonna kick ass here, my foot does the kicking. Everybody clear on that?"

Bellflower, always one to like a man with sand in his shorts, lifted a palm in the air and said, "After you, Captain."

Fresco looked at Ridge. "Let's have it. Straight," Fresco said.

"I went to watch Lopez's house, on my own, and found Detective McCullers already there," Ridge said.

"So it was not a romantic rendezvous," Fresco said.

Ridge hesitated only an instant before he said, "No sir."

Fresco looked at Cully.

"Not at all," she said. "And I resent the implication of—"

"I think we're all aware of everything you resent, Detective," Fresco said. "We'll leave that for a minute. Right now tell me why the hell a bunch of gang kids show up and try to kill you."

"We've only got a theory," Ridge said.

Fresco winced in impatience. Doubting Thomas's theories were as good as anybody else's proof.

"We—Detective McCullers and I—think the gangs are scared shitless. Why else would they do something so paranoid as opening up on two people sitting in a car, just because it's parked outside the house of a man whose daughter they kidnapped? They were so jumpy they didn't even stop to ask themselves if we were cops!"

Ridge looked at Bellflower, and then in deference addressed himself again to Fresco. "We think the kidnapping of Victoria Lopez and this war between Los Malos and the Two-Tone Bloods are related. Somebody wants to bring a big shipment of illegal substance into this country, and they kidnapped Victoria to get her father's cooperation in making a safe run. Los Malos did the kidnapping, but they don't have any supply, and the Two-Tone Bloods are getting cocky, moving into the Malos turf. They seem to think they're gonna have plenty of supply, real soon. And it would make sense, wouldn't it? They've got national distribution.

"We think the Malos have figured that out. They don't know when the shipment's coming in either, so they decided to watch Lopez too."

Cully broke in. "We can get Victoria Lopez back alive. We can do it. We've just got to be careful. We stay on Lopez, we pick up the shipment—but we don't bust it."

"Don't bust it? A truckload of coke?" Bellflower burst out. But then he looked at Fresco and said, "Excuse me."

"Of course we bust it," Cully said, "I mean not right away. Whoever is bringing in this shipment is gonna stay with it. Some way, he's gonna ride shotgun, until he's sure it's been delivered. Then he's gonna split. Ridge and I follow him, right back to Victoria. When we've got her, you bust the shipment."

Fresco shot a glance at Bellflower. "Dangerous to leave that much dope alone for very long," Fresco said.

"But the longer you wait, the more of the distribution network you roll up," Ridge said.

"But haven't we already blown it?" Bellflower said. "With this little war tonight, right out in front of Lopez's house, isn't the big cheese on this dope deal gonna roll off?"

"Who's gonna tell him it happened?" Ridge said. "Lopez? Not if he wants his daughter back. Los Malos? No chance —it's the same as saying they were shooting at him. And to everybody else, it was an arrest on an Encino street. We're the only ones that know it had anything to do with the home of Esteban Lopez. And if anybody in the press asks about the coincidence, you'll just have to request they not mention it."

Bellflower's eyes flickered toward Ridge, a silent reference to their secret of Ridge's anonymity.

Fresco lowered his head and pinched his temples. "I don't believe this. You two go off like cowboys, you get into a shoot-out, you tell us to fuck ourselves, and now you ask us to keep the whole thing secret."

"Only if you want to bust a ton of dope and save the life of a girl."

Ridge's mouth had been open, but the words came from Cully's. Ridge looked at her, and then they both smiled at Fresco.

"Son of a bitch," Bellflower said.

Ridge and Cully started to walk out, but Fresco blocked the doorway, coming eye to eye with Ridge. "One more thing," the captain said. "I want it straight, and I want it now. You two fuckin' each other?"

A dead silence, then Ridge's fist cocked back and flew; but only for an inch as Bellflower snatched his wrist before the punch exploded. Ridge flushed red and spun around to glare at Bellflower's eyes, big and steady as golf balls.

"Had to ask," Bellflower said. And after Ridge and Cully had stalked out he looked at Fresco and said, "I guess he told us."

It was nearly dawn when Cully and Ridge stepped out of the station. Ridge walked her to the departmental Dodge she was driving home, and opened the door for her. She got in, and looked back up at him. "When do you think it's going to happen?"

"When what is going to happen?" he said.

"The shipment."

"Oh. I don't know. It's got to be soon."

"Yeah," she said.

"Good night." He closed the door.

She rolled down the window. "See you about noon."

He nodded. He watched her as she drove off, wondering if she would look back at him in the rearview mirror.

She did.

THE SEVENTH DAY

CHAPTER FIFTY-NINE

Ridge looked up and saw Cully, standing in the doorway facing his desk.

Her hair was loose and brushed back; it fell past either cheek and onto her shoulders in blonde arcs. She wore a white blouse with lace in a deep V from a high collar and square shoulders to a point below the waistline. The fabric on her arms was transparent, with more lace at the cuffs; her skirt was pale blue, and stopped at her knees. She wore high heels and her legs were taut beneath chestnut-colored hose. The other guys in the detectives' section had stopped what they were doing to watch her walk past; they were still staring as Cully stood in the doorway of the cubicle.

But Cully did not see them. There was something sad in her eyes as she moved to Ridge, and sat down—not at her desk, but in the guest chair against the wall, facing him like someone who has come to deliver bad news.

"What?" Ridge asked, not blinking.

"I . . . was just at the church," she said. "At the meeting of the ladies' group. I thought I should . . . you know, dress like them."

"I'm surprised they didn't claw out your eyes."

She tried to ignore the compliment. "I figured I could ask them questions more easily if I just went as a visitor. It felt kind of strange, going to a church as a spy. But I knew it was the first time they would have gotten together after hearing about Mary Ann McCready's death, and they would be talking about her and I could find out a lot in one place without trying very hard."

Ridge's eyes locked on hers. He understood that she had done this for him.

"It turned out I didn't have to try at all," Cully went on. "She was all they could talk about. In one way or another every one of them had envied her—she was young, beautiful, talented—and when someone like that commits suicide . . ." Cully trailed off. "The thing was, they all liked her. And that says something, I think, about Mary Ann."

Sometime during the last hour Mary Ann McCready had become a real woman to Cully McCullers; Ridge could see that, and he thought at first that that was the reason for the timbre of grief in Cully's voice.

Cully had stopped talking. Trying to help her over the hump, Ridge said, "You just went there, to the ladies' group, like a prospective member?"

Cully nodded. "I told them I'd heard interesting things about their church, and wanted to visit." What she could not tell Ridge was how she had felt there in the Fireside Room, among women with whom she would have said she felt no kinship. There, within the aroma of vanilla coffee and cinnamon rolls, she had seen the faces of the women whose serenity had been jolted by the news of this suicide, and had realized that their cozy existence was not a given. From the outside it looked as if these women were there to preserve a lifestyle that came to them easily, but from the inside, Cully saw the struggle.

It was plainest to her in the group's program, which was nothing more than a talk by one of the members, over coffee and a roll. The woman was a new mother, Elaine DiCecco, and she was in her early forties. When the woman had begun to talk—the ladies called it "sharing," and the very term made Cully secretly derisive—Cully had thought, *Here's another maladjusted woman, compensating for the failures she's begun to feel and the youth she's begun to lose by inflicting her saccharine affections on a helpless child.* But the talk was different.

Elaine DiCecco had said, with a beaming smile, "When we first adopted Angela, I was ready for so much happiness. What I didn't know was how many moments there'd be when I saw something about life I didn't expect to see."

The other mothers in the room had nodded. Cully started listening.

Elaine DiCecco had gone on, "This morning I gave Angela a banana. She actually got a little of it into her mouth. But mostly she just squeezed it. She was *proud* that she could squeeze it, she was showing off! And then I thought, maybe that's what we're doing, all of us, every day, no matter what we're involved with. Maybe all art, and science, and even business, is us like children, looking up at God and squeezing a banana."

Cully sat there, a spy among lambs, and felt the clarity of innocence.

Now she realized Ridge was watching her.

"They had a little program, and after that they went onto the patio and had more coffee and just chatted. That's when I found out . . . what I found out."

Cully took a breath. She thought it might be best if she could just come right out and blurt it to Ridge, but she had to lead him up to it.

"Mary Ann loved children, they told me. She used to pick theirs up whenever the babies were around, and she had a way with them, and the ladies were always trying to set her up with eligible men they knew, which they knew was strange to be doing because Mary Ann was so pretty and could have lots of men, but never seemed to be dating anybody."

"Did you find out who her boyfriend was?" Ridge said suddenly.

Cully shook her head. "Some of them had hoped they might set her up with Reverend Crowell. But that never happened, they said. They put them together once or twice, but Mary Ann and the pastor never seemed to connect. That was too bad, they said, because he was such a wonderful man. And they gave me an example.

"Elaine DiCecco, the mother I'd just heard speak, had wanted desperately to have a baby. She had miscarried four times, the last one in the sixth month of pregnancy. So they had started trying to adopt, but they were having trouble finding a baby—Elaine's age, and her husband's lack of much extra income made it almost impossible. The grief of that was about to kill her. I'd overheard Elaine saying the same thing, in the context of the gossip about Mary Ann's suicide; she was one of the ones who said she understood how a person could come to that kind of despair."

Cully paused again.

"Yes?" Ridge said.

Cully leaned forward, and took hold of his hand. "So," she said, "Reverend Crowell . . . found them a baby. A month ago. His story was that the baby came from Mexico. The mother had gone down there to sell the baby, because there are plenty of lawyers both there and here who do business that way, but the mother realized at the last moment that she couldn't do such a thing. She couldn't keep the baby herself, but she wanted a good home for it. One of Crowell's old friends from the seminary was working down there and came across the mother, and called Crowell about it. Crowell worked out a legal adoption for Elaine DiCecco and her husband."

Cully stared at Ridge's face. He was pale as a grave marker. He understood what Cully had figured out an hour before.

She had found Mary Ann McCready's baby.

CHAPTER SIXTY

Now Rojos's flaming hair was covered in black dye, and he wore the coat of a doctor, and he sat in an office in downtown Mexico City. On the door of the office was a sign, "Dr. Andrais Cortez, Cirujano Plástico." Rojo checked his watch. His client was late.

He stepped to the door into the outer office and listened. It was just as he thought; his patient had arrived already and was taking time to flirt with the receptionist, a pretty Mexican with peroxide blond hair.

Rojo's "patient" was Ricardo Flores. He was mumbling to the receptionist and she was giggling. They both looked up and saw Rojo scowling, and Ricardo made a face like a smug bad boy called to see the principal. The receptionist stood primly and ushered Ricardo to the door of the inner office. When she had closed it behind them she moved back to the closet behind her desk and switched on the equipment hidden there, activating a voice mike and video recorder hidden in the wall of Rojo's office.

"You're late," Rojo said in Spanish.

"He wanted to watch a movie," Ricardo Flores said, and sat down in the chair in front of the desk. "He likes watching American movies on videocassette. If I leave too soon, he gets suspicious." "He" was Guillermo Montoya, and Ricardo would answer any question about him and even volunteer information. The one thing he would not do was refer to Guillermo by name; that, for some reason, made him feel disloyal.

"No," Rojo said, "if you *don't* leave he gets suspicious. You've told him you're having plastic surgery. It is sensible that you'd be nervous about your appointments. Next time tell him you have to go, no matter what he wants to do."

Ricardo considered this; what Rojo said made sense.

"How is the girl?" Rojo asked. "Victoria Lopez," he added, since he had to be specific when asking Ricardo Flores about women.

"Pretty," Ricardo said.

"Will he hurt her?"

To Ricardo Flores, this was a stupid question. If this man from the American DEA would ask such a question, he did not deserve to be told the truth. Ricardo shook his head.

"Where are you keeping her?" Rojo asked.

Ricardo shrugged. "The girl is my security that you will keep your part of our bargain. If I tell you where she is, you might cheat me."

"So when does it happen?"

"Tonight."

"You're sure?"

Ricardo laughed, and propped his feet up on the desk. "Am I sure. Of course I am sure."

Rojo stood slowly, moved around the desk, and sat down by Ricardo's feet. "Don't laugh," Rojo said. "We're talking about a lot of paste."

Ricardo knew he should keep a serious face, but he couldn't keep from grinning as he nodded again and said, "I am sure."

Rojo grabbed Ricardo by the ankles and jerked him out of the chair; Ricardo's back bounced against the floor, knocking the wind out of him. Rojo bent down over Ricardo's face and whispered, "Get control of yourself, my friend."

Ricardo got the message.

CHAPTER SIXTY-ONE

"Crowell knows who the father was," Ridge said, stating the obvious in his surprise.

"Yeah," Cully said.

"Let's go," he said.

They had just stepped from their cubicle when a detective in the CRASH pen covered the mouthpiece of the telephone he was holding and hollered, "Ridge! McCullers! I got Michaels here! He says to tell you that in twenty minutes they're hitting a house where they think Two-Tone is staying!"

It was an apartment in central Los Angeles, two stories of stucco with a courtyard in between, like five hundred thousand other apartment buildings in the city. This one had black children playing on the grassless lawn in front, and a new white Mercedes parked in one of the spaces in the back. "That's his car," Michaels said, from the head of the back alley where they were stopped. "These guys ain't known for being subtle."

"Is there a lookout?" Ridge said. He was in the front seat, beside Michaels; Cully was in the back, with one of Michaels's men.

"Get this. The lookout's on the car, not on the apartment," Michaels said. "And one of my guys was supposed to take him out already . . ." Down by the back of the apartment, a black man in a U.S.C. sweatshirt, another of Michaels's men, stepped into the alley, stretched, took his Trojans baseball cap off with one hand, and wiped the sweat from his forehead.

"That's it!" Michaels said. They left the car sitting squarely in the alley entrance; as soon as the bust went down, they would radio their backups who would seal off the street with squad cars. But for now the drill was motion. The four detectives hustled down the alley, hugging the walls of the buildings, and filed up the stairs, where four other plainclothes officers waited with their guns drawn, outside a doorway. A radio somewhere played rap music, and at the other end of the hallway, a black woman in her sixties was holding a plastic pail and using a brush to scrub at the graffiti on the walls. She looked up and saw the cops gathered outside the doorway and said, "It's about time."

The detectives stopped. Their hearts were throbbing louder than the drums from the radio music, and here was an old woman who knew drugs were dealt up and down the hallways but still she was scrubbing the walls because this was where she lived, and every cop there thought, *This is why I'm a cop*.

"Calvin," Michaels said, and one of the black cops moved down the hall and steered the woman toward the front stairway.

"Kick 'em in they butts," the woman said. "I done prayed for 'em, now you give 'em what they need!"

The cops, high on adrenaline, struggled not to laugh. "Do it!" Michaels said, and two of his men used the steel ram they call The Key to the City to slam the door off its hinges, and the detectives poured through.

Inside there was lots of screaming, mostly from the detectives. "Hit the floor!" they were yelling. "Face down! All fours!" Ridge and Cully were inside three seconds after the door broke, but Michaels's men already had three people on the carpet with guns to their throats. Two were women, no older than twenty, and both wore shirts and nothing else. A man in his mid-twenties, heavily muscled like the one who had gotten Cully the name Bull Barrel, was on his face and being cuffed. On the coffee table were bags of white powder, and the air smelled sweetly of marijuana.

Michaels's men were dodging through the one-bedroom

apartment, covering the kitchen, the bedroom, the bathroom, beneath the bed. "Where is he?" Michaels shouted at the man on the floor.

The guy with the muscles didn't say anything. Every detective in the room looked at the louvered door of the livingroom coat closet, the one door they had not yet opened. "Come here," Michaels said, and grabbed the guy by his Afro-Mohawk, pulling him to his feet. Two more detectives flanked the handcuffed man, and shoved him to the closet. "*You* open the door, asshole!"

"Don't shoot, Tone!" the muscled man yelled. "It's me!"

"Open it! Open it!" Michaels yelled, standing back.

One of Michaels's men snatched open the door, and there stood 2-Tone. He dropped an Uzi to the floor as soon as the door opened. His nose was flattened from boxing, his lip crooked from a repaired split, his forearm scarred from a knife fight. He wore a Nike T-shirt, jeans, half-laced basketball shoes, and a Rolex. He raised his hands slowly, and not very high, wanting to show the women he was not afraid of cops.

"Come out of there! Come on!" the cops yelled.

The man moved slowly forward, nodding and saying, "Uh huh. Uh huh," in a way that meant, "I understand absolutely everything about this, and it doesn't bother me even a little."

"Two-Tone?" Michaels said.

"Who that?" 2-Tone said.

"That's you, asshole!" Michaels yelled.

"Not me," 2-Tone said. "My name Peter Michael Gregory—"

Michaels shoved him, driving his shoulder against the door jam.

Two-Tone threw a left hook. Michaels stepped inside it and slammed his forehead against the bridge of 2-Tone's nose. Before anyone else in the room could react to join the fight, Michaels was behind 2-Tone and had him in the classic LAPD choke hold, the inside of his left arm rammed against the carotid artery, right hand gripping left for leverage. As the other cops in Michaels's unit looked on in admiration, watching an artist at work, Michaels slung 2-Tone to his knees and rode him to the floor like a wrestler.

One of the girls being ignored on the floor piped up and said suddenly, "Tone, you just relax now, it gonna be all right, you just goin' to sleep is all."

The detectives laughed, and watched 2-Tone's head sag and his arms go limp.

And then Michaels applied the masterstroke. He loosened his grip for just a moment; 2-Tone's head came up and he involuntarily sucked in a huge breath; before he could exhale Michaels clamped down again and every muscle in 2-Tone's torso squeezed against a chestful of air with no place to go, and he shit loudly in his pants.

"Ah," said one of Michaels's men when he heard the noise, "the coup de grace."

Michaels let 2-Tone's limp body slide to the floor, then rolled him over and pulled his shoulders up against the wall, so he would sit in what he had done. In less than a minute 2-Tone had come around. "Aw, Tone," one of the girls said, curling her nose.

"Get 'em out of here," Michaels said, and the detectives cleared the room of everybody but Ridge, Cully, Michaels, and, of course, 2-Tone, whose eyes were rolling around still, and finally settled on Michaels, who knelt before him.

"Why are you shooting up Mexican gangs?" Michaels said.

"I want my lawyer," 2-Tone said.

Michaels laughed. "So he can shit in his pants too?"

"I wanna make a deal."

"Oh, you mean because we found a pound of cocaine over there? That's nothing, I don't care about that. We can send you to prison, but I'd just as soon put you back on the streets, with your friends telling everybody what you do as soon as the cops grab you. Hey, I know, maybe we'll just make you eat what's in your britches, and forget the whole thing!" Michaels threw his head back and laughed again.

Cully was sure Michaels really was enjoying himself. But suddenly his face turned hard, and his eyebrows peaked again. "Why are you shooting up the Mexicans?"

A street man with a strutter's ego, now squatting in his own excrement, 2-Tone sat humiliated, exactly as Michaels wanted him. Desperate to salvage his pride, 2-Tone had no reluctance to talk. It was just the opposite; he needed to tell them how big a man he was. "I got a deal," 2-Tone said.

"A deal? What kinda deal?" Michaels demanded.

"Big deal."

"With who?"

"Guillermo Montoya."

"Who's that?"

"The man. Big man. Mexico."

Cully and Ridge exchanged a glance. If this Montoya was such a big figure in the drug trade, why had no one in the DEA recognized any of the men Cully had killed as his associates, when he sent out the Crime Net notices after the shootings?

"What, this Guillermo Montoya hires you to shoot Mexican gangs? That's stupid," Michaels said.

Two-Tone shook his head. "Big shipment 'a 'caine comin' in. And the beans don't get any."

"A Mexican," Ridge said, as if he thought everything he was hearing was a lie. "And he's gonna give a big shipment of cocaine—"

"Big?" 2-Tone said. Like every criminal spilling his guts to a cop, he had a need to be believed. "Shit! This here is *cow* tits!"

"He's gonna give a big shipment of cocaine to you and your gang? Now why would a Mexican do that?"

"We can move it. Ev'body knows the beans ain't the ones for movin' 'caine to the white man."

"So why shoot the Mexicans?"

"Montoya said to. They ain't gonna roll when we push 'em out, so he said go ahead and fuck 'em now. He been in that kinda mood since his brother killed."

"His brother?" Michaels said.

"Brought in a load of coke from Mexico City, him and a bodyguard. Got shot up with two of our brothers, 'bout a week ago." Two-Tone looked from one cop to another. He took their silence for disbelief. "It was in the paper!" he pleaded.

Michaels looked down at the prisoner's eyes and shook his head. "Two tons from 2-Tone," Michaels said. "It's amazing how much shit you have to listen to in this job."

CHAPTER SIXTY-TWO

Ricardo Flores wore a new light gray silk suit, with a lavender shirt, a lavender tie, and a lavender pocket scarf. He wanted to look like a businessman.

He caught Aeromexico flight 260 and landed in Los Angeles on schedule at 10:43. He carried no luggage. He brought along a passport—a legitimate one. He was not concerned that his entry and departure would be logged in the U.S. Customs computers; he only cared that he not be profiled as a possible smuggler, and thus followed, but he need not have worried about that either. He had told El Rojo that he was coming, and his protection had been arranged.

He was met at the airport by a blond, blue-eyed young man in a pinstriped suit, who recognized Ricardo from a picture and shook his hand as if they were old friends. "How are you, Ricardo," the young man said loudly. "Great to see you again!"

As they walked into the parking lot Ricardo asked, softly, "What's your name?"

"Just call me Mormon," the young man said. "Everybody else does."

Ricardo told Mormon to drive into downtown L.A. The traffic was heavy, the buildings shading out the fierce sun into an oily, midday twilight. "Now where?" Mormon said, as they inched through the noon traffic.

"Fifth and Hill," Ricardo said, with the deliberate enunciation of one who knows an address but not its location.

Mormon made a couple of turns. Blue reflective signs announced the intersection. "Now what?" Mormon said.

"*Muchas gracias*," Ricardo said, and hopped out of the car.

"Hey!" Mormon called. The light in front of him went

green, and the cars behind him started honking. Ricardo turned back toward the open window of Mormon's car.

"Tell El Rojo not to worry," Ricardo said in Spanish. "The shipment is coming, for sure. But I can't have you watching me."

The horns behind them multiplied.

"Hey!" Mormon yelled again.

But Ricardo disappeared into the pedestrian jumble of the street.

"God damn it!" Mormon said.

The pedestrian tunnel was where they had told him it would be. Ricardo walked through the tunnel and into the underground parking structure. Reuben and Jesus were waiting in their van.

"Good morning," Ricardo said, climbing in as Jesus opened the back door for him. Ricardo's eyes twitched, and he jerked out the lavender handkerchief, sneezing into it. "This fucking smog here, you know? It's worse in Mexico, but I'm allergic to this shit you got here." He kept the scarf in his hand as he closed the sliding door, and Reuben circled the van up through the levels of the lot, toward the exit.

The lot attendant was afraid of them. A small Hispanic, he recognized the chromed barrio affluence of the van and the fighting-cock confidence of the two young men in the front seats. He knew they were gang members, leaders, and operated the drop gate without reaching for their entrance ticket. Reuben acknowledged the tribute with a lowering of his eyelids, and slid the van out into the glare of Sixth Street.

Ricardo saw that Reuben and Jesus were wary. They said nothing until they were out in the middle of the traffic and Reuben finally asked, "Where to?" Neither of them looked around, but both watched Ricardo in the mirrors on their lowered sun visors. Ricardo knew they each had a pistol ready within easy reach, so he kept his hands up where they could see them.

"The airport," Ricardo said, and leaned back in his seat. "And hey! Relax!" He grinned, a wolfish grin that turned into a laugh.

"Why did you come here?" Jesus asked.

"Guillermo wanted me to talk to you, to tell you our plans for you, and give you all the details of why we wanted Victoria Lopez, and how she is going to make us all very rich men." Ricardo felt them relax, and saw them trying not to reveal their relief. They kept the posture of bantam cocks, showing their pride.

"We knew there was a big plan," Reuben said.

"You're smart," Ricardo said. "Monto sees this. He likes it. You're here and we're there, that's why he has big plans for you. You have to make decisions. Hey, find me an auto parts store, before I forget. Monto needs a special oil filter for his new Ferrari, and it's hard to get them in Mexico."

They had reached a neighborhood where autoparts stores occurred every block. Reuben slid the van over to an outlet of a chain he knew to carry foreign parts. Ricardo hopped out and hurried into the store.

He was right back, with a new oil filter in a sack. He sneezed again, and pulled the door shut with the handkerchief still in his hand. "Fucking smog," he said.

"Yeah," Reuben said, and they started off again.

Ricardo started a tale that lasted until they reached LAX. He told them of Montoya's plan to bring in a monstrous shipment of cocaine, tons of it. He confided in them the details of how Montoya had gathered a huge stockpile in Mexico and how he hoped to squeeze out competition so that his network was the only network. He emphasized the importance of Los Malos to this whole plan, and by the time they reached the airport Reuben and Jesus felt like maximum gangsters.

Ricardo checked his Rolex. "I've still got thirty minutes and I got more to tell you. Park, and let me finish."

Reuben pulled into one of the covered lots, and took the time ticket out of the dispenser like a good citizen. They had to wind all the way up to the fourth level to find a space.

Ricardo told them how much they would matter when everybody was forced out of the cocaine trade except the Hispanics—specifically Guillermo Montoya and his partners in America, Los Malos. There would be no black dealers, no Asians, no whites, just Hispanics. Reuben and Jesus did not stop to think that this was impractical and were imagining what they could buy with the sums of money they would be making. They felt honored by Guillermo Montoya's trust.

All this time Reuben and Jesus had been sitting in the front seats of the van and now they twisted around to face Ricardo. They saw Ricardo check his watch again. "I gotta catch my plane," he said. He picked up the oil filter, and looked at it closely. "Hey, I hope this is the right one." He slid the filter back into the sack and said, "By the way, Monto asked me to check the pistols you are using. He wants to send you some special exploding ammunition from Europe, and he wants to know what kind of pieces you like to carry."

Reuben drew his .45 Magnum while Jesus pulled the automatic from his coat. "Let me see," Ricardo said, and Jesus passed the pistol back to Ricardo. Ricardo smiled, pointed the pistol straight up, and quickly slid the oil filter over the end of the barrel. Holding the filter with his left hand and pointing the pistol with his right, he shot Reuben in the neck. He put the next round into Jesus's mouth as it flew open in shock. The oil filter was a perfect silencer.

He put two more bullets into each of them, wiped the gun with his handkerchief, lit the oil filter box with his cigarette lighter to destroy any fingerprints and to make his purchase harder to trace, and left everything in the van except the handkerchief he had come with.

He walked into the terminal and caught his plane back to Mexico.

CHAPTER SIXTY-THREE

Cully could barely wait until they were back out in the alley and clear of Michaels's men. She turned toward Ridge but he shook his head to keep her quiet and pulled her to their car, and had her inside with the windows rolled up before he let her talk. "My God, Ridge, you think that's for real?"

"Sounded real to me."

"One of the men I shot last week is the brother of a major drug supplier?"

"It makes sense. The Mexicans were bringing in a sample to show the blacks what they could deliver. You messed up that deal." Ridge saw where this was going, and trailed off.

But Cully saw it too. "So this guy Montoya had Victoria kidnapped to ensure safe delivery of the shipment!"

"I don't think—"

"It's obvious! Montoya lost his own brother! He wasn't about to take any more chances."

"You're worrying about the wrong thing," Ridge said.

"Is that right?"

"You're trying to convince yourself it's your fault Victoria's where she is, because of the guys you shot. You should be worrying about something else."

"Yeah? What's that?"

"Why didn't we know this before?"

CHAPTER SIXTY-FOUR

Ridge clamped the magnetic bubble light on top of the car and used it all the way through the rush hour traffic on the Ventura Freeway. When he passed the Van Nuys exit, where they would've gotten off to go to the station, Cully said, "Where are we going?"

"Oxnard," Ridge said.

"Oxnard?"

Oxnard is a town up the Pacific coast between Los Angeles and Santa Barbara. Condo developers and land speculators come and go there, but Oxnard—maybe because of its name—clings to its identity as a place of farms and pickup trucks.

The trip took thirty minutes. All Ridge would tell her

was that they were going to visit a friend of his; the rest of
the time they talked about real estate prices. The sun was
low and in their eyes when they reached the Oxnard exit
and turned off the Ventura Freeway. After some searching
Ridge found an unmarked dirt road on the outskirts of town,
and said as he turned up it, "I hope he's home."

"Who's home?"

"My friend."

"Another guy like Louie?" she asked, but Ridge didn't
answer. Cully's irritation was growing; Ridge was nervous
and she did not know why. "You hope he's home?" she
said. "You don't know? Why didn't you call him to be sure,
before we drove all the way up here?"

"He doesn't have a telephone," Ridge said.

They reached a white frame farmhouse with a chain link
fence around a side garden and a barn in the back. A pickup
truck sat on a concrete block in front; there were no other
vehicles in sight. As Ridge turned off the ignition and the
engine died, they heard the sound of chickens behind
the fence. Ridge and Cully got out. Ridge started toward
the house, but was interrupted by the sound of another
engine, and they turned back to watch the arrival on the
same dirt road of a little Japanese car, driven by a slender,
olive-skinned beauty with blunt-cut brown hair. "Tom!"
she squealed, and threw the car into park and jumped out
without taking time to shut off the engine. She threw her
arms around Ridge's neck. They hugged tightly, with closed
eyes.

The woman looked at Cully. "And who's *this*, Tom?" she
said, her voice bright and her mahogany-colored eyes spar-
kling with hope.

"My partner," Ridge said.

"Your partner!"

"Detective McCullers," Cully said, offering her hand.

"Oh," the woman said with disappointment, as she shook
Cully's hand.

"Emma," Ridge said, "this is Detective McCullers. Detective McCullers, Emma Ryles." Ridge hugged the slender
woman again.

"Tom," Emma said, "it's so good to see you."

"How is he?" Ridge said.

Emma took Ridge's hand and moved it toward her belly; before it was halfway there Ridge knew what she was telling him. "You're pregnant? That's great! I thought it was just country living making you look voluptuous!" She laughed and hugged him again.

"He's not here?" Ridge said.

"Back in the shed," Emma said. "Come on."

She led them around the house, through a chicken yard, past a goat pen, to an unpainted shed. The whine of a power saw penetrating a plank blotted out the other barnyard noise, and Cully figured whoever was cutting the wood must have been doing it when they drove up or he would have heard Ridge's engine. Emma stopped and smiled, letting Ridge push open the shed door. It admitted a sharp shaft of sunlight into the wood dust of the air and illuminated a man with yellow hair. He was a six-footer with slightly sloping shoulders, strong arms, and a ruddy Irish face that went electric when he saw Ridge.

"Yaaa-yoh!" he said, in one of those noises that begin in the youth of a male friendship and survive every change afterwards. He dropped the plank he was mitering and came toward Ridge with his fists bobbing in the air like a man mocking a boxing bear, and the two met in the center of the room and did a hug dance.

Cully glanced at Emma, who was glancing at her, and the two of them smiled about the men. "Tommy-Tommy!" the carpenter said. "How are you?!" And with a quick look at Cully, the kind of look that takes in everything at once, he said, "Whoa! You're doing okay, I see!"

"No, uh, this is Detective McCullers," Ridge said, emphasizing Detective in a way that stung her, because it sounded so much like the way she said it herself. "Cully, this is William Dews. My friend." William nodded quickly to Cully and turned back to Ridge.

They bumped shoulders like linebackers, they grunted in rhythm. The walls of the shed were lined with clocks, all ticking, making a sound so steady it was like a faint sizzle.

"So you've gone from Wilbur the farmer to Wilhelm the clockmaker, huh?" Ridge said.

"To Willie the babymaker," William said. He smiled at Emma. She took his hand and squeezed it. A shadow passed over William's face, as if he could not look at happiness without it contrasting to some memory. Whatever the dark recollection, he fought it off and looked back to Ridge. "Stay for supper?"

"Please do, Tom!" Emma said.

Ridge had seen the shadow too. "I'm sorry," he said, "we have to get back to L.A. I've kidnapped Detective Mc-Cullers without the department's permission."

William understood something instantly; Cully saw he was like Ridge in that way, noticing some detail that immediately showed him a whole picture. William said, "Come on, I'll show you how the spread's doing," and he led Ridge out the door.

The women, clearly excluded, stepped out of the shed and watched William Dews and Thomas Ridge draw off together to lean against the goat pen and talk in hushed voices. Emma glanced again at Cully, looking at the men, and said, "Would you like some tea cakes? Made this afternoon?"

Cully followed Emma into the rear service porch, glassed in on three sides, with a concrete floor and fruit jars full of dark preserves stacked around on shelves. A low wooden table and two matching chairs, all newly painted in gloss white, stood in the center of the porch. "Have a seat," Emma said, and stepped through the back door into the kitchen. She left the back door open and called out, "The chairs are more comfortable than they look. I guess with the baby coming, Will's gonna have to make a couple more." She returned with a coffee pot and two mugs. "This is our dining room. We don't get much company." She poured them each a cup, sat down beside Cully, and reached back to one of the shelves, where a plateful of tea cakes lay beneath a layer of waxed paper.

Cully had been absorbed in watching Ridge and Will, standing like two farmers leaning against a fence, but when she bit into the first tea cake, the taste and texture swarmed over her. She looked at Emma in surprise. Emma raised her fine dark eyebrows and said, "Good?"

"Mmm," Cully said in admiration. "And still warm. And chewy!"

Emma smiled, flattered. "The sun out here on the porch keeps them warm and soft." She found a chipped porcelain sugar bowl among the shelves and put it on the table. "Oh, I forgot milk," she said, and started to stand up.

"Don't worry, I don't need it."

Emma ate a tea cake. They sipped their coffee. Neither spoke. Cully felt Emma studying her, and suddenly Emma said, "He's attracted to you, you know."

"Who?" Cully said.

"Who. Tommy! Who. I like that. Who! Like you don't notice." Emma was as familiar as a sister.

"We're partners," Cully said.

"You're lovers. Or about to be." She paused, like an old doctor readying himself to lecture a naive girl on the facts of life. She looked down into her coffee cup, into a dark well of remembrance, and said, "He's attentive—amazingly so. His brain vacuums up little details. Not just about his work; he catches everything about you too. His moods shift so suddenly you wonder what you said or did. But you know what it was; you said or did something that showed yourself, that made him jealous or afraid, and you know you're doing it when you do it. Outwardly he ignores you and you feel as though you couldn't get his attention if you set yourself on fire. And then you realized he hasn't missed anything about you, he's been so tuned into you that he smells your breath, and tastes your skin, even though he won't touch you."

Emma took another sip of coffee, and went on, as Cully sat dumbstruck. "That's Tommy's way of being in love." To Cully it seemed that Emma spoke from personal experience. Emma smiled again and said, "Please don't be shocked. I know I'm being rude." She looked down and brushed away some crumbs from her belly—or maybe she was thinking of the baby growing inside. She looked up again, directly at Cully. "Will was in the CIA. Now he's not. It was a dark experience that Tommy helped him out of. He helped us both; he introduced us when we both needed somebody desperately. I'm a little blunt with the truth now. Truth is dangerous but it's like chemotherapy. Sometimes it tastes like poison, but it's all that keeps you alive."

Cully stared wide-eyed at Emma, not knowing how to take her. Only two kinds of people are as direct as Emma was: saints and psychotics, and on meeting either, no one is ever sure which is which. But a psychotic would have seemed more calm, and a saint less benevolent; Emma simply seemed to care about Ridge. All sorts of wild possibilities flooded Cully's mind, and she said, "You're not telling me . . . that . . . your baby is—"

Emma's eyes flew open. "Tommy's? Oh, no, no, I didn't mean that. No, Will and I are happily married, thank you. I didn't mean—" Emma looked down again at her lap, and laughed at herself. She leaned toward Cully, and took her hand. "I'm sorry. We're out here a long way, and I don't get to talk to another woman very often, not like this."

"Neither do I," Cully said.

Emma sat back. She glanced toward the two men still talking by the fence. "Will and Tom grew up together," she said. "They were in the service at the same time, and then Tom came out here to California, and Will went into intelligence work.

"I knew Tom before I knew Will. So I loved him first. I mean, not exactly like I love Will. I mean in my heart, they're alike. Tom actually introduced us, at a time we both needed somebody. And now there are times when Will turns distant, or he leaves home without notice and comes home without explanation, and I need somebody to lean on. And, uh . . ." She looked again at Cully's eyes, too intense to hide her interest. "No. What you're wondering, that never happened. We both knew what could have happened. But we, I, he, realized how much he loved Will too."

Cully glanced again, out at Ridge's back.

CHAPTER SIXTY-FIVE

Ridge and Will were talking. Only they weren't talking, they were standing together sharing a silence, as only old friends can do. Ridge spoke first. "Emma looks great."

"Yeah," Will said.

"You better be taking good care of her."

"Or else what?"

"Taking care of her is the way you take care of yourself. You don't take care of her, I come back here and whip your ass."

Will laughed, just one guttural grunt.

Ridge took another long moment. "I think I might have me a problem, William. Thought you might help me out." Ridge pulled a set of photographs from his pocket. It was a group of individual face shots of four different men, lying dead on coroner's slabs. Will took them and fanned them out like a man glancing at a poker hand. "Know any of 'em?" Ridge said.

Will looked first at Ridge and then back to the pictures before he said, "Sure." He folded the fan and handed the pictures back to Ridge. "Second one from the top." Will shifted his eyes toward the goats, hobbling around the barnyard. Anybody watching through binoculars would have thought he was telling Ridge he didn't know nothin' about nobody. "Alejandro Montoya. He's—he was—the big brother of Guillermo Montoya, but Guillermo's the senior partner. Big mover of cocaine. What you'd call a major independent. What he wants is power. What he likes is killing to get it."

Ridge put the pictures back into his pocket and didn't say anything. Will glanced over and stared at him a moment, longer than he should have, and then said, "Oh, shit."

Ridge knew Will understood everything: How did Tom Ridge, a senior homicide detective, have a major drug figure on a slab in the city morgue, and not know who the corpse was? If the same pictures Will recognized so easily had been distributed to the DEA, why the fuck had Ridge been left in the dark?

Will sighed. "Maybe it's a paperwork screwup. Or maybe to them he was so recognizable they didn't bother to file a rejoinder with you guys, even though you wouldn't know him. You know, a mental mistake. God knows they get made."

"No way," Ridge said. "Their report was, 'We don't know these victims.' A secretary called me and made the report verbally, and said she was trying to speed up the paperwork."

"So you got nothing written, nothing to prove the DEA misled you."

"Right," Ridge said.

"I don't know, Thomas," Will said. "If you got Guillermo Montoya's brother on a slab, you got some shit happening. How'd you get him, anyway?"

"We had a pilot program going, picking up potential mules at the airport and following them in. One of the detectives trailing them got pinned up and had a fluke shootout. Killed all four of them."

Will blew out a long breath. "This is heavy, Thomas."

"Yeah, I know."

"If you need me . . ."

"Yeah, I know."

Ridge straightened up, and brushed off the elbows of his sport coat where they had rested on the fence. Will looked away, into the distance of the barn shade. "Hey," Ridge said, "I'm sure it's some bureaucratic goof somewhere."

"Sure," Will said, with just a touch of resentment in his voice at being invited into the case and then invited out again. He turned his back to the fence and rested his elbows on it and kicked a heel up onto the lower slat. "Who's the girl?" he said. "The detective who killed the four drug dealers?"

"She's the one."

Will raised his eyebrows, then said, "Healthy wench, ain't she."

Ridge smiled, and they walked back toward the house.

Cully saw Will and Ridge approach the porch and knew her conversation with Emma was over.

They said their good-byes, Will and Ridge shaking hands, Ridge and Emma hugging. Then when Emma hugged Cully Ridge gave Emma a sideways, penetrating look, as if to ask how much she had told Cully.

Emma grinned softly, the queen of hearts.

CHAPTER SIXTY-SIX

Ridge drove back up the pass, the blue-green farmland stretching out unseen behind the big sedan as it ate up the hill, the twilight thickening ahead of them, the city twinkling, and Ridge's eyes fixed motionless upon it, as if the highway were a gunsight, and he could smell death lurking.

Ridge kept his eyes on the road and his foot on the accelerator, while his brain raced like a runaway engine. He could not stop the flow of thoughts; he could not latch onto anything and know that it was solid.

The more he thought about what Will had told him, the more jumbled his thoughts became. Cully had killed the brother of a man who was a vicious murderer, and a warlord in the drug trade as well as the kidnapper of Victoria Lopez. The facts should have been connected all along, and would have been, if the people who had the information about the dead brother's identity had passed it along. Why hadn't they? Ridge didn't know; and he felt himself growing less and less able to figure it all out.

The proximity of Cully to a killer like Guillermo Montoya made Ridge afraid. No man can think straight when he cares too much, and Ridge was surprised and confused by how much he cared.

But hell, did the great Tom Ridge know everything? Maybe it was just like Will was saying, some foul-up that would turn out to have an easy explanation.

But Will didn't believe that, and neither did Ridge. Something was wrong in all this, and Cully was in the middle of it. Ridge's only fear was that he would fail to protect this woman sitting beside him.

And Ridge, who had given up on praying many years before, who had thought of the Divinity as benevolent but inaccessible, now heard in his fevered brain the echo of a prayer he had long ago hurled into the void: "Lord, give me the power to . . . the power to . . ." And he could not remember what he had once wanted power for. But the chant of that memory thrust him back to a tent in Tennessee, on a July night, as he stood beside his grandmother and sang beneath the yellow light bulbs and the brown canvas:

> "There is power, power, wonder-working
> Power
> In the blood of the Lamb
> There is power, power, wonder-working
> Power
> In the precious blood of the Lamb"

And Ridge knew that to an outsider, the hymn would seem only the brutish imagery of an ignorant and superstitious dogma. But to Ridge, who had felt the majesty of dirt farmers bellowing those words into the summer night, singing not of riches in glory but of glory in sacrifice, and who had felt the flesh of that faith in the warmth of his grandmother's arms, they meant something.

When he had asked himself, *Who loves me now like my grandmother did?* the answer was *Nobody*. But now the question was turned around. Now the question was, *Whom do I love like my grandmother loved me, when she held me in her arms and would have given her blood for mine?*

And the answer to *that* question was: Cully McCullers.

Cully sat beside him, hearing again in the silence Emma's declaration: *You're lovers—or will be soon.* She looked at Ridge, and was so absorbed with Emma's prediction that she was blind to what was happening to him; she studied his face, his isolation, and thought, *Emma's right, and maybe I knew it before she did.*

But Ridge drove for a long time without speaking or turning to look at her. "Tom?" she said. "Tom? You're . . ." She didn't understand the reason for what she was seeing, so she doubted at first that she was seeing it. "You look . . . scared!"

"Cully," he said, and took a breath. "One of the Mexicans you killed in that shoot-out was the brother of that big-time dealer, Montoya, that Two-Tone mentioned. He's a heavy hitter. Will knew it, so the DEA does too. Somebody's holding back information on us. I'm not sure who or why. But guys like Montoya, they sometimes . . . kill for revenge."

He glanced at her, and glanced back at the darkening road. He switched on the headlights. The dashboard lit dimly. In its light his face looked gray.

Cully realized his fear was not for himself but for her.

CHAPTER SIXTY-SEVEN

"God damn it, Ridge, slow down!" Bellflower said. "Tell it slow enough for us no-brains to follow!" Bellflower stood with all the immmoveable majesty of a cigar store Indian, arms folded across his chest, the fluorescent lights of Fresco's office bouncing off his ebony skull. Fresco sagged in his desk chair; Ridge and Cully paced like twin tigers in a zoo cage.

"It's real simple, Leonard!" Ridge snapped in frustration. "I'm going fast 'cause we don't have much time!"

"So you told me, when you got me out of bed to come down here," Bellflower said, through closed teeth.

"We've got a way to save Victoria Lopez," Cully said.

"And give you maybe a billion dollars worth of cocaine," Ridge said. "But if you don't want the bust, go ahead and make it tough on us."

Bellflower was about to unleash his temper on Ridge, when Cully jumped in. "Here's what we've got. Victoria's kidnapping was engineered by a man named Guillermo Montoya."

"In the major leagues of the drug trade, he's rookie of the year," Ridge said.

"Montoya has been sending up dry runs," Cully said, "just to make sure the route is safe. When he brings in the real stuff, he's gotta ride shotgun on it himself, it's just too big to trust anybody else with."

"We pick up that shipment at the border," Ridge said. "We wait until Montoya leaves it, then some of our people stay with the dope, and we tail Montoya to Victoria Lopez."

"And you let this guy go?" Fresco said.

"We bust him!" Cully said.

"In Mexico? Where you've followed him?"

"We'll pretend to be newlyweds," Cully said. Nobody smiled.

"You're talking about Mexico!" Fresco hollered. "Come on! How many guys is he gonna own down there? You'll never make the Federales cooperate to pull the bust!"

"Yeah, we will," Bellflower said quietly. "If we've got pictures of Montoya with the dope, if we can prove publicly, without the slightest doubt, that Montoya was bringing cocaine into this country, the Mexicans will help us, with a vengeance. They don't like to be embarrassed."

Cully glanced at Ridge. They had them.

Bellflower turned back to them. "But how do you guys know which truck this shipment is gonna be on?"

"We have . . . a friend on the inside of Lopez's operation," Ridge said.

"A snitch?" Fresco said. He was supposed to be kept informed about snitches and their compensation.

"More like a consultant," Ridge said.

Just then Fresco's desk phone rang. He answered, listened, and said to Ridge, "It's for you."

Ridge took the receiver and said, "Yeah?"

"Mr. Ridge!"

"Louie?"

"Mr. Ridge, where the fuck are you?"

"I'm at the station, Louie. You called me here, and I answered, so where the fuck you think I am?"

"You ain't where it's happening, amigo."

"Where what's happening?"

"Where *it's* happening!" On the other end of the line, as Louie talked, Ridge could hear traffic passing; Louie was calling from a booth somewhere near a freeway. "There's a shipment going down tonight, and it's something big. Really big. It's gonna happen."

"What's gonna happen?"

"Whatever it is," Louie said.

"How the fuck do you know anything is gonna happen?" Ridge demanded into the telephone.

"Because Lopez's son is driving," Louie said, and paused as a truck thundered past on the freeway. "He doesn't work in the company. He goes to college, man, he's gonna be a lawyer! But along about four this afternoon he shows up at the warehouse, and some of the guys on the dock, they point him out, tell me about him. Good guy, like his father. Hey, I gotta talk fast, he's coming out! He stopped at a Jack in the Box for dinner, and I gotta take off if I'm gonna stay with him!"

"Don't lose him, Louie!" Ridge said so sharply that Cully sat up.

"I ain't gonna fuckin' lose him, Mr. Ridge!" Louie said with a chuckle. "I followed him here, didn't I?"

"Yeah, you did," Ridge said.

"Oh, he's goin' to take a piss, I'm all right for a coupla minutes. So anyway, there's the son, and he don't drive for his father or work in the business. Guys on the dock say he used to do a little of that in the summers, but even then he mostly worked in the office. So I'm thinking, Mr. Ridge said notice anything unusual, right? And this is unusual. So I ask the foreman if I can stay in the late crew and work another shift. I need the money because my wife's pregnant, I say.

"And the other guy, you know, the cop I saw, he don't notice the son and he don't ask to be there working. He just gets back in his old truck, and moves on. Hey, did I tell you, I helped him fix his truck?"

"Get on with it, Louie!"

"Oh, yeah. Well, I get to work the late shift, and I see the son again, and he's with his father, and they're standing beside a Lopez Produce truck, and they're looking at it like they're studying it. Then Mr. Lopez and his son, they hug. And the son gets into the truck and takes off. The father watches him all the way from the dock. I gotta tell the foreman I'm having cramps in my back—which is fuckin' true, Mr. Ridge—and can I get off. So he lets me, and I run out and get into my car and follow that semi to this place."

"Where is that?"

"Freeway exit."

"What exit, Louie?" Louie was intentionally drawing this out, reminding Ridge what a great job he had done.

"Oso Parkway, off the San Diego freeway."

"That's over an hour from here!"

"What, you want me to stop someplace closer and call you? I didn't want to lose him, and this is the first place he's stopped."

"And the rig he's driving is empty?"

"I helped unload it myself an hour before he took it. And it was a sweet rig, too, man, a year-old Mack, probably their best."

Ridge thought a moment. "Louie. Listen, Louie, stay with him. Don't let him out of your sight, but don't let him know you're following him."

"Mr. Ridge—"

"I know, I know, you're king of the tiptoes! But don't get caught. Go into Mexico if you have to. I'll get you out somehow, I'll square it with everybody."

"Hey, man, this is Louie you're talking to. You think it's hard for me to get in and out of Mexico?"

"Next chance you get, call the station, ask for Ragg Wilson. Tell him where you are, and I'll meet you there."

"Gotta go," Louie said, and hung up.

Ridge hung up the phone and looked at Bellflower. "You got calls to make, Commander. You gonna make 'em?"

CHAPTER SIXTY-EIGHT

The trip took them two hours. They stopped at an all-night service station to gas up, before they drove across the border. Ridge pumped the gas while Cully went to the toilet. When she returned Ridge looked up and said, "That's disgusting."

"What?"

"That you can look so fresh just from washing your face and combing your hair."

"Emergency surgery," she said. "I feel like a dead clam."

"Cully," he said slowly, "I don't want to let you down."

"Let me down?"

"Victoria. I want to bring her home alive. For you."

He kept his eyes down on the gas nozzle for a moment, and when he looked up their eyes locked. They just looked at each other, beneath the harsh lights of the service station, the hose from the gas pump hanging between them. But whatever it is that makes memory was at work then. For some people, romance smells like roses. For others it is perfume, or the smell of hay. But for the rest of Cully's life, whenever she smelled raw gasoline, this moment would glimmer.

CHAPTER SIXTY-NINE

They waited at the border, slumped in the sedan, beside the Customs building. The Customs guys let them park within the shadows of the west structure, where illegals who have been caught are detained before being sent back across the border. They also allowed Cully to buy coffee and peanut-butter crackers from the vending machines in their employee lounge.

Ridge sat dozing at the wheel. Cully sipped the metallic coffee and rubbed her eyes. The border control gates lay in an orange blister of illumination beneath humming sodium lamps, blotting out the stars and the black emptiness of the desert all around. With the desert so dark and the gates so bright, it seemed impossible that anyone wanting to smuggle anything would try to do it through these gates, but the desert was as formidable as the Great Wall of China would have been. With the Coast Guard sweeping the sea and the Air Force sifting the air, the easiest—and for a big load, possibly the only—way into the United States from Mexico was the sandy blacktop that Cully was watching.

There were eight gates—five for passenger cars and three for trucks. All but one of the five automobile gates were empty, but the truck gates were working at full capacity and still not keeping up. Trucks—bearing tomatoes, cantaloupe, watermelons, grapefruit, oranges, bananas—stacked up in a long queue stretching from each of the gates back toward Tijuana. Cully watched the endless ritual as each driver stopped at a gate, showed his manifest to the customs agent there, then pulled forward to the scale, halting every few feet as the wheels reached the balance and each axle was weighed.

Cully's thoughts tumbled. The agents were cops like her, investigators too, in their own way. What they did seemed superficial, even futile; they couldn't possibly check every one of the twenty thousand grapefruit on a single truck, and how many trucks came through every night? How much tar heroin could be hidden inside a single grapefruit, buried at the bottom of a pile? How much coca paste in a cantaloupe? But the agents had their weapons. Experience was one: They knew, nearly to the pound, what the truck would weigh, and how heavy its cargo should be. They knew the kind of drivers each company employed, and after spot-checking enough sleeping compartments, tool boxes, and driver's seats, they knew who would be carrying the untaxed tequila and the counterfeit wristwatches.

She sat up. A truck was pulling through the middle gate. It was loaded with watermelons; the striped green rinds mounded above and bumped out between the three horizontal slats of wood surrounding the load and forming the truck bed. The slats, painted red, bore the words from top to bottom: Lopez Produce Company.

Cully nudged Ridge in the ribs and said, "Hey." Ridge came awake instantly.

"That's it," he said. At that moment they saw Louie. He was crossing the pavement in the shadow of another Customs building where he had parked his car. He walked up to Ridge's sedan, grinned, and slid into the back seat.

"You owe me big for this one, Mr. Ridge!" he said.

"You ain't just a-woofin', Louie," Ridge said.

"He parked at a warehouse in TJ," Louie said. "There was another truck there, Mexico City license. They didn't bother to load from the warehouse, they just took what was in the Mexico City truck and put it into the Lopez truck. Then they packed in some produce they had waiting on the dock. Whole switch took less than ten minutes."

"They didn't see you?" Ridge said.

"If I don't smile, nobody sees me," Louie said.

"Okay, Louie," Ridge said. "When I get back to L.A., we'll keep you smiling. Right now I want you to get out of here." He turned and slapped hands with Louie, and Louie swam into the night.

CHAPTER SEVENTY

They watched the agents run the mirrored carts beneath the truck, checking for migrants clinging underneath. From where they were they could not see the driver's face, but they could tell the customs officer was chatting casually with him.

"What happened to Armando?" the agent was saying.

And the driver had to answer, "Sick. Back tomorrow."

Across the way, in the shadows, Cully glanced over at Ridge. "Only one man in the cab. Where's Montoya?"

"In the back, with the melons? Maybe dressed like a worker?" Ridge wondered aloud.

The customs agent waved and the truck groaned forward,

toward Los Angeles. Ridge shifted into gear and drove out the access road. He fell in among the late-night traffic, a quarter mile behind the truck. He did not turn on the lights of the sedan until they had gone a mile, and another car filled the line of sight between them and the Lopez truck.

"This is spooky," Cully said.

"Just a precaution," Ridge said. The traffic, at three-thirty in the morning, was light but steady, and moving at ten miles an hour above the speed limit they were able to keep the lights of the truck in sight. It was easy; the truck wasn't moving quite as fast as the rest of the traffic, and on the five-lane freeway it stayed in the second lane from the right.

"Ridge . . ." Cully said.

"Yeah."

"What's the biggest drug bust you ever heard of?"

"Actual street value? Maybe two hundred million. That's the biggest in LAPD history. What, you planning on making history?"

"No. I was thinking how little that matters to me. All I want to do is get Victoria back."

Ridge nodded.

"Ridge . . ." she said again. "If you were going to ride shotgun on that kind of shipment, would you do it inside the truck—or outside?"

"What are you getting at?"

She looked around again. Ridge looked at her. "Shit!" he said, as it hit him, "you think they've got an escort?"

"I don't know. But that beige van up there is staying mighty close. And there are a couple of cars behind us that aren't going any faster than we are."

Ridge checked his mirror. He was about to say something when the night turned to day around the truck. Cully looked up into a blinding stab of light; she shielded her eyes and then heard the hacking din of two helicopters as they descended from the blackness overhead and threw twin million-candlepower spotlight beams onto the freeway. Peering forward like an Indian scout on a sunny plain, she saw a whole team of cars from the San Diego County sheriff's department switch on their blue revolving lights in front of the truck and nose to a stop, forcing the truck driver to hit his air brakes and turn his tires to blue smoke. Traffic behind the truck ground to a stop. The plain beige van that had been rolling along beside the truck stopped with it and disgorged a SWAT team in full battle dress. The team sprang across the concrete and jumped up to the cab, covering the driver.

"Ridge—" Cully said.

"It's a bust!"

"What do we do?" Instinctively she grabbed her Beretta and snapped back the action, jacking a round into the chamber.

"Put that away!" he shouted. "Those guys'll shoot at anything!" He meant the SWAT team, standing on the grooved concrete of the freeway and gawking around with wild eyes, holding their assault rifles at the ready, prepared to fend off the counterattack of an entire army. "Get out your shield and open it," he said, and they both got out of the car, their badge wallets open to display their credentials, and walked toward the back of the Lopez Produce Truck.

"Halt!" one of the SWAT gunmen barked, dropping his center of gravity six inches and pointing his M-16 at them. Ridge and Cully froze, keeping their badges up, and remained in that ridiculous posture as other members of the assault team, oblivious to all else, cut the lock on the back of the trailer and slid the door open. Floodlights and the muzzles of their guns leaped into the trailer. They saw melons, and crates behind them that would prove to be full of cocaine—but no Guillermo Montoya.

Ridge and Cully approached the head of the SWAT team, a wiry blade of a man with captain's bars on his shoulders, who frowned down at their badges and then at them. "Who the hell are you?" he demanded.

"LAPD," Ridge said. "Who's in charge?"

The SWAT captain pointed toward a sedan parked on the shoulder, where a tall man with red hair and a red beard was talking on a mobile radio. Ridge and Cully hurried up to him and flashed their shields. "Ridge and McCullers, LAPD," Ridge said.

The man, El Rojo, looked at them through amber eyes and said nothing.

Then they heard a sound, something like air escaping from the pinched throat of a balloon, darting through the still air all around them.

The sound came from the cab of the truck, from the young Hispanic man at the wheel. The noise unraveled into sobs, and then into a single word, repeated over and over: "Victor-i-a! Vic-tor-i-a!!!"

CHAPTER SEVENTY-ONE

Edward Lopez, Victoria's brother, told his story in the interrogation room the San Diego Police provided in their south station. The family reluctance to depend on the police had been demolished; the boy—he was barely twenty—sat with his head down and his elbows on his knees and repeated every detail of what he knew.

He would repeat this story a dozen times that night, for the interrogators and tape recorders of a half dozen different law enforcement agencies—the FBI, the DEA, the U.S. Department of Customs, and even the San Diego Police Department. But Doubting Thomas Ridge and Bull Barrel McCullers could only stand to hear it once.

He was a junior at Pomona College, he told them. The kidnappers had known his box number at the college station; it was clear they had checked him out too as a possible hostage. The psychology was effective; it was like saying, "We got your sister, and we could get you anytime we want to."

Their first contact was simple. They mailed Edward an envelope, with nothing on it but his address, handwritten. Edward suspected immediately that this letter might contain ransom instructions because he knew already what the kidnappers wanted. Several times before his father had refused threats and pressure to carry drugs, and when Victoria was taken Edward and his father had agreed they had no choice but to stay calm and do what they were told.

When the letter appeared in his box at the school post office, he took it back to his dormitory room. Thinking it might be a letter bomb, he held the envelope up to a bright light. Inside he saw something square and flat. So he opened the envelope, and found a second envelope. He unfolded the second envelope and held it up to the light. He saw that in this one there was no writing, just something round and blunt, something like the eraser broken off a pencil.

So he opened the second envelope. And sure enough, the thing inside looked like an eraser, a little dried out. He was trying to figure the symbolism of this dried-out pencil eraser when it hit him this wasn't an eraser at all.

For months and even years afterward, Cully would not be able to shake from her mind the picture of Edward Lopez, when the tears welled up in his eyes and instinctively he sought the one woman in the room to say, "It was one of my sister's nipples."

CHAPTER SEVENTY-TWO

Cully and Ridge waited in a hallway papered with Just Say No to Drugs posters and fliers for Neighborhood Watch. Ridge stood rock still; Cully paced, seeing the eyes of Edward Lopez scream "Help me! Help Victoria!"

"Ridge!" Commander Bellflower and Captain Fresco came barreling up, still in high gear from a race down the San Diego freeway. Bellflower pumped Ridge's hand and said, "We heard on the car radio that they got the drugs."

"Yeah," Fresco added, "they were saying there was so much they were going to take it to Sea World and weigh it on the scales they use for Shamu."

"Yeah," Ridge said, "but they didn't get Victoria Lopez."

Bellflower and Fresco looked at each other. When they looked back, their faces—so polished by victory, by the dramatic results that brought headlines, budget approvals, promotions—suddenly dulled in shame.

"We heard it was her brother driving the truck," Bellflower said.

"First Montoya . . . got his attention," Ridge said. "Then he communicated all his instructions—about the produce truck, where and when he was supposed to cross the border, everything—through the mail, to the brother."

"But Montoya wasn't on the truck," Bellflower said. "Nothing in the back but melons and cocaine."

"That's right," Ridge said. "The DEA had its own play going."

"I thought we checked that out!" Bellflower boomed.

"They lied to us!" Cully blurted. "They intentionally kept us in the dark to protect their operation!"

"Son of a bitch," Bellflower said. "But you really can't blame them. For a billion dollars worth of—"

"I can blame them," Cully said. "They've just killed Victoria Lopez."

"Fresco!" somebody called out, and they all turned to see a freckle-faced, forty-year-old Tom Sawyer in a San Diego Police Department uniform with captain's bars on the collar come striding down the hallway. He grinned, slapped Fresco on the shoulder, and yelled, "You drive all the way down from Smogtown just to congratulate me on our bust?"

"Whatta ya mean *your* bust?" Fresco said.

"Let's go talk to the DEA" Bellflower said to Cully and Ridge. "Maybe they can help." They left Fresco and his San Diego counterpart in the hallway.

The DEA had set up their own little operations in one of the offices the San Diego Police had loaned them for the evening and from there they were dealing with the aftermath of the bust. Bellflower, with Ridge, and Cully in tow, reached the office and found the door open. Inside four men were gathered around a single desk and were shouting about when they could file their reports with Washington. Bellflower reached in and knocked on the open door.

No one looked at him; they kept shouting. So Bellflower led his team into the room and boomed, "You guys want to give the LAPD a minute?"

They looked around. The guy standing behind the desk, a pale paunchy man in his mid-forties, nodded to the others, who filed out into the hallway to continue their argument. Cully shut the door behind them, and the pale man behind the desk introduced himself. "Tacks," he said, "Regional Director, DEA."

"Bellflower, Commander, LAPD." The two men shook hands. "I believe we've crossed operations," Bellflower said.

Tacks glanced at Ridge and Cully. "Yes. Apparently," he said. "But that's okay. No harm done."

"No harm done!" Cully exploded, but Bellflower held up a big hand to silence her.

"I'm afraid we do have a problem," Bellflower said. "There's the matter of the kidnapped girl. Victoria Lopez."

"Yes," Tacks said. "We're aware of that situation."

"We'd like your help," Bellflower said. "Do you know where she is?"

"I'm afraid I can't comment on that," Tacks said.

"Listen!" Cully yelled, and Ridge had to grab her by the shoulders to keep her from charging; but Tacks stood there, unimpressed.

"I have people in place," he said. "People. In. Place. Do you know what that means?" Bellflower started to speak but Tacks overrode him. "I've lost agents from successful busts. From bureaucrats celebrating. From congressmen announcing too many details. I appreciate the jeopardy this girl is in; but I have ordered my agent in this to return undercover—for his own safety, and the sake of our ongoing operations."

"You know where Victoria is!" Cully said.

"Detective, I can handle this," Bellflower said sharply. Then to Tacks he said, "You do know where she is?"

Tacks only looked at him.

"You listen to me!" Cully shouted.

"Detective!" Bellflower barked back.

But Cully would not back off. "You know where that girl is! You've got a man inside Guillermo Montoya's operation, and you know where they're keeping her. And we're gonna save that girl!"

Tacks would not look at her; he fixed his gaze on Bellflower. "We have no desire to see an innocent girl hurt. We'll help her all we can," Tacks said.

Ridge said, "Just let me talk to your guy, cop to cop, off

the record. Whoever you've got who's working Guillermo Montoya."

"Guillermo Montoya?" Tacks said, looking straight into Ridge's face as he lied. "Never heard of him."

CHAPTER SEVENTY-THREE

Ricardo Flores sat playing backgammon with the other *capitáns* in the basement bunker, next to the concrete room where Victoria Lopez lay sleeping. Guillermo had learned the game and taught them to play when he heard it was popular in Los Angeles. None of the *capitáns*, including Ricardo, was very good at it, but that was not surprising. When they played with Guillermo they always angled to lose, and were nagged by the fear that something would go wrong with the dice and they might accidentally win.

But all those fears, Ricardo thought secretly, were now over.

The other *capitáns* expected a phone call at three in the morning to tell them that everything had gone well and the shipment had arrived safely. Ricardo took secret pleasure in being the only one to know this call would not come. The secret made him feel powerful.

"What is the matter?" Ricardo said, checking his watch at 2:46. "He should have called by now!"

"The traffic could have been heavy," Arturo said.

Ricardo shrugged; he didn't want to overplay his hand.

Three o'clock came and went. Then 3:10, then 3:20. At 3:22 Ricardo said, "Something is wrong. Very wrong."

The door to the bunker opened and Guillermo Montoya walked in. His skin was drained of its normal chestnut color; his forehead was lined from lack of sleep. Ricardo's jaw literally fell open. "What's wrong, Ricardo?" Guillermo said. "You look surprised to see me."

"I . . ." Ricardo stammered. "I was worried about the shipment. Is everything all right?"

"The shipment? You mean the thousand kilos of pure coca powder, that I paid thirty million dollars for? And

would have made one billion dollars on? That shipment?"
Guillermo's rage was so fierce that he was smiling.

"Something *has* gone wrong," Ricardo managed to say.

"Oh. Yes. Something has gone wrong."

All the *capitáns* were looking at Ricardo. He then realized
that he was the one who had been wrong; he was the only
one who had not known the secret. Guillermo Montoya had
not accompanied the shipment.

"The Americans took the truck as soon as it had cleared
the border," Guillermo said, his voice shaking. "They at-
tacked it, with helicopters, jets, a submarine! Like a war!"

"Money . . . and drugs . . . we can get more of," Ricardo
stammered. "Thanks be to God you did not go along."

"You suggested I go," Guillermo said.

"No!" Ricardo said, with more force than he believed he
possessed at that moment. "You wanted to go! You suggested it. I volunteered to go, but you said you should be
with the shipment! I remember it!" He nodded at the hard
killer faces of the other *capitáns*, trying to encourage them
to endorse his point. They just stared back at him.

"Yes," Guillermo said. "Maybe you volunteered. But you
didn't notice something about me. You didn't notice how I
began to worry about this trip north. My brother was killed
there, the last time he took powder in. The closer the time
for the trip came, the more I thought about that. I became
afraid. I could not eat. You did not notice that either, did
you, Ricardo? And then, the last time I slept, three nights
ago, I dreamed of Alejandro's face, white and dead. Looking
at me, and shaking his head. Then . . . then when the truck
was loaded, and I had taken my place among the melons,
as they shut the door I saw a flash of light! Alejandro's face.
Warning me. So I got out; the truck left without me."

The other *capitáns* kept staring at Ricardo.

"And then," said Guillermo, his eyes blank, "the shipment was taken. Alejandro was right. And I was right to
listen to him. So I sat alone in my office all night, and talked
to him. I asked Alejandro: 'Alexandro. My brother! Who
could have betrayed me? Not Esteban Lopez! Not his son!
I have Victoria in my pocket! My *capitáns*? Only three of
them knew! And who could have informed the DEA?' And

Alejandro looked at me from his grave and said: 'The DEA?' "

Guillermo's unfocused eyes swiveled toward Ricardo. "Where did you bury Rojo?" Guillermo asked.

"What?" Ricardo said.

Guillermo laughed.

And then the world went black for Ricardo Flores.

When consciousness returned he was hanging by his hands, bound by a chain hooked to a bolt in the ceiling. Victoria Lopez stood with her back to the far wall, her soft brown eyes like pancakes in her fear. Ricardo was naked, and he was crying.

Guillermo Montoya walked into the room, followed by his other two *capitáns*—the only two left, after the death of Ricardo; Ricardo already counted himself a dead man.

But he tried to smile. "Guillermo," he said, "how can you think to do this to me?"

Guillermo stretched his hand toward Arturo, the man whose eye he had put out, the man who was still the most loyal and deadly of his *capitáns*. Arturo uncovered the object he had carried into the room beneath a blanket. It was a chain saw.

Guillermo, holding the saw low and in one hand so that it pointed out toward Victoria like an erection, looked at the girl, and started the motor. She opened her mouth but no one could hear her scream because of the roar of the engine. Guillermo only looked at her because he was conscious of her as his audience. His focus was Ricardo. "This is for Alejandro," Guillermo said. "My brother."

CHAPTER SEVENTY-FOUR

Detectives Ridge and McCullers returned to their office cubicle at the Van Nuys station. It was midmorning when they arrived, and they remained through the rest of the day.

They spoke hardly a word, and could not look at each other.

They waited for some word of the fate of Victoria Lopez. Every hour Cully checked for reports from both Mexico and Southern California. No word came.

When it was long past dinnertime Ridge looked at his watch and then, finally, looked at her. "We haven't slept for . . . how many hours?"

"I don't know," she said.

"Let's go home. If we . . . do get any leads, we want to be fresh enough to follow them."

They both knew it was a false hope, but they were tired enough to believe it.

Outside they were surprised to see that night had fallen. They walked toward their cars, parked at the far end of the parking lot beneath a sodium vapor light. They both stopped suddenly when they saw the figure step from the shadows of the shrubbery surrounding the lot, and stand beside the car, not moving, hands hanging free at his sides, waiting for them to approach.

They moved to him. The sodium vapor light gave his red hair and beard a greenish cast. Maybe it was why he looked so pale. "Ridge?" El Rojo said.

Ridge nodded.

"And you're McCullers."

"Yeah," she said. "And you're the phantom of the DEA."

Rojo looked toward the station. The lot was quiet. Everyone on shift had returned from dinner, and the new shift wouldn't be arriving for another two hours. "I wanted to come see you," he said, his voice weary, and tinged with the stretched-out accent of west Texas. "I felt like I owed you something. Or maybe I just owed Victoria Lopez."

They stood there looking at each other, all of them accepting the past tense, until Rojo said what he had come to say. He took a breath and put it bluntly. "I had a man inside. I recruited him personally. Ricardo Flores, he was Montoya's top guy. I had made him a deal. He was gonna give me Montoya, and the bust of the century. I was gonna give him six months to make Montoya's organization his own. It was a chump deal for him, but he didn't know that. Of course that doesn't matter now. What does matter is that I thought I could get Montoya. Shut him down forever."

Rojo paused. Ridge and Cully just stood there. A homicide cop learns that when somebody is confessing, all you can do is wait. Rojo went on: "I knew Montoya had her. I didn't know where she was, Flores kept that from me. So I had our station in L.A. put in an agent at the Lopez Warehouse, to tip us when he thought the shipment was going down." Ridge nodded; that was the undercover cop Louie had spotted. Rojo went on: "I could have done it differently from the way it came down. Coulda jawboned the Mexican police into a full search. I figured that wouldn't't've worked anyway. Montoya woulda had a man in the police force just like I had a man on his team, and if I had guessed right enough about where to look for him, he mighta suspected my man, and then I woulda lost him without getting Montoya.

"That's how I figured it, anyway." He stopped again. "I wanted Montoya. Two years ago he tortured one of my agents to death. I wanted him bad. But that's not why I did what I did. I chose what I chose 'cause I thought it was best but . . . Anyway, none'a that matters now. I'm just here to tell you, I'm the one held up the Crime Net report that the guy you had up here dead was Montoya's brother. I didn't want you people gettin' too close, while I had the man inside. And, uh . . ." Rojo looked away, and took a long breath.

Cully couldn't wait any longer. "Have you found her? Her . . . body?" she said.

Rojo's amber eyes cut toward her. "No," he said. "Not yet. But I found the man I had inside, Ricardo Flores. He was cut in pieces with a chain saw. They threw hunks of him around the slums in Mexico City. The street dogs were gnawing on him, but we found enough to identify." Rojo paused again. "I, uh . . . I just wanted to tell you. If Victoria Lopez doesn't make it, blame me, not yourselves."

Rojo walked away, into the night from which he had come.

THE NEXT DAY

CHAPTER SEVENTY-FIVE

Lake Hollywood. The night stinking of ozone. A layer of fog drifting like a waltzing ghost over the surface of the water, smooth and dead. Seeping up from the water, the damp. The cold. The darkness.

And then, a face. It is the face of Victoria Lopez, and it rises to just below the surface. The mouth comes open, as if to scream, but from the throat erupts blood and water.

Ridge cannot move his own body. The nightmare holds him paralyzed. He struggles; his limbs are without strength and will not respond. But he is too horrified; he must move. The first part of him to wake is his voice. "Vih," he moans. "Vih." The sound becomes "Victoriiuuhh," and his eyes open.

He lies panting, terrified, his eye sockets puddled with tears. He rolls over onto one elbow and claws the liquid from his eyes. He struggles to control himself.

He lies back, afraid to return to sleep. He stares at the ceiling.

Ten minutes, lying in a cold sweat stupor, it hits him. He knows how the Lady of the Lake got the scratches on her forearms.

He rolls out of bed, dresses, and drives to the Van Nuys station for a hundred feet of nylon rope and a set of grappling hooks.

He reaches Lake Hollywood just before dawn, beating all the joggers. He pulls the barrier pipes from their vertical sleeves and drives to the spot where Mary Ann McCready climbed the fence. He doesn't bother with the climb itself; from his trunk he takes wire cutters and makes himself a door in the chain link.

It takes him twenty minutes, and almost fifty casts. On the forty-eighth, the hooks catch something heavy.

Ridge pulls it in. It is what he knew it would be, a cinder block, coated with sludge from the lake bottom.

Suddenly he feels the urge to weep, but it is easy for him to resist.

CHAPTER SEVENTY-SIX

Cully slept in numb oblivion. She woke without moving anything except the lids of her eyes, to see the sun brightening the edges of the curtains, and she lay in the warm cocoon of the covers.

She rolled her eyes enough to see the bedside clock: 5:52 in the morning. That early, time was her own. She let her mind drift, and it drifted to Ridge.

She thought of Ridge in bed beside her. Her thoughts tumbled into pictures of his naked body, arching, taut, unleashing its pent-up passion. In that half-dream of morning, parts of her own body tingled, wanting to be touched. Her images of Ridge became so lurid that she knew they must be wrong. Ridge? Her partner? Getting lost with him, so that all either of them felt was physical drive, was the quickest way to take her life apart. It's just so easy to want the wrong thing, first thing in the morning, when it feels as if you have started but the rest of the world is a step behind.

Deal with life, Cully. Deal with Victoria Lopez, she told herself.

Victoria Lopez. Did she have any life to deal with?

She was dead. But was she? Was Cully wrong? Maybe this drug dealer, Guillermo Montoya, who had just lost a billion dollars worth of addictive white powder, would see no purpose in killing her or keeping her, and would just let her go. Maybe he would be rational, gracious, a humanitarian; maybe he didn't act from raw, self-centered, cruel instinct, like every other criminal Cully ever encountered.

Ridge. Ridge. Ridge beside her, Ridge inside her. Ridge. *Victoria, Cully, Victoria! If you don't keep trying, keep hoping, then who will?* She had no idea what to try now, but she had to try something. Not for herself, but for the sake of . . . her client. *When you're a homicide cop, you're supposed to be working to protect innocent people from further killing, but what you always feel you're doing is working for the victim.* Did she just come up with that herself, or was it something she heard Ridge say?

Ridge again! Always Ridge!

The more awake she became, the more her confusion grew. She threw back the covers and got out of bed. Her body ached; was that from fatigue, or unsatisfied passion?

She stood in the shower and let hot water pound against the back of her head and cascade down her face. Cully McCullers, Detective, swirling in the case of Victoria Lopez and the mystery of Thomas Ridge.

And the more her thoughts tumbled the more she realized: she could not solve the one, until she had solved the other.

CHAPTER SEVENTY-SEVEN

In less than an hour Cully was bouncing down the rutted gravel road to the white frame house in the lost hills outside Oxnard, where Emma and Will lived.

Emma opened the door for her before she could knock, and greeted Cully by gripping her by the elbows, like a country woman would welcome an old friend. "Cully!" she said, "you came back! Will's not here, he drove a calf to town after breakfast. But he'll be back soon, I know."

"That's okay," Cully said, "I came to talk to you."

Emma's eyes shone. Cully imagined she got no company, and a visitor was a welcome relief. Emma led her into the living room and offered her everything from ham to tea to pecan pie, but Cully wasn't hungry. Emma moved to her spot on the couch, the yarns of her knitting strewn out beside her. Cully wondered then, as she looked at this pretty young woman who wore her hair like a Shaker and her skirts to the floor, what had driven Emma to so embrace a country style of living that clearly was not native to her, and yet seemed natural when you saw her in it. "Me?" Emma declared, sitting down. "So you want to talk about Tommy."

"Yeah," Cully said. "I need to know something about him."

"I bet you do," Emma said, smiling like a matchmaker.

"It's not like that," Cully said, knowing those weren't the right words but not knowing how else to put it. "I'm just . . ."

Emma's smile faded. She was a smart woman; she heard the concern in Cully's voice. "What is it you want to know?" she said.

"What I want to know . . . I'd ask him myself, but . . . some things he stays away from, he won't talk about, as if it hurts him too much to think about them, but I need to know."

Emma nodded, waiting, open.

Cully took a breath. "I guess the first thing I want to know is what happened to his wife."

"His wife. Well. They just sort of . . . left each other. About a year ago. He was faithful to her, if that's what you were wondering."

"No, I—"

Emma had no patience for anything but the heartwood; she didn't listen to Cully's disclaimer. "It just turned bleak for them, and she didn't handle rough times very well. Her father had a little too much money and she was spoiled. And when . . ."

Now Emma stopped, unsure how far to go. She had to tighten herself, from the inside, to make herself go further. "Do you know about Bobby?" she asked.

"Bobby?"

"His brother." Emma took a quiet breath. "He died. And when Bobby died, Tommy was . . . he was Tommy, you know, he was always serious and quiet and thoughtful, but now he was pretty raw inside, and she wasn't happy, and . . . their marriage didn't last."

Cully looked at the floor—weathered oak, mopped clean and waxed. "Is he . . . over Bobby yet?" Cully sought Emma's eyes. "I have to know, because you were right. I am in love with him. And it's probably a mistake, doesn't love always seem like a mistake? But I love him, I think. But I'm not thinking too clearly right now, and I've probably already gone too far, but I have to know about him, to keep from hurting him and hurting myself. I mean, things go on inside Ridge, hidden things. He feels and thinks in ways I don't understand, and . . . I think maybe I let my first husband down, and I don't want to let him down too."

"What was the question?" Emma said, smiling.

"I don't remember . . . . Is he over Bobby yet."

"Oh, yeah. I can't tell you that, unless I tell you about Bobby."

"Tell me."

"Bobby . . . was younger than Tom, about three years. And he was a minister."

A minister. Ridge's rage at religion howled in Cully's brain.

"They were raised by their grandmother, and they grew up going to tent revivals," Emma went on. "They were both normal kids, both great in school, and not very much more religious than other families where they grew up. But something about religion reached them. Knowing them both, I'd say Tommy was really the more spiritual, ethereal one. He got chills over the music they sang in church and he tried to figure out the deepest meanings behind Biblical stories.

"Bobby was the pragmatist. At least that's how it always seemed. He used to say it was obvious that the church was one of the most influential organizations in human civilization, and shouldn't be left to the bigoted and the stupid." Emma smiled in fond remembrance, giving Cully the impression that Robert Ridge had been as outspoken with his thoughts as Thomas Ridge was discreet with his own. "And Bobby was a motivator. He did things that appealed to people in our generation. Like, when everyone was trying to raise money to stop world hunger, Bobby recommended, from the pulpit, that everybody in his church skip one meal a week and donate the money to feed the poor. He said, 'Do just this much, and the next time you pray, *Give us this day our daily bread,* you'll know that you've done just a little something to help God make some-one else's prayer come true.' "

Emma paused, her eyes fixed on some distant spot in the past, and in them was a reflection of admiration that still lived inside her. "Bobby, he was . . . he was beautiful. And he looked up to Tom, and asked Tom's advice about things like church politics. But Tommy was always saying, 'It's not about politics, Bobby. First and last, it's about integrity and the truth—trying to find the truth that sets you free.' And Bobby would say, 'It's not that simple.' But he always felt better after talking with Tom.

"Bobby had a big church. I mean a little one that had once been a big one and was becoming big again. He had a nice home—a parsonage with a swimming pool! He put in a Jacuzzi, and had the youth groups and the deacons and even the blue-haired old ladies over to swim. Everybody supported him, or seemed to.

"Then one night Bobby and his wife were out in the backyard. With the lights off, by the way. And they were making love in the Jacuzzi.

"Next door to them lived a woman—a lonely old spinster. And it turned out that she liked to peek through a chink in the redwood fence and watch them. And on this night, she saw them. She told everybody about it. 'The preacher is out in the backyard, every night, screwing like a dog.'

"Well," Emma went on, her face stiff, "you wouldn't think something like that would get so out of hand, but . . . it ruined Bobby. He overreacted, I guess, and told people what he did in his back yard was none of their business, as long as the woman was his wife. When he saw they didn't like his answer, and they came at him harder, he struck back with some pretty angry sermons from the pulpit. Eventually they fired him. A couple of nights later he went out and got drunk, and hit a tree on his way home." Emma brushed her patchwork skirt, though there was no lint there. "I guess that's all I can tell you, about that," she said.

"Is that why Ridge runs away from publicity?"

"Does he do that?"

"A detective like Ridge could be famous, if he had the slightest instinct to work the press. Some cops do. They get their names into headline stories, they go on talk shows, they even get movies made about them. Ridge is the exact opposite. He ducks it, and covers, like he's hiding a wound."

Emma nodded. This was news, but it did not surprise her. "I'm sure Bobby's part of it," she said. "Tommy's a private man, and he thinks that if you expose too many feelings that belong in your private heart, then you diminish them somehow. I know he wouldn't welcome any public discussion of the losses in his family and how they might motivate him to be who he is.

"But," Emma said, after a slight pause, "if that's true, then the biggest reason would have to be his parents." She studied Cully's eyes. "You don't know about them either."

"No," Cully said.

Emma sighed. "They were killed. Or committed suicide. No one knows. That's why Tommy and Bobby were raised by their grandmother. They were staying with her when it happened. It was . . . it was Tommy who found the bodies. When their uncle drove the brothers back to their house, Tommy went in first and noticed the smell and found the bodies. He ran back and kept Bobby from ever seeing what he had seen.

"They were in bed, both shot through the head. The pistol—which had belonged to the boys' father—was on the floor in a pool of blood, and first the uncle and then the sheriff handled it and wiped it, and of course there was no hope of fingerprints after that. Nobody ever knew if it was a double murder, or a murder-suicide, or even a double suicide. Nobody ever will know.

"If Tommy's hiding something that he doesn't want talked about, then that's it. I admit I've wondered myself if that wasn't the biggest reason he's a detective, and such a good one. I'm sure he doesn't want to open himself up to that kind of speculation." Emma paused, and looked at her softly. "But bottom line, Cully, is that he is what he is."

Cully sat, as the breeze pushed open the shade, and

clicked it against the blue paint of the window sash. Like that persistent breeze, a wild thought was rattling in Cully's brain. Maybe she was getting like Ridge, thinking with her gut and not her mind; Emma had a link to all of this, something deeper than just friendship.

"One more question, Emma," Cully said.

"Anything," Emma said.

"Were you Ridge's wife?"

"Tommy's?" Emma said. "No." She smiled. "I love him, of course. But I wasn't his wife." She stopped smiling. "I was Bobby's."

CHAPTER SEVENTY-EIGHT

And so, Cully thought as she drove back up the mountain toward Los Angeles, the central fact of Thomas Ridge's life was a mystery.

Knowing this, she felt strangely at peace.

Her visit with Emma had left Cully quiet in her center, strangely clearheaded and determined. At peace with the Mystery of Ridge, Cully was ready to face the facts, and the fact was that Victoria Lopez was either dead or alive. If alive, Cully was going to save her. If dead, she was going to get the man who killed her.

Either way, she had one more card left to play.

When she had topped the crest of the western rim of the San Fernando Valley, she punched Ridge's home number into her carphone. There was no answer, so she called the Van Nuys station. The desk sergeant answered. "This is McCullers," Cully said. "Is Ridge there? I need to talk to him."

"Yeah! McCullers!" the sergeant said. "Ridge called, he's looking for you! He left a message, sounded kinda urgent."

"What?"

"He says he's going to Crowell's church. He said to tell you he's got the Lady of the Lake's killer, whatever the hell that means. Who knows with Ridge?"

Cully punched off the call and checked her watch. It was 10:45. Sunday services were starting at the church in fifteen minutes. She hit the gas.

CHAPTER SEVENTY-NINE

Sunday, clear and bright. Men in neckties, women in hats, girls in crinoline, and boys in black leather shoes. Organ music filtered out to the side street above Ventura Boulevard, and to the bank parking lot across from the church, which took the overflow of cars. Doubting Thomas Ridge entered the wide church doors, accepted the morning bulletin from a smiling usher in a bow tie, and moved silently up the side stairs to the balcony.

It was not until the second hymn that Reverend Crowell spotted the detective, back in the second pew behind the guardrail. The congregation was singing "He Leadeth Me," and Ridge knew the words. That may have been why Crowell missed him the first time as he scanned the crowded sanctuary to nod at the familiar faces, and to note the unfamiliar ones to greet after the service and extend the warm pastoral hand of friendship and invitation. Led by the choir and the powerful vibrations of a heavy organ, the congregation sang,

> "He leadeth me, oh blessed thought
> Oh words with heavenly comfort frought
> Where'er I go, where'er I be
> It is God's hand that leadeth me"

They sang with their hearts, and surged into the chorus. Crowell's eyes passed again over Ridge, then snapped back to him, like a heel caught on bubble gum. The two men stared at each other for a moment. Then Ridge resumed singing, without looking down at the hymnal; but Crowell had lost his place.

He glanced away at nothing, then smiled at nothing. Gradually the brightness of his smile returned. As the congregation reached the final verse, he tried to look again at Ridge. The words of the hymn were:

> "And when my time on earth is done
> When by Thy grace the victory's won
> Even Death's cold wave I will not flee
> For Christ through Jordon leadeth me."

And at the words "Even Death's cold wave I will not flee," it was Ridge who smiled.

Outside the sanctuary the music sounded distant, and as natural to the stillness of a Sunday morning as the chirping of birds on the telephone wires. Then car tires squealed at the end of the street and Cully's BMW surged up the pavement.

She saw Ridge's sedan parked in the restricted zone on the church side of the street and slid to a stop beside it. She backed, snugged up to the curb behind it, and hurried into the sanctuary's entrance foyer.

The congregation had stopped singing. They were sitting quietly as a deacon ran through the morning announcements. An usher handed Cully a bulletin, but as she reached to open the inner door Cully shook her head and whispered, "Thanks, but I'm looking for somebody." She saw Crowell on the carpeted platform behind the pulpit but she wanted to spot Ridge before she positioned herself.

Looking through the glass of the sanctuary's rear door she scanned the congregation but did not see Ridge. As Crowell approached the pulpit and began the morning prayer, she tiptoed up the stairs into the balcony.

She found Ridge—head unbowed, eyes unclosed—and slid into the pew beside him. He greeted her with a steady look, then stood and led her back to the top landing of the balcony staircase, so they could whisper.

"I've got him," Ridge muttered.

"Crowell?"

He nodded. "He was the father of Mary Ann McCready's

baby. That's not something I can prove, it's just something I know. What I can prove is that he killed her."

The prayer ended, and the congregation began its offertory hymn. Ridge pulled Cully farther from the noise, but kept glancing through the door into the balcony to be sure Crowell was still on the pulpit. "I don't know why it took me so long to see it," Ridge said, talking so quickly he could barely get the words out. "Crowell was lonely and attractive, and so was she. She got pregnant. And marriage was out of the question. An actress is the wrong wife for an ambitious young minister, especially if she's a few months pregnant—she probably waited too long to tell him because she knew what he would say. So now she doesn't want the baby but she can't accept an abortion. And he comes up with a solution. He finds a place where she can go away for six months to have the baby. She tells everybody she's away making a film—the congregation never knows. Crowell even finds the baby a home! A great, loving home, with somebody in the congregation! So Mary Ann can see the baby and know it's being loved. What a stupid, naive miscalculation!

"Because then . . . then something happens. Mary Ann McCready sees her baby, in the arms of another woman. Before it was just a thing, an idea she didn't want, but now it's a baby, full of promise and bliss! Mary Ann's life suddenly lacks every shred of that. And Crowell's wise, sensitive advice starts to look a little like calculated, self-serving manipulation. And remember, she's in the physical aftermath of pregnancy; her hormones are going wild, she's in a deep depression, maybe suicidal.

"She tells her lover, her minister, her friend, that one thing can save her. Her child. She's got to have it back. Crowell tells her that's impossible. He knows she went to a priest when she was first considering an abortion; he can't risk her going to anybody for a second opinion about this. He tells her to look at the lives she'd be ruining. Not just his, and hers, but the baby's, and the happiness of the people who adopted the baby. And the serenity of this whole church!

"And Mary Ann McCready is caught. Her desire to hold the child, to love it, becomes unacceptable in her eyes. But it won't stay down. And that does drive her to suicide. And Crowell . . ."

Ridge grit his teeth. The hymn ended with the singing of the doxology as the ushers brought the offering plates forward and Crowell blessed the gifts to the service of God. Ridge continued, whispering, "Crowell told her he would help her. Help her end it. They went to the lake together. He gave her a cinder block from the retaining wall of his new house. I dredged it up this morning."

Cully's eyes were still and wide.

"He threw it over the fence for her, and climbed over with her. He helped her stick her arms through the holes in the block, and hug it to her chest. That's how she scratched her forearms. Then he led her into the water, like a baptism.

"But at the last moment, she wanted to live. She wouldn't breathe the water into her lungs, she couldn't do it. And so he helped her. He pressed her neck down, into the water . . . ."

Ridge looked toward the sanctuary. He was pale. Cully knew she must be too.

"When are you going to take him?" she said.

"As soon as the service is over," Ridge said. "Come on. Let's hear him preach."

Cully grabbed his arm. "Ridge. Are you okay?"

"Sure." There was something like a blank smile on Ridge's face.

"I just hope he runs."

CHAPTER EIGHTY

John Crowell stepped up to the pulpit. He tried to take a deep breath, but his chest was constricted and his abdomen shook with the effort. What air he did get into his lungs, he let out in a long sigh. "I come to you today," he began, in a rich, somber baritone, and stopped. It was as if he was hearing himself, and pondering the significance of his being a preacher, standing before that congregation on this morning.

"I come to you today," he repeated, "with a heart near to breaking. Mary Ann McCready . . . is dead. And . . . and . . ."

Cully was convinced that whatever Crowell had been planning to say in that sermon, he had abandoned. A stack of note cards lay on the lectern before him, and they would remain there, unread and untouched. Crowell bowed his head and pressed his palms into the sockets of both eyes, as he sought new words within the darkness of his mind at that moment. What prompted this spontaneity, Cully couldn't say for sure. It could not have been simply Ridge's presence there; Crowell could not know what was in the detective's mind, or out in the trunk of his car. Could he?

The congregation was apparently used to emotion and sincerity flowing from the pulpit, but this seemed to capture them too; they sat nearly breathless, watching and listening to the passion of their pastor before them. "She met death," he said, "in Lake Hollywood, this past week. And I, as your pastor . . . and hers . . . must tell you that I did not help her live. I know I helped her die."

Cully felt Ridge beside her, all coiled and taut. He was far into the contest all detectives of homicide feel, in the ultimate hunt of individual human combat. He did not want Crowell to volunteer his own guilt; he wanted to demolish the preacher's pride and twist a confession from his guts. Was he about to be cheated of his victory?

"Many of you here this morning are feeling the same thing. The news of her death has shocked you and made you think of every word you said or didn't say to her. Should you have perceived her secret thoughts, or sensed whatever demons tormented her? You feel you failed her, that maybe you could have saved her. I must tell you that none of you failed her as completely as I have."

His voice was shaking. "Mary Ann was alone in life. Her parents died when she was young, and so did her only sister. Her only family was here. All she had was you. And me.

"She asked herself questions. 'Am I really a Christian?

Am I really an actress? Am I . . . a worthwhile human being?' I . . . didn't help her find those answers. I tried but . . . And in the end she asked herself, 'Should I be alive?' And . . ."

Crowell began to cry. His body shook with silent sobs. Many in the congregation, both men and women, wept as they were moved by the sight of him.

Whether a confession would save Crowell's soul, Cully could not have said. She knew it might save his life. But she saw then that Crowell wanted to tell the truth, especially with Thomas Ridge there listening to him, but he could not do it, he could not stand before them and confess everything. Maybe if he had been able to be that honest, Mary Ann McCready would still be alive.

". . . And . . ." Crowell sobbed, "she decided the answer was no, and took her own life."

Crowell wept like an innocent man, and sealed his fate.

CHAPTER EIGHTY-ONE

Crowell stepped back to his chair and buried his face in his hands. The associate pastor, a twenty-two-year-old intern, stepped forward, announced the closing hymn, sang it, and prayed the closing prayer. Crowell stepped out during the benediction, to compose himself before the Fellowship Hour held on the patio every Sunday.

Ridge led Cully down through the crowd and into the corridor of the church offices. He was about to knock on the door when the church librarian said, "We try to give him a few minutes to himself, after a sermon." Ridge only glanced at her, and knocked sharply at the door.

When there was no immediate answer, he turned to Cully and said, "Get around back! Make sure his car's here, he must have a marked spot."

She hurried out and Ridge knocked again, harder this time. "Yes, who is it, please?" came Crowell's voice through the heavy door.

"Mr. Crowell, this is Thomas Ridge, Homicide, LAPD."

"Could this wait until later?" Crowell called, without opening the door. "I need this time to prepare for the fellowship after the service."

"Sorry, Reverend Crowell," Ridge said. "There's just this little matter of a cinder block I pulled out of Lake Hollywood this morning. And it can't wait."

Ridge heard a shuffling from within the room. "Open the goddamn door!" he shouted, as the librarian turned to gawk.

Ridge kicked the door. It gave only a little, and cracked instead of flying open. Ridge shoved it, and found it blocked by a heavy office chair, wedged between the door and the desk. The back window, high in the wall over the bookshelf, was open. Ridge yelled out the window, "Cully! Stop him!" and ran out into the hallway.

Cully was just stepping into the parking lot when she heard Ridge, but she did not see Crowell at first. Then she heard a car start and turned to spot Crowell behind the wheel of a new Buick. He drove toward the lot's exit and she ran to cut him off. She pulled her pistol and screamed, "Stop!" He could not have heard her but he saw her blocking the street in the direction of the freeway, so he reversed the car, moved backwards over the curb, and headed east.

Ridge stood in the street with his pistol drawn, and left Crowell one way to go—up the curvy road of a mountain.

Ridge and Cully met at his car. He drove in pursuit, as Cully called for backup.

"Where's he going?" Cully shouted, full of adrenaline. "He can't get away on Mulholland!" The road along the crest of the mountains, separating the San Fernando Valley and the Los Angeles Basin, was slow and bottled up easily. Any escape routes down the canyons were widely spaced.

"His house is up here!" Ridge said suddenly, and hit the brakes to double back to the long drive they had already passed.

They found Crowell's car, with the driver's door still open, in front of the half-finished house. "Take the back!" Ridge said, drawing his pistol again. "And don't get hurt."

CHAPTER EIGHTY-TWO

Cully, Beretta drawn, eyes wide, circled the house, across the bare earth and the strewn cinder blocks that matched the one in Ridge's trunk.

Ridge found the front door of the house open, just as Crowell had left the car door. Ridge stopped with his back to the outer wall and shouted, "Crowell!"

There was no answer. Ridge darted into the foyer, and called again. He heard a noise inside, a strange sound he could not identify. He slid over to the far wall, next to the livingroom, and heard the sound again. He whirled into the broad livingroom portal, dropping to one knee and leveling his gun.

Crowell stood in the center of the living room, surrounded by the half-papered walls. Between the thumb and index finger of his right hand he held one of the razor blades he had been using to trim the Country Manor wallpaper he had been hanging himself on weekends and evenings. The sound that Ridge had been hearing was a high-pitched groan, coming from within Crowell's chest.

Ridge looked at the razor blade and nearly laughed; what a feeble weapon! But it was not a weapon against Ridge's pistol, it was a weapon against Crowell's guilt.

The minister plunged the bright edge of the razor blade into his own jugular vein.

Ridge screamed something—just a sound. It covered the brief moan that squeaked from Crowell's throat. Blood shot from his neck as from a garden hose and slammed against the plaster wall in a great crimson blossom.

Crowell collapsed to the bare plywood floor just before Ridge got to him. Crowell's eyes rolled up at him, twitching, pleading. "No!" Ridge was screaming. "Don't! Don't!"

But the blood pumped out in three great chugs, and Crowell's blue eyes stared up at Ridge, and the light in them went out.

When Cully reached him, Ridge was sobbing. Hugging

the dead minister to his chest, Ridge was saying, "Oh, Bobby . . . Bobby . . . Bobby . . . ."

CHAPTER EIGHTY-THREE

Dugan arrived in his own car, with an unmarked coroner's van behind him, just as Cully had instructed him in her phone call.

Woger's boys only glanced at Ridge, sitting on the passenger side of his sedan, parked at the far end of the driveway away from the house. They entered the front door and found Crowell's body alone on the livingroom floor.

Only Dugan got close to the sedan. Cully led him over, and Dugan saw that Ridge was covered with blood. Dugan drew up short and said, "My God, was he hit?"

"No," Cully said. "The guy in the house murdered the Lady of the Lake. Ridge came to get him, and the guy killed himself with a razor blade."

Dugan looked from Cully to Ridge and back to Cully.

"The guy was a minister, Rosie," she said. "He preached a sermon at his church just before he did this. We were there, he saw us, and he ran. Ridge tried to stop the bleeding, and he ended up like that."

Dugan moved over to Ridge's window, leaned down, and said, "Ridge. How do you feel?"

For a long moment Ridge did not speak. He stared with unfocused eyes toward the violet mountains across the San Fernando Valley. Then he turned to Rose Nose Dugan and said, "It's bad enough for them."

"For who?" Dugan said.

"The people in the church. It's bad enough for them that their minister committed suicide. Nobody has to know he did it because he was a murderer."

"You sure that's how you want it, Ridge? You've always been a stickler for setting the record straight on victims like the Lady of the Lake. If she was murdered, and not a suicide—"

"She left a baby, Rosie. Adopted by some people in the

church. That baby's got to grow up." Ridge paused, then said, "Maybe it's better for him if he doesn't know what happened to his parents."

Cully walked to the driver's side of the car, and said across the top to Dugan, "I'm gonna take him home and get him cleaned up. Here are the keys to my car. It's parked on the corner of Ventura and Moorpark. Have somebody drive it back to the station lot. Oh, and Rosie? I won't be in for a few days."

"No? Where you going?"

"The Cayman islands."

"Vacation time? Unannounced?" He looked back toward the coroner's van, where Woger's boys were taking out the stretcher and a new body bag. "Okay," he said. "But this is a favor you owe me."

"You ain't seen nothin' yet."

He shrugged, and leaned down to the window again and slapped Ridge gently on the shoulder as she got behind the wheel. She had already pulled out of the driveway when he thought, *Now what did she mean by that?*

CHAPTER EIGHTY-FOUR

When they reached Ventura Boulevard Cully said, "Where's your apartment, Ridge? North Hollywood?"

He glanced at her, and gave her the address.

His apartment was on the front corner of a building on Kling Street, behind a Gelson's Market. Though it was midday the Sunday streets were nearly empty, and Cully was able to get Ridge into the courtyard and up the stairs with no one noticing the dry dark stains all over his clothes.

Ridge stopped at the door to his apartment, fumbled with his keys, and paused again just before he entered. "Think Oriental," he said.

Inside, the livingroom was bare except for a chair, a lamp, a well-stocked bookcase, and a small television on a crate. "It's . . . serene," Cully said.

Ridge wouldn't look at her. Staring at the dull shag carpet he said, "Thanks for . . . everything. Back there."

"Yeah. Sure." She checked her watch. "You get some sleep. I've got to get going."

"Not without me."

"What?"

"You said you were going to the Caymans. That's what you told Dugan."

"I was joking," she said.

"That's where Guillermo Montoya keeps his money. Most all the big dealers do. You're going after him."

"Ridge—"

"Not without me." He looked at her. "Not without me."

"Then you better shower. And pack a bag."

"You gonna call Fresco? Or Bellflower?"

"I'll do that from the plane."

CHAPTER EIGHTY-FIVE

On a DC-10 bound for Miami, Cully inserted her credit card into the new in-flight telephone system and brought the receiver back to her seat. "Some day he'll laugh at this," Ridge said. Cully dialed Bellflower at home.

After a long pause, and with a good deal of static, Bellflower answered. "Uh, Commander," Cully said, "this is McCullers."

"You got a bad connection, McCullers, call me back."

"Umm, this is as good as it's gonna get, sir. I'm calling from an airplane."

No response.

"Detective Ridge and I, sir, are on a transcontinental flight. We're on our way to the Cayman islands." She paused again.

"You better pick the pace up a little, Detective," Bellflower said.

"Uh, yes sir! The way it breaks down is this, Commander. Guillermo Montoya has had a street loss in excess of a billion dollars. Maybe his net loss is only a tenth of that, a hundred million. Or just one percent of the street value, ten million dollars! In either case he's been hit, and he's going to rebuild, and to do that he's got to go to his bank. And that's in the Cayman islands. It's a little place, sir, with one airport. We'll go there and wait for him. When he shows, we'll follow him, and when he leaves we'll trail him. He'll lead us back to where he lives—and to Victoria Lopez."

No response from Bellflower.

Cully said into the receiver, "Sir? Sir?"

"Fresco doesn't know about this, does he?"

"Uh, no sir. We had to catch this plane to be there before the banks open Monday morning."

"It'll work," Ridge said toward the receiver.

Cully said, "It's very simple. Montoya was betrayed by his right-hand man so he's gonna be paranoid about who else in his organization might skip out on him. But he's got to have cash and he's got to get it from his account in the Caymans. He knows the DEA is hot for him—they're the ones that turned his best friend against him—so he won't transfer the money by wire because he won't trust the technology; he'll figure the DEA can trace the transfer and find him at the end of it.

"I'm just trying to think like this guy," Cully went on, glancing at Ridge for encouragement. "He's stayed alive so far because he's so cautious. He hasn't flaunted his identity—the DEA knows his operatives but they don't know him—and he'll figure he can go to the Caymans himself. All we have to do is be there when he gets off the plane. We stake out the airport. We—"

"Wait a minute," Bellflower broke in, "that's a resort, there's bound to be lotsa flights coming in there from all over, and this whole thing depends on an accurate make at the airport."

"All the big commercial flights between Mexico and the Caymans stop over in Miami," Cully said. "And Montoya won't risk that. He'll have to charter a plane, but he'll land at the main airport and come in like any legitimate traveler because he won't trust any government besides his own to shelter him from extradition if he were caught. And if he' got to fly anywhere near the Bermuda Triangle in a light plane, he sure won't do it at night. That's a big dangerous stretch of water with a lot of superstition about it, and he's already spooked. So all we've got to do is stake out the airport from midmorning to sundown."

"But you'd have to recognize Montoya and we don't even have pictures of him, nobody's ever seen him."

"I've seen his brother," Cully said. "I saw him in the sights of my pistol, and I'll never forget his face. Now we're on our way, Commander. You want us to turn around in Miami, or you want us to go to the Caymans, and bag Guillermo Montoya, and maybe bring back Victoria Lopez?"

"I'll have the paperwork drawn up and ready to serve the Mexican government," Bellflower said. "If we tell them exactly where Montoya is, and show them the evidence we already have on him, including the statements from the Lopez family, we can force them to help us raid him."

Cully shook her fist at Ridge and mouthed the word *Yeah!*

"Keep your receipts," Bellflower said. "And you keep me or Fresco posted. And only us."

"Yes, sir. Thank you, sir," Cully said, and cut off the call. She looked at Ridge and said, "He's gonna reimburse us."

"You didn't tell him about the first-class tickets."

"He didn't ask."

CHAPTER EIGHTY-SIX

They landed in Miami and caught their connection to Grand Cayman island, landing ten minutes ahead of schedule. They stopped by the tower and told one of the air controllers that they had a friend who was flying over in a small plane and they were just wondering when he might land, and the controller told them there had been some severe Carribean turbulence at lower altitudes and all small craft had been grounded for 24 hours. Ridge and Cully thanked the guy and walked outside into the sunshine before they stopped and exchanged a look. If Montoya was coming at all, he would not arrive until the next day.

Ridge and Cully took a cab to the Cayman Elegante, and walked in carrying their complete luggage: one bag apiece, each containing toilet articles, two changes of clothes, and a pistol stripped into its pieces. At the desk the concierge, a coffee-skinned beauty, smiled at Ridge and said, "Good evening, sir. Do we have your reservation?"

"Uh, no," he said. "We'd like . . . two rooms."

"Two rooms, sir? Yes, sir." She took two keys from the rack as Ridge signed the register, and handed them across to him. "These face the sunset," she said. "And they have a connecting door."

Ridge handed the keys to Cully, waved off the bellboy, and carried her bag and his into the elevator. On the tenth floor, one from the top, they got out and moved to the first room. Cully opened the door and Ridge carried the bags inside. Cully followed him in, switching on the lights. Ridge set her bag on the bed. The door closed and latched automatically. They both turned and looked at it. Then they looked at each other.

Ridge said, "Tenth floor. Must be . . . a nice view." He opened the curtains. In the west, the sun set pink between an azure sky and a cobalt ocean. Cully moved over and stood beside him. He looked at her. The pink light warmed her hair and tinted her skin.

She turned and looked at him.

They kissed.

When a man and a woman come together, society demands an answer to one question: Is it sex or is it love? Sex and love, two human realities, as elemental as flame and water.

Cully McCullers and Thomas Ridge plunged onto the bed and reveled in each other's flesh as if love and sex were not two things, but a single wildfire they could contain only by giving up their bodies to be burned. And when the wild hot part was over, they lay quiet and satisfied, not intoxicated but sober, as if they had drunk from the fountains of heaven.

CHAPTER EIGHTY-SEVEN

Back in Los Angeles, during the night, a delivery had come to the home of Esteban Lopez: a wooden crate, with waxy caulking. It was brought by an overnight carrier service, originating from one of their San Diego shipping centers.

The Lopez family had been through enough; they had not been expecting such a box, and they did not open it. They called the police.

Fresco handled the situation personally. He sent a bomb disposal unit to the Lopez house.

It took the defusers twenty minutes to determine that the crate seemed to contain no triggering devices or explosive compounds. In the time it took them to be sure the box was not likely to be a bomb, there were already reporters at the house.

The defusers opened the crate. They were hit by an unmistakable odor.

Beneath the lid, cushioned by the green paper that protects oranges on their way to market, they found the source of the stench.

CHAPTER EIGHTY-EIGHT

Cully slept, but not one unbroken void. She woke several times to find Ridge still beside her, sleeping in peace.

When she did sleep, she had a dream. Not of pistols, not of corpses, not of drug dealers, and not of dead girls.

As she drifted toward the dawn, through the small quiet hours, she dreamed of babies, and a home. Homemade teacakes, warmed by the sun.

She opened her eyes when the dawn was still only a pink promise at the edge of the sea. She rose silently and stared at Ridge, lying on his side, still in his own dreams. She soundlessly picked up her bag, slipped into the adjoining room, showered, and dressed and then picked up the phone and asked for room service to bring fresh bread, fruit, and coffee to Ridge's room. She went back into the room, and found Ridge still sleeping. Quietly she opened the hall door, to pick up the morning paper to read while she waited.

CHAPTER EIGHTY-NINE

Ridge, like most cops, had trouble falling asleep; but once he was gone he was slow to come back. As he was rising back to consciousness he had a dim awareness of shuffling going on in the room, and when he finally opened his eyes he was sure someone had just knocked on the door.

He looked around. No Cully. "Yes?" he croaked at the door.

"Room service!" a musical island voice called.

Ridge slid into his pants and opened the door. The bellboy brought in the tray and set it on the table as Ridge scrounged up a tip. When the bellboy left, Ridge checked the bathroom, then opened the door between the two rooms they'd taken, to see if Cully might have gone into the second. The towels were there, and her bag, but she was gone. On a hunch, Ridge checked her bag. Her pistol was gone too.

Ridge moved back into the first room. The coffee was steaming aroma. Ridge sat down at the table to wait, figuring Cully had just run downstairs for something. He noticed the fresh newspaper on the food tray, with the coffee and the breads. Then he noticed another paper, lying on the chair beside the table. Ridge leaned down, flipped the paper open, and saw the headline: *Girl Dismembered in Los Angeles Drug War*.

Ridge grabbed for his gun.

CHAPTER NINETY

Guillermo Montoya stepped off the plane, squinting into the bright light of morning.

Three other men climbed down the plane's stairs behind him, carrying leather shoulder bags—Montoya's and their own.

They walked across the sunbaked tarmac and into the little terminal.

Montoya saw her first—the tall shapely American sitting on the stool in the bar beside the walk. He noticed her because of her looks: the kind of gringo woman who likes rich men and likes to party, Montoya thought. She noticed him staring at her and smiled. He nudged one of his guards; they smiled, but she kept smiling at Montoya. Something about her looked familiar.

Guillermo was feeling renewed, powerful, potent. He had had bad luck with the drug shipment, with Ricardo, with Victoria Lopez, but he had solved all his problems, he would rebuild. The idea of meeting a new woman appealed to him. He moved toward her, across the thin burgundy carpet. The woman opened her purse, and reached inside it.

"Montoya!" a voice shouted. It was Ridge.

Guillermo looked across at the tall man who had just run into the terminal. Guillermo suddenly understood where he had seen the woman's face. It was the picture. She was the one who had shot Alejandro, his brother. Guillermo dug into his coat.

As an extra precaution against unexpected safety checks, he and his three bodyguards all carried the new plastic pistols that would not set off the metal detectors at airport security stations. The guns were expensive and not as accurate as conventional weapons, but they used mercury-injected bullets that exploded on contact. When they saw Guillermo's panic, his bodyguards crouched and groped for their pistols too, and had them out before Guillermo did. All of them aimed at Cully.

Her world popped like a balloon that has no sound. And in that silent zone, everything was slow motion. She saw the four men. She reflected that once before she had been in this situation, with four guns rising toward her, and as it had been then, it was now. In a microinstant, she reflected on many things: eating popcorn with her father; watching him shake and sweat and clutch at his stomach; her graduation from the academy; the night she prayed with two ladies for God to spare the life of Victoria Lopez. And she made a conscious decision to discount three of the men before her now, and to focus only on the space of skin between the eyebrows of Guillermo Montoya.

Ridge already had his pistol out. Still on the run, he started pulling the trigger. One of his wild shots hit the first bodyguard, and then another dropped the second. The third got off a round that tore a chunk of wood from the paneling behind Cully.

She never flinched. She had forever. She stayed calm and balanced. She could not miss.

Ridge's shoulder slammed against Cully, driving her into a cocktail table, just as two mercury-tipped bullets cut the air and exploded a bowling-ball-size hole in the mahogany counter where she had stood.

The ammunition in the plastic pistols was devastating, but they were slow to fire. The investigating authorities in the Caymans would later discover that the last bodyguard, pulling his trigger too quickly, actually caused his gun to jam.

But Ridge had a well-oiled Beretta, and he saw his last shot punch through the bodyguard's heart. Then Ridge's pistol clicked empty. Cully, from the floor, saw his finger move the last time on the trigger, and nothing flash from the muzzle. And then she saw Ridge draw himself up to full height, so he loomed as an unmissable target, and point the empty pistol at Guillermo Montoya.

Montoya was no marksman; give him a knife, an ax, or a chain saw and he was an artist at mayhem, but a gun battle confused him. Since this one began his eyes had darted back and forth and his hands had lagged behind, so he had shot where he was not looking. But now Ridge's form was irresistible.

Cully's first and only shot hit Guillermo Montoya in the left eye and blew off half of his skull.

CHAPTER NINETY-ONE

Esteban Lopez had waited at the office of the Los Angeles County Medical Examiner through a long day and a long night. His wife had come to urge him to go home with her, and he had sent her home alone. Several hours later she had sent the undertaker, the who had done such a beautiful job on the neighbor's son who was killed in a motorcycle accident, but still Esteban would not leave his daughter. Even if all he had of her was her head, he would not leave until the authorities released the head to him, and then he would go home and die.

All through the night he waited. Police officers came and went. One of them, named Fresco, approached Esteban about midnight and apologized for all the time it was taking and said they would not be long now. At four in the morning this man Fresco returned with a doctor by his side. "Mr. Lopez," Fresco said slowly, "this is Doctor Pollard, he's our forensic specialist. I'm sorry this has taken so long, but we had to be sure. You've been through so much already, and before we told you this, we had to be sure . . ."

CHAPTER NINETY-TWO

The young man from the Ministry of Justice possessed the musical name of Jonathan Kajingles. He was barely twenty-two years old, and indignation flared wonderfully in him. He had been to law school in America; he had also, when he was a boy, danced in the streets for the quarters rich tourists would throw.

And now he was angrier than he might have been because he seemed to be the only one on the island who was out-raged at these two detectives from California who had brought weapons into his country and held their own private war. The constables who had first arrived at the scene of the shooting had treated Ridge and McCullers with def-erence; amid the chaos, the American detectives had con-trolled the crowd and displayed a slick professionalism that the locals recognized and appreciated. The constables who drove the Americans down to the Ministry Building had not handcuffed them; they had not even taken their guns!

But the young prosecutor had made up for all that. And when the young chargé d'affaires from the American con-sulate showed up, he found the detectives disarmed and shackled.

Except that the American chargé was white and the Cay-man prosecutor black, they could have been brothers, or teammates at polo. They understood each other; and as soon as they squared off in the office, the prosecutor's anger was no longer emotion, but position.

"Here is the problem," the prosecutor said. "Americans condemn drugs, they make them illegal, and at the same time they consume tons of them every day. The wave of filth washes over us on its way to America. But you want to treat us like *we* are the problem. And now you even bring your violence here."

The American chargé, whose name was Dellforth, nod-ded as if in agreement, but what he said was, "From what I understand from my conversation a few minutes ago with the chief of police in Los Angeles, these officers didn't bring Guillermo Montoya here, Jonathan. They followed him."

"They came—"

"They followed him because he brought his money here."

"Well within our laws, he brought his money here."

"So you're telling me you don't ask yourself where a twenty-eight-year-old Mexican with a peasant's education gets five hundred million dollars a year to run through your banks?"

"I know where he got it! He got it from you! Don't accuse us of hypocrisy, until you have—"

The telephone on Kajingles's desk rang, and he interrupted himself to answer it. He grunted a couple of times in reply, and handed the telephone to Dellforth, who answered it by speaking his own name.

As the chargé listened, Cully and Ridge sat on an oak bench against a windowless wall, their hands still shackled, a uniformed policeman standing guard over them, presumably to keep them from killing Kajingles with their feet. As the phone call droned on, they stared at the floor.

Dellforth put the phone down on the desk and looked at Kajingles. "May I let them speak? This is their commander in Los Angeles."

Kajingles shook his head. "They are in custody," he said.

Dellforth sighed for Kajingles's sake, and sat down again. "Jonathan, please understand, we regret this incident and will express our regret in writing. But if you ask us to beat our breasts in guilt, you're making us look like the bad guys, instead of the dealers. These officers came here with a legitimate purpose. And this has been an emotional case! The girl's kidnapping, the misreporting of her death . . . It's given everyone a sense of urgency!"

Cully's eyes snapped up. "Wait a minute!" she said. "The *misreporting* of the girl's death?"

Dellforth ran his tongue around his lips. "Ahm, yes," he said. "Your commander informed me that their first conclusions were invalid. The teeth had been knocked out of the head that was delivered to the parents, so the girl's dental charts weren't as helpful as they would have been. But the medical examiners in Los Angeles were finally able to determine that the jaw configurations didn't match. Who it was, they don't know. But it was not Victoria Lopez."

"Son of a bitch . . ." Cully mumbled.

"Excuse me?" Kajingles said.

"Son of a bitch!" she screamed. "Get these goddamn handcuffs off me! Get 'em off!"

She jumped to her feet and the uniformed cop moved over. Kajingles gestured as if violence was unnecessary and said, "Madam, it's this kind of outburst that makes restraints advisable."

"Come on!" she screamed. "I'm a cop! A cop!"

Kajingles looked at her eyes. He motioned to the uniformed officer, and he removed first Cully's shackles and then Ridge's. Cully grabbed the telephone and punched out Bellflower's number. "Commander!" she said, as soon as he picked up the receiver.

"McCullers?" Bellflower said.

"Is it true? That Victoria is alive?"

"I don't know. We do know the head didn't belong to her. Probably a hooker from Mexico City, that's our guess."

"I'll call you right back," Cully said, and hung up.

She moved back to Ridge. The two of them huddled in a corner, talking in heated whispers. Kajingles and Dellforth watched them, mildly amused.

The detectives moved back over to the desk, and Cully asked Kajingles, "May I use your phone?"

He gestured in kingly assent. She picked up the receiver and dialed Los Angeles. "Commander!" she said sharply. "You're going to have to get in touch with some people. For starters, a DEA man with red hair, Tacks will know his name. And then the mayor, the governor, and the President of the United States if you have to!"

"You in that big of a mess?"

"No," Cully said, looking directly at Kajingles. "The prosecutor here wants some respect, but he's on the right side. He'll help us."

"Help us what?" Bellflower said.

"Ridge and I have a plan."

THE LAST DAYS

CHAPTER NINETY-THREE

It was twilight in Mexico City, a place that has no day. In the dimness of the evening, beneath a smog-dark sky, in the murky shadows of an unfinished government building across the street from a pile of earthquake rubble and the new high-rise beside it, El Rojo huddled with Ridge, McCullers, three Special Weapons members of the DEA, six members of the S.S.V., Mexico's version of the FBI, and Caesar Augusto de la Puente, Minister of Public Safety, who had expressed such concern for the girl that he insisted on being there himself.

Everyone except Cully wore clothes the color of dirty water. She was in a red dress, skintight except for the waistline bow that hid her pistol.

All they had had to go on was the word of one of Montoya's bodyguards, dying in a Cayman hospital with a bullet in his gut. *But he hopes he might live*, Cully assured herself for the hundredth time, *so maybe he told us straight, huh?* But could it really be true? Was Victoria Lopez, this beautiful girl from north of the border, a challenge to Guillermo Montoya, someone he had hoped to seduce eventually, and to own, as if that would make him legitimate?

Cully tried to focus on Rojo, a commanding presence in front of the jittery assault force. He was saying, "All we can figure is that these men don't want to kill her. If they've heard Montoya's dead they've killed her already and moved on. If they haven't heard they'll try to keep her alive, but if they smell an assault they'll know they've got a built-in hostage. If our surprise works, we've got the advantage. So keep your heads."

They checked their weapons silently and moved into their

positions. Rojo stayed behind with de la Puente, to watch from the dark empty room. Cully picked up a yellow gift-wrapped package the size of a hatbox, and walked across the street to the entrance of Montoya's highrise.

The guards waited—three men in the foyer, smoking cigarettes and watching the lights come on in the street. It made them feel as if they were outdoors, after spending so many hours in the underground room. Guillermo would be away for three days, or maybe for three hours. They were never sure. They were, in their way, like Ricardo; they all dreamed of having their own organizations someday, so that they could kill and grow rich for themselves.

Arturo would not allow Ricardo's name to be mentioned, no matter how tired and bored they became. Arturo was the new prince, the only man Guillermo Montoya would trust to remain behind and take charge in his absence, and it was Arturo who first saw the blonde in the flashy dress, swinging across the street toward them.

"Hey," Arturo said, punching the man next to him. They did not bother to pull their guns. The man Arturo punched opened the door for Cully, and Arturo said, "Whatever you're looking for, we have it here."

The blonde smiled. "Guillermo told me to come here. He said you would let me in."

Outside the door, a beggar hobbled by. He stopped and lifted two fingers to his lips, trying to bum a smoke. When no one responded, he tapped on the glass, and one of the guards snapped, "Get out of here or we'll put your eyes out."

Arturo glanced at the gift-wrapped box. "Guillermo?" he said. "Who's that?"

"We spent the night together, last night in the Cayman islands. I flew in this morning and he told me to meet him here."

Looking at her, Arturo could believe it. But Guillermo had a fast rule that he never invited women to this place. He hesitated.

"If you don't believe me," the blonde said, undoing the bow on the hatbox and lifting off the top, "ask him yourself."

She held the box out toward him. Inside it was the head of Guillermo Montoya.

Arturo recoiled, away from the blonde and toward the panic button beside the elevator door.

The beggar shot Arturo through the front glass. Men poured inside, and slammed the other two guards to the floor.

They ran down the hallway as quickly as they could move and still be quiet, the DEA commandoes in the lead, the Mexicans in the rear, Cully and Ridge in the center.

The man at the end of the tunnel, when he saw the police coming, dropped his shotgun and raised his arms.

On the other side of the door, they found a hot moist room. Against the far wall was a cot, and on the cot was a naked girl. She lay perfectly still.

It was Victoria Lopez; Cully knew without seeing her face. Cully moved over to her, and touched her softly on the shoulder.

Victoria Lopez turned, and her brown eyes rolled up to meet Cully's.

Epilogue

Victoria Lopez had been raped. A young man she thought she loved had been killed before her eyes. The girl Cully and Ridge brought back to her father was not the same one he had sent away to college.

But Thomas Ridge, as he watched their reunion, felt a secret sense of victory. In his own experience he saw hope for the pain, hope that Victoria herself, right now, could not see. Ridge had come to believe that behind the suffering and confusion, behind the nightmares and the doubt, lay the ambush of joy.

For Cully McCullers, the moment was not as exhilarating as she had expected it to be. She saw the grieving in the Lopez family, not for their own pain but for the pain they knew each other had felt. The sight of this grief made the reunion bittersweet for Cully.

She had one other personal reaction, and it was, like Ridge's, a dark secret. Ridge had thrown himself in front of a bullet to save her, an act neither of them would ever mention in each other's presence. It was a willingness to sacrifice, an act of love, that frightened her to consider.

For weeks and months afterward, Cully McCullers felt her own life had been bought for her at a price, for some great purpose. But, try as she might, she could not figure out what that purpose was.

ABOUT THE AUTHOR

A native of Jackson, Tennessee, Randall Wallace graduated from Duke University. Currently, he writes and produces scripts for television and feature films. He is also the author of two novels, THE RUSSIAN ROSE and SO LATE INTO THE NIGHT. He lives in Los Angeles with his wife and two sons.

Praise for Joseph Wambaugh

"Joseph Wambaugh's characters have altered America's view of police." —*Time*

"Wambaugh is a master artist of the street scene." —*Publishers Weekly*

"Wambaugh is a writer of genuine power." —*New York Times Book Review*

"Perhaps better than any other contemporary writer, Wambaugh is able to convey just what it is that makes cops different from the rest of us and, more important, why." —*Library Journal*

Nobody Writes About Cops Better Than Wambaugh
Don't Miss Any Of These Bantam Bestsellers

NERO WOLFE STEPS OUT

Every Wolfe Watcher knows that the world's largest detective wouldn't dream of leaving the brownstone on 35th street, with Fritz's three star meals, his beloved orchids and the only chair that actually suits him. But when an ultra-conservative college professor winds up dead and Archie winds up in jail, Wolfe is forced to brave the wilds of upstate New York to find a murderer.